HEART-SHAPED HACK

A KATE AND IAN NOVEL

TRACEY GARVIS GRAVES

CHAPTER ONE

"THE BABIES ARE GOING to starve," Helena said.

"Don't be so dramatic," Kate replied. "No one is going to starve, least of all the babies." But her pinched expression and the way she was jabbing at the keyboard as she refreshed the donations page on their website said otherwise. For the first time in the sixteen months since Kate had left her position as a corporate attorney to open the food pantry, she faced the heartbreaking prospect of turning hungry people away. She couldn't stand the thought of letting down her regulars, especially the young mother of three who relied on the pantry to feed them.

The problem was that Kate's nonprofit organization wasn't the only one in Minneapolis that needed help. Tomorrow was the first of September, and everyone was trying to stockpile whatever resources they could before they headed into the colder months.

"Let's see," Helena said. "We could rob a bank. We could pawn our valuables. You could sell your body on a street corner."

Despite their dire circumstances, Kate cracked a smile. Helena had walked through the front door of the food pantry shortly after Kate opened and said, "I'm sixty-five, and they're forcing me to retire from my job at the insurance company. My husband retired two years ago, and now he's home all day.

That's too much togetherness for us. I have to find something to do outside the house, and you wouldn't have to pay me much." Kate hired her on the spot and had never regretted it.

She swiveled her chair toward Helena. "Why am I always the one who has to sell her body? Why can't you sell yours?"

"Who do you think is going to bring in more money? A gray-haired grandmother of seven or a willowy twenty-nine-year-old beauty? It's a no-brainer."

It was hard to argue with logic like that.

Kate had been so determined not to let down their clients that she'd resorted to begging her ex-boyfriend Stuart—who worked as the executive producer on an hour-long talk show on the local ABC station—to let her appeal to the public during the afternoon broadcast.

"Do you know how hard it is for me to be around you, Kate?" Stuart said when he received her call. "Do you ever think of that?"

"Of course I do. But this is really important to me."

"I used to be really important to you."

Kate remained silent. They'd been through this before.

He sighed in defeat. "Come in tomorrow. I'll squeeze you in after the cooking segment."

"Thanks, Stuart."

The skirt had been Helena's idea. "We need to do whatever we can to grab viewers' attention."

"You mean *I* need to do whatever I can."

"Of course I mean you. You have great legs."

On the day of the broadcast when Helena arrived at the food pantry, Kate said, "I don't remember this skirt being quite so short. I'm actually a little worried about the type of viewer I might attract with it." She tugged on the hem, pulled out her desk chair, sat down, and crossed her legs. "Can you see anything?"

"You'll be fine unless you decide to recross your legs in the middle of the segment like Sharon Stone did in that one movie."

"I can assure you I will not be doing that. The skirt is as far as I'm willing to go. I draw the line at flashing people, not even for the babies."

Kate had paired the black-and-white houndstooth skirt with a black short-sleeve top and her favorite black heels. When she arrived at the TV studio, she ducked into the bathroom to check her teeth for wandering lipstick. Before she left the food pantry, she'd applied a raspberry lip stain that Helena claimed looked stunning on her. That morning she'd curled her long dark hair and then brushed through the curls with her fingers so they draped across her shoulders and down her back in loose waves. She'd used plenty of mascara to play up her brown eyes. The extra primping made her feel a little like she *was* standing on a street corner, but she banished those thoughts. At this point, they needed all the help they could get.

After Stuart snaked the mic up the back of her top, his hands lingering on her skin in a way that made Kate feel sad, he positioned her on a stool and told her to wait for his signal. She kept her legs tightly crossed, and when the light on the camera turned red, he pointed at her and she began to speak.

"Good afternoon. My name is Kate Watts, and I'm the executive director of the Main Street Food Pantry. As we head into the winter months, our needs—and those of all local food pantries—will be greater than ever." Kate stared into the camera, imagining she was speaking directly to someone who might have the means to help them.

"No child should ever have to go hungry, and many of our local residents depend on the food pantry to feed their families. I'm here today to personally appeal to you should you have the ability to help us in any way. The families we assist, and especially the children, depend on your generosity more than you could ever imagine. Thank you."

She ended the short segment with the food pantry's telephone number and street address, and when Stuart gave her the all clear, she reached under her shirt for the microphone and handed it back to him.

"Thanks, Stuart." She gave him a quick hug. "I really appreciate this."

"Sure," he said, looking over her shoulder as if there was something very interesting across the room. "Take care, Kate."

That had been yesterday, and so far only a few additional donations had trickled in. She and Helena spent the rest of the afternoon making calls to local churches and schools to set up additional food drives while continuing to monitor the donations page. Finally, at a little before three, Kate went into the back room to recount their inventory. It was the end of the month, and they were down to their last cases of infant formula and baby food. Almost all the canned vegetables had been depleted, and they were completely out of peanut butter and soup. If it was this bad now, Kate didn't want to think about what might happen when budgets were stretched even thinner by holiday spending. Dejected, she was sitting on the floor, clipboard in hand, when Helena burst into the back room.

"I ran after him," she said, gasping for breath. "But he was too fast. Boy, am I out of shape."

"Who did you run after?"

Helena tossed a brown paper bag to Kate and leaned over, resting her hands on her knees as she took in giant gulps of air.

"The man who dropped off the money. Seriously, I may need supplemental oxygen over here."

Money?

Kate looked into the bag and blinked several times. "Did you lock the front door?"

"Yes."

She turned the bag upside down and watched in disbelief as hundred-dollar bills rained down on the concrete floor. She counted it quickly. "There's a thousand dollars here."

Their website listed four levels for donations with amounts ranging from ten to one hundred dollars. There were higher amounts for corporations, but this was the largest donation they'd ever received from one person, and it was more than enough to replenish their shelves. Kate was already picturing herself pushing a giant cart through Costco. "Did he leave his name?"

"No. He walked up to my desk and said, 'Give this to Katie.' He must have seen you on TV yesterday."

"Young? Old?" *Rich?*

"Young. Early thirties maybe? Tall. Blondish-brown hair. He was in a real hurry to leave. I chased him out the door, but he jumped into the driver's seat of an old blue car."

"An old car? Are you sure?"

"I think it was old. It didn't look like any car I've ever seen. It had stripes on the hood. And then he burned rubber."

"Why would someone who drives an old car drop off a bag full of money?"

"I have no idea. But whatever the reason, he just saved us."

CHAPTER TWO

IT HAPPENED AGAIN THE NEXT month.

Kate was conducting a client interview when Brian, one of the high school kids who volunteered in the afternoon, approached her desk. "Uh, Kate? A guy said to give this to you." He thrust the paper bag into her hands, and she stifled a gasp when she looked inside. She shoved the bag into her desk drawer and locked it.

"Thank you, Brian."

It hadn't occurred to her that the previous donation would be anything other than a onetime thing. In addition to the monthly allotment of food Kate received from food banks, which operated on a much larger scale than food pantries, they also received recurring donations each month. But they were smaller amounts and were typically comprised of food from can drives or other collection methods. Though she appreciated it all, cash donations were what Kate cherished most. She had a knack for hunting down bargains, and cash meant being able to buy in bulk, which helped the money stretch even further. Tomorrow she would make another trip to the discount warehouse and fill her four-year-old TrailBlazer to the roof.

Curiosity regarding the man's identity consumed Kate. Was he some kind of philanthropist? A self-made man who owned a successful start-up? Maybe he'd developed an app or video game and sold it for millions. Maybe he was a lottery winner. Maybe he just liked to pay it forward on a grand scale.

She could hardly wait until the end of the day when all their clients were gone and she and Helena were alone. As soon as Kate locked the door, she turned around and said, "He did it again."

"Who did what again?" Helena asked, picking up her purse and getting ready to leave.

"The man who dropped off the money last month gave us another thousand dollars. Look." Kate handed her the bag of money, and Helena looked inside.

"Well, I'll be darned. Are you sure it was the same person?"

"It's the same amount. And it was brought in on the last day of the month, just like last time. It's got to be him."

"Looks like we've found ourselves a mysterious benefactor. If you don't mind my saying, Kate, I think the skirt really helped."

CHAPTER THREE

KATE AND HELENA WORKED OUT a plan. The first donation had arrived on August thirty-first and the second on September thirtieth. Today was October thirty-first. Kate had no way of knowing if he'd come again, but she and Helena had begun watching the door as soon as the food pantry opened. If their mysterious benefactor showed up while Kate was in the back room or with a client, Helena was to detain him and dispatch one of their volunteers to find her immediately.

"Maybe he won't come since it's Halloween," Helena said.

Kate smiled. "Because he'll be too busy haunting a house?" But she'd had the same concern, and when he hadn't shown up by two thirty, her hope started to fade. When the food pantry closed at three, Kate sent Helena home and began to lock up.

She was crushed but tried to buoy her spirits by thinking of how fortunate they'd been to receive the previous two donations. Kate had spent the money wisely, and they were doing fine. Not great, but no one who was hungry would be turned away in the coming months, and that was all that mattered.

She'd locked the door and was halfway down the street when she heard the footsteps. She slowed her pace, and when she looked nonchalantly over her shoulder, she observed a man trying to open the door of the food pantry. He rattled the doorknob in irritation and cursed under his breath as he turned to go. She scanned the street. Every meter was full, but there wasn't an old blue car in sight. Maybe he'd left it in the ramp around the corner.

Afraid he would leave before she had a chance to talk to him, she started running, meaning only to reach out and grab his sleeve. Unfortunately, she was wearing ballet flats that didn't have much traction, and since she'd built up a bit more momentum than she'd anticipated, she slid right into him. In an effort to maintain her balance, her arm became wrapped around his throat.

"Gah!" he yelled. "You're choking me."

"Sorry," Kate said. She disentangled herself and took a step back.

He massaged his throat. "What is *wrong* with you?"

"I'm just excited because I thought my plan had failed, but it didn't. It worked!"

"Your plan?"

"To catch you in the act of making another donation. You *are* here to make a donation, aren't you?"

"That was my intent, yes."

Kate clapped her hands together excitedly. "Now I finally know who you are. Oh, Helena is going to be so happy for me."

"Is Helena insane too?"

"I'm not insane. I'm determined."

"I'll say." He looked at her warily. "So, what's my name? You said you know who I am."

That took a bit of the wind out of Kate's sails. "I don't actually know your name. Not yet. But I know what you look like."

And speaking of that.

How in the name of all that was holy could Helena have failed to mention so many crucial details about his appearance? Helena had guessed his age as early thirties, and Kate would agree. Helena had said he was tall, and that was also true. Kate was five nine, but even if she were wearing heels, he'd still have several inches on her. Helena had been right about his hair being somewhere between blond and brown. Dirty-blond, Kate decided. It was long enough to cover his ears and graze his shirt collar, but too artfully messy to be called shaggy. The scruff on his face was also carefully cultivated; this was not a man who was simply between shaves. His eyes were a mesmerizing shade of green, and they stood out against his fair skin. He was wearing jeans, an untucked white button-down shirt, expensive-looking loafers, and a brown leather jacket.

He was stunning.

"How long have you been trying to... catch me?" he asked.

"This is my first attempt," Kate said. "Initially I'd assumed your donation was a onetime thing. It was only after the second one that I realized there was a pattern. I've been waiting for you all day."

He seemed to be considering the information. "I see."

"What's with all the secrecy?" she asked. "Why have you never given me the opportunity to thank you?"

"I hadn't decided whether or not I was going to introduce myself."

That was a strange thing to say. "But you did see me on TV, right? That's why you're making the donations?"

"When you wore the short skirt? Yes, I saw you."

Kate's face grew warm. "That was Helena's idea. We figured it couldn't hurt. We were desperate."

"Do you frequently employ the use of sex appeal for personal gain?"

"It was for the babies. And shall I point out that it worked? You're here, aren't you?"

He smiled. "Ah, you're feisty. I like that."

Kate's eyes narrowed. "Who are you?"

"Just a man with a mission."

"Independently wealthy, or does the money grow on a tree in your backyard?"

"I steal from the rich to give to the poor."

"So, your name? Is it Robin Hood then?"

"Clever, but no. My name is Ian."

"Ian...?"

"Just Ian."

"I'm Kate Watts."

His expression was quite patronizing. "Yes, I know. You were looking right into the camera when you said your name."

"I wasn't sure you caught it."

"I did, Katie. I catch everything."

"Kate," she said firmly. Katie made her think of pigtails and strawberry lip gloss. Sneakers and training bras. Kate was partial to lipstick and blowouts. She wore the best lingerie she could afford under her jeans and casual tops, and when she dressed up, her stilettos were sky-high.

"So, *Katie*," he said, handing her a paper bag. "I trust you can put this to good use."

"I can. We desperately need it, and I'm truly grateful. I told Helena that if you made another donation I wouldn't get upset if I didn't get the chance to thank you. But since I have, I want to tell you how much this means to me and especially to the people who count on this food pantry."

"You're welcome. Glad I could help." Lazily, he looked her up and down. "You look good in jeans, but I like the short skirt better. I'll see you around, Katie."

She stood there openmouthed as Ian laughed and made his way down the street, and she watched him until he turned the corner and disappeared.

CHAPTER FOUR

KATE WAS TAKING A BREAK and having coffee and a muffin at Wilde Roast Café when Ian slid into the booth and sat across from her. He was wearing a lightweight cream-colored sweater with a tan-and-green-patterned shirt underneath, and he smelled good.

"Hello again."

Confused, Kate looked around. "Where did you come from?"

"I walked in the door like everyone else."

"Do you live nearby?" Kate lived in the St. Anthony Main neighborhood of Northeast Minneapolis. The food pantry was conveniently located on SE Main Street, which was a short three-block walk from her apartment. The quiet brick-paved street was lined with restaurants, shops, and a movie theater and included a stunning view of the Mississippi River and St. Anthony Falls. There were also bars that featured live music and plenty of green space in nearby parks.

He shook his head. "Not really."

"Then why are you here?"

"I felt like talking to you again. You're seated, so you probably won't try to strangle me this time."

"How did you know where to find me?" She was tucked away in a back booth instead of one of the tables near the windows that looked out over SE Main, so it wasn't like he'd walked by and spotted her.

He held a steaming cup of coffee and blew on it to cool it. "I tracked your credit card activity. According to Capital One, you bought a cup of coffee and a muffin here twelve minutes ago."

"You tracked my credit card?" Her voice sounded rather loud and shrieky.

He held a finger in front of his mouth. "Shh, Katie Long Legs. That information is for your ears only. How's your coffee? Would you like a refill?"

Kate did not appreciate being shushed, but she lowered her voice. "Are you some kind of cyberthief?" she whispered. And since when were criminals so well-dressed and impeccably groomed?

"I did not *steal* your credit card number. I simply accessed your account to see where and when you'd used it last. Then I came here."

"If you wanted to talk to me again, why didn't you just go to the food pantry?"

He looked at her like it was obvious. "Because you're not there. You're here at this café."

"If you're not a cyberthief, then what are you?"

"I'm a hacker."

"Is there a difference?"

"Most definitely."

"When you said you steal from the rich to give to the poor, I thought you were kidding. Is that how you get the money?"

"I don't steal it. I appropriate it from people who shouldn't have it in the first place. Then I give it to those who are more deserving."

Kate twisted her napkin. "I can't keep the money. I've already spent the first two donations, but if you come back to the food pantry with me, I can return the most recent one. It's still locked in the safe because I wasn't planning on going shopping until tomorrow."

"No, Katie. I don't want it back. It's for you. It's *for the babies.*"

"It's wrong," she said quietly.

"Is it?"

"It's against the law."

"Trust me when I say the people I took it from don't want the law involved any more than I do."

"What are you saying? That you're a thief who steals from other thieves?"

He wrinkled his nose, and it was adorable.

Stop! Thief!

"It sounds so distasteful when you say it like that. I prefer master appropriator of ill-gotten funds. You can call me master for short."

"I have lots of things I'd like to call you. Master is not one of them."

"That's okay, Katie Brown Eyes, as long as the other names are favorable."

"Stop that! We are not on a nickname basis."

"After seeing how riled up you're getting? Not a chance."

"Am I supposed to accept that this is okay because you're stealing money that has already been stolen once? Instead of giving it to charitable organizations, why not give it back to the people it was stolen from in the first place?"

"I only wish I could, but it's a bit more complicated than that."

"I'm pretty sharp. I can probably keep up."

"I've no doubt that you could."

"But you're not going to tell me."

"Not right now."

Kate let out a frustrated sigh.

"I assure you that you can spend the money with a clear conscience," Ian said.

"You can't assure me, because now I know it once belonged to someone else. And there lies my ethical dilemma."

"You'll have to take my word for it then."

His word? Was he crazy? "I'm just trying to help people, Ian. I don't like the position you've put me in."

"Please don't be upset with me. I really do want you to keep the money. For the babies."

Kate picked up her muffin, but she'd lost her appetite so she put it back down and brushed the crumbs from her hands. "You said you felt like talking to me again. Why? What do you want?"

"I thought maybe we could be friends."

"A few days ago you hadn't decided whether you even wanted to introduce yourself."

"Clearly I've made my decision."

"Why would you want to be friends? You hardly know me."

"You'd be amazed at what I know about you, Katie."

Oh, yes. The credit card. She'd have to cancel that immediately. And she'd choose a new, stronger online password that Ian would not be able to crack.

"I appreciate the donations very much, and I will spend the last one because my clients desperately need it, but I don't want any more of your money. And I really don't see us becoming friends."

Kate had been harboring some fairly romantic fantasies about running into Ian again, but in not one of those fantasies had she ever cast him as anything other than the hero, and certainly never the villain. He had ruined everything.

"I'll win you over eventually. I'm very charming that way." As he got up and walked away, he turned and said over his shoulder, "Until next time, Katie."

CHAPTER FIVE

KATE ARRIVED AT VIC'S FIFTEEN minutes before her one-o'clock lunch date. After regretfully admitting to herself that there was nothing to pursue with Ian—on account of the fact he was apparently some kind of felon—she'd moped around for a week and then scrolled through the inbox of her online dating account. After deleting multiple stomach-turning requests for casual sex and naked pictures, she sifted through what was left to see if anyone interesting had messaged her. So far she hadn't had the best luck with online dating, but Kent, the man she was meeting this afternoon, sounded promising. He was thirty-six, handsome, and worked as a stockbroker for Morgan Stanley. He loved cooking, animals, and long hikes in the woods. They'd been exchanging e-mails for several days, and the last couple contained mildly flirtatious comments from Kent about how attractive she was and how much he was looking forward to meeting her in person. He seemed nice enough even if he did want to spend what Kate felt was a bit too much time discussing her physical description, especially her body type. She was one of those enviable women who was long legged and slim hipped but still in possession of full breasts. And they were real. Even so, she worked hard to stay in shape. She attended a Pilates class several times a week, and she walked everywhere. For her profile photo, she'd had Helena take a full-length picture of her standing next to the sign for the food pantry. She was wearing jeans and a sweater, and her long hair was pulled back in a ponytail. Kate wasn't interested in false advertising, and she wanted the men who looked at her profile to know exactly the type of woman they'd be meeting. Apparently it wasn't enough, because Kent had sent not one but two messages yesterday asking for additional clarification.

Do you count calories or follow a specific diet plan? he'd asked. What the hell was that all about? Frankly, she sometimes ate like a truck driver because she was hungry, dammit. And hunger was a bit of a hot button for Kate, considering she spent her days making sure people got enough to eat. That message was followed up with *What kind of clothing would you say highlights your best features?* What did that even mean, and why did he care what kind of clothes she wore?

Ian likes short skirts, and that didn't seem to bother you.

Ian just liked to push her buttons. And besides, Ian was no longer in the picture.

Kate glanced at her watch discreetly. Kent was now five minutes late. Just then her phone vibrated to signal an incoming e-mail. Kent was probably reaching out to let her know he was running behind. Very thoughtful.

She opened her e-mail and smiled. The message *was* from Kent.

I changed my mind. I'm not interested.

What?

In addition to confusing, Kate found the message rude and unacceptable and fired off a reply.

You're a tool.

His response came ten seconds later.

You're just bitter because you're fat.

Kate stared down at her phone as if it somehow held an explanation for the bizarre exchange. She was so deep in thought that the scrape of a chair being pulled back startled her.

"It would never have worked out," Ian said, sitting down across from her. "You were already fighting over e-mail."

"We were not fighting. We were having a discussion. And how would you know?"

"Loves cooking, animals, and long hikes in the woods? *Please.* Do you want to know what Kent really loves? Threesomes. Kent loves threesomes. Also hard-core porn and occasionally cocaine. Is this the dating pool you want to swim around in? I mean really, Katie."

"Oh my God. You did *not.*"

"I'm going to order us a drink. A bourbon sounds excellent on this crisp fall afternoon." Ian signaled for the waiter. "Against my better judgment, I'll order you a glass of wine. According to your credit card statement, you had a staggering amount of chardonnay delivered to your apartment last month. I think you might want to take one of those 'Could I Be an Alcoholic' quizzes the next time you come across one, just to see what it says."

Kate logged on to her online dating account. Her profile picture had undergone a significant change because she now had two chins and giant puffy cheeks. Even her eyelids looked bloated.

"You FatBoothed me?"

"He seemed awfully concerned with your figure. That just goes to show what kind of man he is. Already micromanaging your wardrobe and diet before he's even met you. If he had just been patient, he would have seen you in person and realized he had nothing to worry about. It's his loss."

Kate peered closer. "What is that above my lip?"

"It's a mustache. You dark-haired girls have to be so careful about that kind of thing." Ian gave their drink order to the waiter.

Kate didn't speak. Her brain was trying to process how everything had gone so wrong in such a short amount of time.

"Katie? Are you okay?" He sounded genuinely concerned. "On a scale of one to ten, how mad at me are you, with one being you still like me and ten being you'd like to castrate me with a pair of rusty scissors?"

"When did I ever say I liked you?"

"It was subtly implied."

"All I'm trying to do is find a nice guy to spend time with," Kate said, stunned. "It should not be this hard."

The waiter brought their drinks. Kate picked up her wineglass and took a rather large gulp. She started to set it down, changed her mind, and took another drink.

"Can I be honest with you?" Ian asked.

"I don't know, can you?" Kate leaned forward, resting her elbows on the table while she massaged her temples.

"You're quite beautiful, so I don't understand why you'd waste your time with online dating."

Kate should not have cared that Ian said she was beautiful, but she did.

"I use dating sites because I don't want to go to bars and my girlfriends all work sixteen hours a day. Helena claims her clubbing days are over, so that doesn't leave me with much. If I meet someone online, at least I have the opportunity to vet them first."

Ian snorted. "These men all want one thing, and they'll lie to get it. Using a dating site to vet them is going to get you roofied. It's really not safe, Katie."

"That's why I only meet them in public places. I don't let them take me home, and I don't invite them in until I've gotten to know them. And *I'm* not lying. Everything on my profile is true."

"Congratulations. You're the only one telling the truth."

"Well, how do you usually meet women?"

"They have a way of suddenly appearing. Like the birds in that song."

She had to think about that for a minute. "You mean 'Close to You' by the Carpenters?"

Ian snapped his fingers. "That's the one."

"How convenient for you."

He smiled. "Isn't it?"

"Are you dating one of these women now?"

He sipped his bourbon. "I'm currently between lovers."

Kate took another big drink. Her glass was more than half-empty, so Ian signaled the waiter for another.

"I feel conflicted," he said. "It's like I'm just contributing to your drinking problem now."

"I do not have a drinking problem! There was a buy one bottle, get one half off sale, so I stocked up."

"Denial. That's a shame. Let's go back to your dating woes."

"I don't have woes. I'm just having difficulty getting back out there." Kate could only admit this to herself, but the thought of jumping back into the dating pool had extended her relationship with Stuart by at least six months.

"Maybe there's something wrong with you."

She shook her head. "There's nothing wrong with me."

"There could be. Tell me about your most recent lover."

"Stuart was more than my *lover*. We broke up six months ago after dating for five years."

"Why, did you sleep with someone else?"

"What? *No.*"

"Did he?"

"Nobody slept with anyone else! We grew apart and weren't the same people at the end of five years that we were when we started dating."

"Was Stuart a nice guy?"

"He was a *great* guy. He's still a great guy."

"If he was that great, you'd still be with him."

"I loved Stuart for a long time."

"But?"

"When it comes to men, you either break up with them or you marry them."

"Stuart asked you to marry him?"

"Yes. And I said no." And she'd unintentionally stomped all over his heart in the process.

"Why?" Ian asked.

The wine had already loosened her up a little, and she answered honestly. "Because after five years there was nothing about him that surprised me." Stuart was like a puzzle with a limited number of pieces; all he really needed to be happy was Kate, his PlayStation, beer, a hot meal, and sex. Kate needed more.

"Ah, now we're getting somewhere. So you want a nice guy, but you don't want him to be boring."

"Yes. Nice and not boring and not into threesomes and no cocaine. I mean, is that too much to ask?"

"No, although I feel compelled to point out that the three-some thing is pretty universal."

"Oh for God's sake," she muttered.

"That doesn't mean we're all going to try to convince you to participate in one. It's just that very few guys would be like, 'Go away, extra girl,' should one happen to climb into our bed when you're already in it. That's all I'm saying."

Kate had finished her first glass of wine, and the waiter arrived with her second. Ian handed it to her and held up his bourbon. "Cheers to weeding out the assholes, Katie."

Kate clinked her glass with his and said, "Cheers."

An hour later, after sharing an order of crab cakes and beer-battered fish and chips, which Ian insisted on because "that dick Kent would probably have made you order a salad," Kate leaned back in her chair and sighed.

"Feeling better?"

"More relaxed anyway," she said. "Probably because I'm stuffed full of fried food and this is my third glass of wine."

"In case you were wondering, I'm having a great time."

"Let me guess. This is all part of your 'let's be friends' campaign."

"That depends. Is it working?"

Kate tried to suppress a smile.

"I saw that, Katie. I told you, I miss nothing."

After they finished their drinks, Ian insisted on paying the tab. "I'll walk you home," he said. Dried leaves crunched under their feet, and Kate breathed in the smell of wood smoke coming from a nearby chimney.

"This is my street," she said a few blocks later. "I'm in the tall brick building."

"I know."

"How do you know where I live?" Kate asked.

He looked at her incredulously. "You can't be serious." He followed her up the short sidewalk to the front steps, and she sat down when they reached the top.

"You're not going to invite me in?"

"You can't be serious," she said, throwing his words back at him. The chill of the cold concrete seeped through her jeans almost immediately.

Ian sat down beside her. "Wow, these steps are really hard and cold."

"Tell me everything you know about me," Kate said. She was tired of being blindsided whenever he spouted some new personal detail.

"Let's see… you turned twenty-nine in September. You have a dentist appointment next week, and the book you placed on hold at the library is ready for you to pick up. You receive a disturbing number of messages on your dating account from men trying to hook up with you or asking to see you naked, which you delete immediately. I have to say I'm truly shocked at what men deem appropriate behavior in the modern dating world."

"You," Kate said, pointing a finger at him. "*You* are shocked."

"I am. I'm not sure how you women put up with it."

"The struggle is real. Go on."

"Your e-mails all include emoticons, usually hearts and smiley faces, and your Netflix queue consists mostly of romantic comedies. Oh, and you're a 34C. That's just the stuff I can remember offhand. I'm sure there's more."

Kate was horrified. "How do you know my bra size?"

"I scrolled through your order history at Victoria's Secret."

"Well, that's not at all creepy," she deadpanned.

"Did you know there are items in your shopping cart? Sweaters. Lots of thick, long, skin-covering sweaters. Frankly, it confused me."

"Maybe I already own plenty of lingerie. Considering I walk to work, sweaters are much more practical. Plus they're awfully cute."

"I added a few things to your cart and checked out for you. I paid for it with *my* credit card. Expedited the shipping too, so you should have it by Monday."

"You *added* a few things?"

"One hint: not sweaters."

"How wildly inappropriate."

"Kid in a candy store. Couldn't help myself."

"How?"

"Excuse me?"

"You've obviously hacked into my computer. How did you do it?"

"I came in your backdoor."

"I'm certain you did not."

"I assure you that I did."

"Without even discussing it with me first? No preparation? No warning? Don't you think that's incredibly bad form?"

Ian grinned. "Are we still talking about your computer? Because I find you utterly delightful right now."

"I'm waiting."

"A backdoor is just a way to gain remote access to a computer. It took me all of two minutes to take over yours."

"You have access to my computer?"

"Yes."

A panicked expression appeared on Kate's face. "Can you see my browsing history?" She'd recently clicked on a link to an article about how to pleasure a man orally, telling herself that it was always prudent to keep one's skills sharp, especially now that she was single again. That link had led to a plethora of other links covering a host of similar topics, and Kate had spent a rather enjoyable evening sipping wine while clicking and reading.

Ian winked. "I can, and I must say the more I learn about you, the more I like you."

"And to think I was once bothered by you tracking my credit card activity."

"Those were the good old days, huh?"

"Do you know what I think? I think you've fallen into the habit of relying on your money and the way you look to excuse your appallingly intrusive behavior."

"You're absolutely right. There aren't many problems my money can't solve, but let's talk more about the way I look. What exactly do you like the most?"

Kate feigned indifference. "I'm sure you're very appealing to some, but I don't happen to find you all that handsome."

"Yes you do."

Kate decided a subject change was in order. "You owe me some information."

"Quid pro quo, then?"

"It's only fair."

"Go ahead."

"Age?"

"Thirty-two."

"Hometown?"

"Amarillo."

"Really? You have no trace of an accent."

"I'm a man of many personas, darlin'." He said the words in a thick drawl.

"College?"

"MIT. Computer Science. Top of my class, of course."

"Naturally." Kate pulled her jacket tighter. Her butt had gone numb. "How long have you lived in Minnesota?"

"A little over two months."

"How long are you staying?"

"Not sure yet. I move around a lot."

"Where do you live?"

"That's top secret."

"Who do you work for?"

"I work for no one."

"What's your last name?"

"I can't tell you."

"You can't tell me your last *name*? Are you kidding me?"

"Nope. By the way, my ass is freezing."

"What do you do all day?"

"I hack."

"I know that, but who or what do you hack? Besides me, that is."

"I hack whatever I want or need to hack."

"Pretty good at it then?"

"I'm the best there is. No one can keep me out. Why did you stop practicing law?"

Kate knew it would have taken him no time at all to unearth her education and former profession. "I'm supposed to be the one asking questions."

"I'm just curious."

"I wanted to help people. I couldn't do much of that stuck in a tiny office filing briefs. At the food pantry I at least have tangible proof that I'm helping others."

"Is that why you rebuffed me that day at the café? Because you believe the law is black-and-white and I work in a gray area?"

"I rebuffed you because I didn't want your stolen money. Plus you violated my privacy in a way that was very off-putting and not okay. And, I might add, you've continued to violate it."

"I know you probably don't believe me, but I'm actually a really nice guy. As such, I have a proposal for you."

"I can't even imagine what it might entail."

"I propose that you forget about online dating and go out with me instead."

"Why would I go out with you? You engage in frequent illegal activity, and you have *horrific* boundary issues."

"Because I promise you that spending time with me will never be boring. And isn't that what you're really after? Someone who can inject a little adventure into your life?"

There was no way she could ever take Ian seriously, but he was spot-on about the boredom. No matter how inexcusable his behavior, the few conversations she'd had with him had been the most stimulating exchanges she'd had with a man in a very long time.

"We are on a vastly uneven playing field," Kate said. "You know things about me, embarrassing things. Conversely, my efforts to find out anything substantial about you have crashed and burned. Nothing you've told me is personal. If you don't want to answer something, you don't, yet you did not extend to me the same courtesy. Do you want to know how that makes me feel? Naked. I feel like you have stripped me completely bare."

"I like the direction this conversation is going."

An idea slowly worked its way into Kate's thoughts. At first she rejected it, but then the logical side of her brain took over. Retribution of some sort was absolutely necessary. Her solution was bold for sure, but it was the only way for her to gain any equilibrium. She yanked on Ian's jacket and said, "Come with me."

"Oh good, we're finally going inside where it's warm."

Kate led Ian into the elevator. She punched the button for the fourth floor, and when the door opened she led him down the hall. Once they were inside Kate's apartment, she pulled a small canister of pepper spray out of her purse and flicked off the safety button.

"This just took a weird turn," Ian said.

"Take off all your clothes."

"Excuse me?" The shocked look on his face told Kate she had finally managed to rattle him.

"You've shown no remorse whatsoever for your all-encompassing and blatant invasion of my privacy. Because that makes me feel naked, I've decided it's only fair that you should feel naked. Also, get out of my computer immediately. I'm willing to move past the fact that you hacked me, but it ends now."

"No more backdoor?"

"No more backdoor."

He appeared crestfallen. "Ever?"

"Never," Kate said firmly.

"Not even on my birthday or like a special occasion?"

"Are we still talking about my computer?" she asked.

"You probably are."

"Do you really think that's an appropriate topic for us to be discussing right now?"

"You're right. That talk should probably come a little later in our relationship when we feel like spicing things up a bit."

"You did not just say that."

"I didn't? Because I heard the words come out of my mouth."

"Right now you're closer to a restraining order than you are to a relationship."

He looked concerned. "Then I am *really* off my game."

"Because I don't have the technical ability to know whether you've complied, I'll have to take you at your word that you've removed the backdoor. If I somehow discover you haven't, there will be no second chances."

"So if I remove the backdoor and take off my clothes, we'll be even?"

"Calling us even is a bit of a stretch, but okay."

"And you'll go out with me?"

"I suppose I can give this proposal of yours a chance. Trial basis only. If it doesn't go well, I will not hesitate to cut you loose."

"And the pepper spray?"

"That's for my protection. Normally I would not allow a man I'd just met to come up to my apartment. I'm going to remain here next to the door so I can make a fast getaway if you try anything sketchy."

"You seriously want me to take off all my clothes?"

"If you're brave enough to do it, yes."

Ian unzipped his leather jacket and draped it over the arm of her couch. Next he pulled his sweater over his head and let it fall to the floor. Underneath he wore a white T-shirt, and Kate observed the way his muscles flexed as he took it off. He dropped it on top of the sweater and kicked off his shoes.

He lost the jeans next, and her heart rate increased. His abs were absolute perfection, and her eyes were drawn to the narrow trail of hair that started at his belly button and disappeared into his boxer briefs.

"You can leave your socks on," she said. "My hardwood floor's kind of cold."

"Are you sure? Because I can certainly take them off."

"I'm sure." Kate wondered if he'd actually go through with it. But she'd questioned his bravery, and men rarely let that kind of thing go unchallenged. He put his fingers in the waistband of his underwear, and as soon as they were down around his ankles, he stepped out of them.

Well goddamn.

Here was a man who was utterly secure in the way he looked naked, and with good reason. His imposing height and athletic build showcased muscles that were well defined but not bulky. Broad shoulders tapered to a narrow waist, and his long legs looked sculpted and strong. Kate was not a fan of overly hairy men, and Ian had just the right amount.

"Six three?"

He smirked. "Four."

"Work out some?"

"Quite a bit, actually. There's a gym in my building."

Kate had to admit he was mouthwatering standing there in all his naked glory. How long had it been since she'd had sex? Six months at least. And it's not like sex with Stuart had ever been especially satisfying. As she pondered that, Ian began to develop a rather impressive erection. She averted her eyes.

"Stop that. This is not about sex. It's about boundaries. It's about equality."

"If you're going to stare at it, it's going to wake up and say hi."

"I wasn't staring."

He let out a chuckle. "Okay."

Kate's shoulders slumped in defeat. "Not modest at all, are you?"

"I can stand here all night if you want me to. Frankly, I'm more concerned about your itchy trigger finger on that pepper spray. I've heard it stings."

Kate snapped the safety lock back on but kept the canister in her hand, just in case. She leaned back against the door. "You're quite stunning to look at, as I'm sure you're already aware."

"Shall I give you a little twirl?"

"Sure. Why not?"

Slowly he turned in a circle, and looking at him was pure torture. *The ass on this man!* All of Kate's recent orgasms had been of the DIY variety, and she was dying for some hot, steamy sex with an actual partner.

"Do you know what I like about you, Katie?" Ian said when he'd turned back around.

"My extreme tolerance?"

"Yes! Most women would not be able to put up with me."

"Most women would probably have you arrested."

"Says the woman who made me take off my clothes."

"I'm guessing it's not all that hard to get you out of them."

"You're a good sport, Katie, and you have legs up to your neck."

"The legs are a big deal to you, aren't they?"

"I'll let you know after I've seen the rest of you. There might be a body part I like even more than your legs."

"A bit assumptive, don't you think? I said I'd go out with you, but you are still firmly in the friend zone. And I don't care what kind of hotshot hacker you are, you won't find any naked pictures of me online, so don't even bother searching."

"Two steps ahead of you, Katie. Already looked and came up empty-handed. It was a sad day for me."

"Aren't there things about me you'd like to find out organically?"

"There are certain things I will never be able to find out about you until we're doing them together. Just think about that. I know I am."

And now so was Kate.

She took one last look at his naked body. "Okay, you can put your clothes back on now."

"I don't know," he said, taking a few steps toward Kate until he was standing close enough that she could identify the notes of his cologne—something spicy and masculine with a hint of citrus—and feel the warmth radiating off his smooth-looking skin. "I kind of like being naked."

"Must you always have the upper hand?"

"Always, Katie. Never forget that."

Kate found it much easier to converse with Ian once she'd finally convinced him to get dressed. "Let's go," she said, grabbing her keys and beckoning him to follow her into the hallway.

"Outside again? But it's nice and warm in here."

"I'm walking you out because we've had enough togetherness for one day." Kate was actually enjoying Ian's company, but she was determined to wrest some control back from him and bring their interaction to a close on her terms. She also wanted to take a hot bath and put on something warm and comfortable, preferably made out of flannel. Then she planned to pop some popcorn and spend the evening watching one of those romantic comedies in her Netflix queue.

Ian followed Kate into the elevator and then back outside to the front steps where he called a cab.

"Where's your car?" Kate was curious why a man who clearly wasn't hurting for money would drive an older model, but maybe it was his frugality that allowed him to give money to charity.

"I elected to leave it at home in case you decided to challenge me to a drinking contest. I'm not positive I would win. Either way, I'd surely be too impaired to drive."

"You're the one who ordered the third round. Believe it or not, I would have stopped at two."

"Sure you would have."

"You're insufferable. I don't like you."

He leaned in closer. "Liar," he whispered.

She pushed him away. "Tell me something deeply personal and embarrassing. Something that's, let's say, on par with snooping in someone's browsing history."

"So this anecdote? It should be of a sexual nature?"

"If it's embarrassing, sure."

"When I was fourteen, there was this girl I really liked. I'd been seeing her for a while, and we'd had some pretty heavy make-out sessions under the bleachers at school and in her bedroom when her parents thought we were studying. We finally reached the point where she said she was ready to go all the way, so I met her at a park by her house. It was dark and we crept up into this covered slide and took off each other's clothes. I got so overly excited that when I tried to put on the condom, I came all over my hand."

Kate's eyes widened. "Fourteen? Seriously?"

"Did you not hear the part where I came on my hand? This is incredibly embarrassing information I'm sharing with you."

"I'm sure it was quite awkward."

"It was, but since I was so young I got hard again about three minutes later. I pretty much nailed it on the second attempt. In case you were wondering, I have much more control now."

"I think there are probably other, more *legitimately* embarrassing, stories you could share. I'm equally sure you're not going to tell me any of them."

"Probably not." He leaned against the metal railing of the steps. "I gather from the plans you made with Kent that an afternoon get-together is an acceptable option for our first date? It just so happens I have a meeting at one o'clock on Monday at U.S. Bank. I'll swing by afterward and take you to a late lunch. How does that sound?"

Why not? she thought. Curiosity had become the driving factor in her decision-making process. Ian intrigued her in a way Stuart never had.

"I suppose that will work."

"Speaking of Kent," Ian said, shaking his head. "He wasn't a nice guy. After I got done going through his online dating account, I snooped around on his computer. Found quite a few videos on his hard drive. In the clips he's having sex with lots of different women. I can't be sure, but it seemed to me by the way he posed them that they might not have been aware the camera was running."

Kate's face fell. She imagined a possible scenario in which she was starring in one of those tapes without her knowledge or consent. Then she thought of those tapes being shared and watched by other men, and her stomach lurched.

The cab pulled up to the curb.

"So I'll see you on Monday, okay?" Ian said. She didn't answer. "Katie?"

"Can you make those videos disappear?" Kate thought of the women who had no idea they were being recorded or how many men might someday view the videos.

"Consider it done." He jogged down the steps, and after he opened the door of the cab, he turned around and said, "You think I'm one of the bad guys, Katie, but you and I are more alike than you realize."

He blew her a kiss, and Kate watched the cab drive away, desperately wanting to believe him.

CHAPTER SIX

KATE DUCKED BEHIND A LARGE potted plant in the lobby of the bank on Monday afternoon at a little before one o'clock. She was curious about Ian's meeting and had decided she'd do a bit of sleuthing under the guise of meeting him at the bank instead of waiting for him to pick her up at the food pantry. When he walked through the front door five minutes later, Kate slid down in her seat. He was dressed in a pair of dark jeans and an untucked green button-down shirt, with his leather jacket on over them. He was also wearing glasses. Kate peered carefully around the plant and watched as he pushed the button for the elevator. As soon as the doors closed, she approached the elevator, and when they opened again she stepped in.

The building had three floors. Kate got out on the second floor and looked around. She spotted the back of Ian's head as he stood at the reception desk in a glass-walled office to her left. A few moments later, a man approached Ian, shook his hand, and they walked down a short hallway together and disappeared around the corner.

Kate opened the door to the office and sat down in one of the two leather chairs that were tucked into the corner facing each other.

The receptionist glanced over at her. "May I help you?"

"I'm just waiting for someone. Thank you."

To kill time, Kate logged on to her online dating account. Ian had modified her picture again. Her face was still fat, but in addition to the mustache, he'd given her a mullet and blacked out one of her teeth. She started laughing so hard she snorted. She was so busy crafting a new bio to go along with her profile picture—a bio in which she stated that any man interested in dating her would need to look within to see all the wonderful things she had to offer—that she didn't notice Ian until he was standing right in front of her.

"Oh, hi," she said.

"Imagine running into you here."

"This *is* quite a coincidence."

"It's not a coincidence at all. I knew you were following me."

"You did not."

"I spotted you hiding behind the plant when I walked into the bank. Plus I could smell your perfume as soon as I stepped out here."

"Did you"—she used her fingers to make little air quotes—"*appropriate* money from this bank?" she whispered.

"Of course not. I do all my work from the Batcave. Believe it or not, I actually bank here. I was just signing some papers."

Kate had never seen a man look so utterly scrumptious while wearing glasses. There was something about the combination of his hair, his scruff, and the semi-rimless designer frames that made him irresistible. "Are the glasses a disguise? Because I totally knew it was you."

"The glasses are real. I often suffer from eyestrain since I spend so much time on the computer, and I was up late last night, working."

"They make you look very smart." She took a moment to imagine how his scruff would feel rubbing against her skin if he were to kiss her.

"I am smart, but I think you mean devastatingly handsome. More so than normal, that is."

"You're so humble."

"Ready?" He walked to the door and held it open for her.

"Yes."

"Follow me." He looked at her and laughed. "That shouldn't be a problem for you."

They took the elevator to the basement, and when the doors opened to the parking garage, Kate followed Ian to a row of cars. He stopped beside one and pulled a set of keys from his pocket.

She gasped.

Ian smiled. "It's a—"

"1964 Shelby Daytona Cobra Coupe."

"'65. But color me impressed."

"My brother Chad was obsessed with this car. He used to have a poster of it on his bedroom wall. There were only six built between 1964 and 1965."

"A bit rare indeed."

The last authentic Shelby had sold at auction for around seven million. Ian's was obviously a replica, of which there were quite a few, but it was still a very notable vehicle with a price tag that started in the low six figures. "Helena called it an old blue car."

He grinned, looking contemplative. "Technically, that is correct."

Kate could not resist running her hand lightly over the Guardsman Blue paint and the white racing stripes on the hood. The Shelby was unmistakably race-car-like in appearance with its aerodynamic design and unique body style. Chad was going to be so jealous. "For someone who values his privacy, isn't this a bit ostentatious?"

"How so?"

"Rakishly handsome playboy who makes grand philan-thropic gestures and drives a flashy car. Any of this ringing a bell?"

"Rakishly handsome playboy?"

"Well, if the Prada loafer fits. Wouldn't you fly under the radar more easily in, say, a Ford Focus?" she asked.

"A Ford Focus? You want me to tool around town in a Ford Focus? Jesus, would I still have my balls?"

"No, they cut them off when they hand you the keys. Of course you'd still have your balls. What kind of question is that? This conversation has gotten way off track."

"You mean because we started out talking about my car and now we're talking about my balls?"

"Are we?"

"I believe so."

"Maybe we should go back to talking about your car."

"You want to drive it, don't you?"

"Why would I want to drive your car?"

"Why *wouldn't* you want to drive my car? Can you handle a stick shift?"

"Yes, and rather competently I might add."

"That's an enormous turn-on. Truly."

She pretended not to hear him. "This is not a good car for Minnesota winters."

"Horrible, I agree. My other car has four-wheel drive, but it's not nearly as fun to operate as this one." Ian dangled the keys in front of her.

He was right. Kate was dying to drive his car and couldn't wait to see how it handled. She took the keys, opened the door, and reached over to unlock the passenger side for Ian. They belted up, and she started the car.

"Please note that I'm already making good on my promise, Katie. Because I assure you, driving this car will be the opposite of boring."

Kate maneuvered the car through the city streets, familiarizing herself with the dashboard and getting a feel for the clutch. To his credit, Ian remained calm, not giving her any pointers or questioning her driving skills in the least. Heads turned as they drove by, and Kate felt like she was on display.

"People are looking at us," she said.

"No one is looking at us."

"Everyone we've driven by has looked at us."

"They're probably just looking at you."

"Yes, I'm sure that's it." She adjusted the mirror. "Do you care if I take this out on the open road?"

"I'd be disappointed if you didn't."

Kate made her way down University Avenue toward the Central Avenue intersection where she would pick up Highway 65.

"My first car was a stick," she said. "I wanted to pull my hair out when I was learning, but now that I drive an automatic, I really miss it. We did a lot of driving back home, and my girlfriends and I spent many Saturday nights driving too fast down dark country roads, looking for the party. I'm from

Indiana. Zionsville to be specific. It's near Indianapolis. I moved here for my undergrad at the University of Minnesota and then stayed for law school. My parents and my brother Chad still live there. Or did you already know that?"

He gave her a look that said *Aren't you cute?*

Kate chuckled at her naiveté. "Of course. What was I thinking?"

"Any plans to move back?"

"Probably not. I like it here, and I see my family often. Either they come to visit me or I fly home. What about you? How does a native Texan end up in frigid Minnesota?"

"I was just passing through and decided to stay. I own a computer security company and work from home, so I can live anywhere I want."

"That's fantastic!" Kate tried to hide her relief at the revelation that Ian was involved in something other than illegal activities, but she wasn't very convincing.

"Oh my God," Ian said. "You really did think I was some kind of common thug."

Kate shook her head vehemently. "No I didn't."

"Yes you did," he said, mimicking her.

Kate decided to come clean. "Well, can you blame me? You're all 'I hack whoever and whatever I want,' and then you swoop in with bags of cash which you freely admit you've stolen."

"I have my reasons for stealing from cyberthieves, but it isn't because I need their money. I have a substantial income of my own, which I obtain via highly legitimate means. And I like cash because it isn't traceable. You really shouldn't assume, Katie."

"So what is it that you do, exactly?"

"I specialize in penetration testing. Pentesting for short. I'm incredibly good at it."

"I've never heard of that. That sounds made up."

"I assure you it's a real thing. Penetration testing is when I hack away at you until I penetrate your defenses. Once I'm in, I go as deep as I can until I'm as far inside as you'll let me go."

"Are we still talking about your company?"

"Aren't we?"

"You said 'penetrate *my* defenses.' And 'get in as deep as you can until you're as far inside me as I'll let you go.'"

"Freudian slip. I meant that companies hire me to penetrate their computer systems so I can identify their weaknesses. I wonder how tricky you'll be."

Kate bit her lip to keep from smiling. "You just did it again."

"Really? That's interesting. Anyway, once I show a client all the alarming ways their computer systems can be compromised, I charge them an exorbitant amount of money to make sure it won't ever happen."

"And they don't mind paying it?"

"People will pay any price when you exploit their weaknesses."

"If you're a legitimate business owner, then what's with all the cloak and dagger? Like not telling me your last name, which is just silly, by the way."

"It's not in a hacker's nature to share personal information. Anonymity is kind of our thing. And sometimes I hack into things I'm not supposed to," he said. "For fun."

"How shocking."

"And *occasionally* I find myself in a bit of hot water, which I prefer to keep other people out of."

"So the anonymity is to protect the people you associate with."

"In a manner of speaking, yes."

"You could have just told me that."

"I've already said too much. For some reason, being around you is like swallowing truth serum. Your beauty disarms me."

"Thank goodness I possess at least one weapon I can use against you."

"Your legs are another."

Kate laughed. "I'll have to remember that."

She increased her speed, waiting until she'd redlined the engine before shifting into fourth. She loved that sound, and there were few things more fun than driving a fast car. She could see out of the corner of her eye that Ian was watching her. It was equal parts unnerving and exhilarating.

She passed the other cars, weaving expertly in and out of the lanes, loving the way the car handled. When the traffic finally thinned out, she pressed down on the gas pedal until the speedometer was just under seventy-five.

"Come on, you can do better than that," Ian said. "How long has it been since you've had a speeding ticket?"

"Years. I can't remember the last time I got pulled over."

"Then what are you waiting for? If you get caught, I'll pay the fine. As long as you keep it under a hundred, you won't lose your license."

Kate loved to listen to loud music when she drove on the highway, and listening to something old-school—Aerosmith, maybe—would be really fun in the Shelby. Purists balked at adding a stereo, but most replica owners installed them anyway, even if it did reduce the true Shelby experience. Ian's car had no radio of any kind in the dash. It didn't even look like there was a place for one.

"You're sure about this?" Kate asked, already easing the gas pedal toward the floor. Whoever built this car had likely spent a lot of time on it, and she was surprised Ian wasn't acting more concerned.

"Positive." He reached over and yanked on her seatbelt to make sure it was tight.

Kate accelerated. There was a fairly empty stretch of road ahead, so she kept her foot on the pedal as the speedometer inched toward eighty-five, ninety, ninety-five. She realized that music would have actually detracted from the experience because the sound of the engine, loud and raw and unbridled, was all she needed.

There were two cars up ahead, one in front of her on the left and one on the right. Luckily, neither of them were police cars because Kate flew around the first and, as soon as she passed it, had to immediately swerve back into the other lane. She lost herself in the sensation, feeling more invigorated than she had in a long time.

"Go, baby, go," Ian shouted.

She continued on that way, passing cars when she encountered them. When she checked her speed, she experienced a moment of exhilarating panic because the needle hovered just below one hundred and ten. A little voice inside her head warned that she would surely lose her license if she came upon a policeman. She told that voice to shut up. Besides, she walked to work.

Kate spotted a cluster of taillights up ahead, which would leave her no room to pass, and she reluctantly began decelerating. She was surprised at how *slow* ninety felt as she brought her speed down to a more acceptable level. A few miles down the road, she pointed to an exit sign which listed several options for gas and food. "Shall I pull off here?"

"That depends. Have you satisfied your need for speed?"

She laughed. "For now. But you might have created a monster."

"Come on over to the dark side, Katie. I'll save you a seat next to me."

Kate nosed the car into a parking space at a restaurant whose sign promised the best charcuterie in Minneapolis.

She followed Ian inside, and after the waitress seated them, Kate said, "That was absolutely incredible."

"I agree. Watching you drive my car was one of the hottest things I've ever seen. The only thing that would have made it better is if you'd been wearing a skirt. But even in jeans it was awesome."

"Driving your car while wearing a skirt might be difficult."

He looked perplexed. "Not if it was short enough."

"You're shameless."

Ian opened his menu. "When do you need to be back?"

"I don't. I left Helena in charge. She's closing up today."

"I promised you lunch over an hour ago. You must be starving by now."

"A little. Should we see if they're right about the charcuterie? There's a sharing platter." Kate had fallen in love with the dish—basically an assortment of salty and tangy cured meat—in college.

"Drives fast, likes meat. I might have to marry you."

Kate looked at him pointedly. "You forgot pretty."

Ian started laughing. "You're like a breath of fresh air. Really you are."

They gave their order to the waitress and asked for tall draft beers to go along with their meal.

"One of the conditions of this date was that you would no longer be accessing my computer. Have you kept your word?" Kate had googled whether she'd be able to detect the presence of a backdoor, but she'd learned it would require more technical knowledge than she currently possessed. And if the hacker who'd put it there was halfway competent, it would be nearly impossible.

"Katie," he said, looking offended. "Of course I have."

"I hope so, because my next browsing session is going to be epic."

His eyes grew big and he leaned forward. "Tell me."

"No."

"It's going to be something dirty, isn't it?"

She gave him her best sultry look. "Boy, is it ever." Kate was actually planning on watching hair tutorials on YouTube, but she couldn't resist the opportunity to tease him a little.

"You can't just dangle things like that in front of me. I'm not that strong."

"You'll have to be. That was our agreement."

"Okay. But you didn't say anything about staying out of your dating account, so I might have made a few enhancements to your profile picture."

"Yes, I saw that and updated my bio accordingly."

The waitress set down their beers, and after Kate took a drink, she said, "How did you remain so calm when I was going one hundred and ten miles an hour?"

He shrugged. "I don't know. You seemed to know what you were doing. Why, would you not be as calm in the passenger seat if I was driving that fast?"

"No. Not even close."

"Don't you trust me?"

Kate shook her head. "Not yet." Strangely, despite the things Ian had done to her that he shouldn't have, she did trust him a little. He'd made sure that Kate's date with Kent didn't happen, thus moving her permanently out of harm's way. For that she was grateful.

"Someday you'll sit beside me and know you can trust me no matter how fast we're going. I mean that," he said, and Kate thought it wasn't only his driving he was referring to.

After they'd stuffed themselves full of prosciutto, duck and chicken liver pâté, serrano ham, and spicy chorizo, Ian paid the bill and led Kate to the parking lot where he tucked her into the passenger seat of his car. It was late afternoon by then, and the November sky had started to darken. Kate was conscious of Ian's movements, especially when he shifted gears. The interior of the car was small, and she couldn't stop thinking about how near his hand was to her thigh when he was holding the gearshift. She momentarily forgot she was supposed to be keeping him at arm's length because all she wanted right then was for him to come a little closer.

He won't even tell you his last name, she reminded herself.

When he pulled up in front of her building, he turned off the car, walked around to Kate's side, and opened her door. "Just so you know, I'm not willing to sit outside this time."

"I'm not either. It's too cold."

When they reached Kate's door, she noticed the Victoria's Secret package lying on the floor in front of it.

"Sweaters!"

"And other things," Ian reminded her.

"I'm scared of what I might find."

"You shouldn't be. I have impeccable taste."

She turned toward Ian and smiled. "Thank you. This has been a really great first date."

"Hasn't it? We've gotten to know each other a little better. I let you drive the hell out of my car. I have not tried to talk you into a threesome, nor have I offered you any cocaine. Honestly, I've been a perfect gentleman. Admit it. You like me. You might not trust me yet, but you're drawn to me like a moth to a flame. It's my mind that turns you on."

What he said was true. Ian was an enigma, a puzzle with a thousand pieces. She'd never met a man who fascinated her the way he did, not that she was ready to let him know it.

"I like really simple men," she said. "In fact, the simpler they are, the more I like them. They're very malleable."

"Malleable."

"Easily influenced. It means I can bend them to my will."

"I know what the word means even when I'm not wearing my smart glasses. But there's no way you could ever convince me you like simple men. I think Stuart was simple, and that's why you're not with him anymore." He moved closer until Kate's back was pressed up against her door. "Would you like to know what turns me on?"

"No." *God, yes.*

"Sure you would. I can see the wheels turning in that pretty little head of yours. You're a risk taker, and nothing revs my engine like a smart, beautiful, *fearless* woman. Any woman who is fearless behind the wheel is going to be open to all kinds of experiences. You left Stuart and you quit your safe job because it wasn't enough for you. You've only scratched the surface of what your life will become. It's the *possibilities* in your future that excite you."

It was unsettling to realize how quickly he'd figured her out. How could he have known that every word of that was true? She looked into his green eyes and said, "Maybe you're right."

Ian took off his glasses and slid them into the pocket of his jacket.

"I like those," she said. "Put them back on."

"They'll only be in the way when I kiss you."

"Who said we were going to kiss?"

"I did. Katie, you must pay closer attention. Besides, this is the end of our first official date. Why wouldn't we kiss? Sharing a kiss is quite common at this stage."

"I know how dating works." Although truthfully, she was a bit rusty and hadn't kissed anyone since Stuart.

"This hallway is awfully bright. I would prefer more romantic lighting, like the kind inside your apartment."

"You don't get to come in again until the second date."

"The only thing I took away from that statement is that we're going to have a second date."

Kate smiled.

It really *was* incredibly bright in the hallway. Kate almost wished Ian hadn't told her he was going to kiss her and that it was a bit darker, because she was suddenly hit with a bout of first-date-kiss nerves that made her fidget.

"I'll just wait until you stop moving."

She made herself stand still. He slid his hands underneath her jaw, and his fingers came to rest behind her ears while his thumbs grazed her cheek. His first kiss was soft and gentle and only lasted a few seconds. He pulled back a few inches and came in again, giving her another soft kiss. The third was firmer, more aggressive, and he dipped his tongue lightly into her mouth. The fourth was soft again, leaving Kate in a heady and intoxicating state of anticipation about what the next kiss would be like. Number five was almost her undoing because Ian pressed his body closer to hers and gave her a deep, open-mouthed kiss while circling her tongue with his. When he finally pulled back, it took her a moment to regulate her breathing. She was holding on to his neck rather tightly because her legs felt like Jell-O.

"You seem a bit wobbly, Katie."

"I've got to hand it to you. Your kissing skills almost make up for your shortcomings."

"I have shortcomings? Really?"

"A couple, yes."

"I'd promise to work on them, but we both know I'm not going to."

He waited until she unlocked her door, and then he bent down and picked up the package from Victoria's Secret. "Bet you'll have this open before I get to my car."

That showed how little he knew. She had it open before he reached the elevator.

CHAPTER SEVEN

KATE HAD ARRANGED TO MEET the girls for brunch at Aster Café at eleven. Their last group e-mail had been circulating for over a month as the three of them tried to come up with a mutually agreeable time to get together. While Kate's schedule was fairly flexible, theirs was not. Brunch had already been moved three times.

Kate arrived at eleven, Paige was ten minutes late, and Audrey didn't join them until ten minutes after that.

"I'm sorry, I'm sorry, I'm sorry," Audrey said as she rushed up to the table, leaned down to hug them both, and plopped into her chair.

Kate and Paige assured her it was okay. That was the way brunch usually began.

Their waiter, who had been hovering in the background, approached. "Can I interest anyone in a mimosa?"

Paige groaned. "I would love *several*, but I've got to head into work to go over depositions as soon as we're done."

"Same here," Audrey said.

This was hardly a surprise because when Kate was still practicing law, she used to work the same long hours they did. If she was going to enjoy the benefits of working less, she needed to find some girlfriends who didn't work seventy hours a week.

"How about you?" the waiter asked Kate.

Even though a mimosa sounded wonderful, it would hardly be any fun drinking one by herself, so Kate said, "I'll just have orange juice."

"You look fantastic, Kate," Paige said. "I love your outfit."

"Thanks." Kate was wearing a pair of black leggings tucked into high-heeled black boots that came up over the knee and laced up the sides with black ribbons. She'd paired them with one of the sweaters Ian had bought her. Made of the softest cashmere, it was tunic length and a beautiful dark plum color. The back had a low scoop neck, so Kate had worn her hair in a messy French twist she'd learned how to do when she'd watched the hair tutorials on YouTube.

When she'd opened the Victoria's Secret package right there on the floor just inside her door, she'd been delighted. Ian didn't know how much Kate had wanted those sweaters and that the reason there were items left in her shopping cart was because she'd given all her disposable income to the food pantry and could no longer afford them, at least not that month. In addition to the cashmere sweater and the two others that were already in the cart, Ian *had* added another sweater, a gorgeous white cable pullover. He'd also bought her a pair of pink flannel pajamas with white snowflakes. They were soft and warm, and she loved them. Of course, Ian being Ian, he'd also bought her a black satin and Chantilly lace babydoll nightie that tied in front and came with a matching thong. It was actually very pretty, and when Kate tried it on, she felt incredibly sexy.

Kate turned her attention to her friends' outfits and offered her own compliments. Paige had dressed in a manner similar to Kate, but Audrey had gone one better and was wearing a ribbed sweater dress that left nothing to the imagination. Dressing for brunch was almost a competitive sport, and one they engaged in willingly. For Paige and Audrey—both attorneys at large, downtown firms—it was an opportunity to dress less formally, a bit funkier than they could during the week. For Kate, who wore jeans on a daily basis, it was the chance to dress up and add some glamour to her otherwise very casual wardrobe.

In an effort not to make Kate feel left out, her friends overcompensated, asking a multitude of questions about the food pantry. Thanks to Ian, she was able to report that things were going very well.

"And how are you getting along without Stuart?" Paige asked gently.

Paige had gotten married last year, and Audrey was engaged. Kate was genuinely happy for both of them. She'd long since worked her way through the various stages of her and Stuart's breakup. At first she'd gone through the crying, self-doubt stage, wondering if she'd made a huge mistake. That was followed by quiet resignation and contemplation, accompanied by a considerable amount of wine. Then she'd completed the healing stage, which allowed her to arrive where she was now, which was the cautiously optimistic about the future stage.

"I'm doing fine, really. I've actually met someone new."

Audrey leaned in. "Do tell."

"He works with computers. Really, really handsome. It's fairly new, but it's going well."

"What's his name?" Paige asked.

"Ian."

"Ian what?"

"Ian…"

Shit.

She was making it seem like Ian was make-believe. Stalling, she put her spoon in her mouth, and after she swallowed, she said, "Smith."

Smith?

Jesus.

"I don't know anyone by that name," Paige said.

"He's new in town." Kate hadn't heard from Ian since they'd gone to lunch on Monday. On Thursday she'd admitted to herself that she was looking forward to seeing him again. By Saturday morning, she'd started listening—and hoping—for a knock on her apartment door.

The rest of the time passed in a blur of catching up on everything that had transpired since they'd last met for brunch. They lingered a while after paying the bill. Kate had the rest of the day to fill and was in no particular hurry to leave the restaurant. But all too soon her friends looked at their phones and groaned when they noticed the time.

"I have to go to work if I hope to get out of there before midnight," Audrey said.

"Me too," Paige said.

They told Kate good-bye, accompanied by a flurry of hugs and promises to get together soon. A few minutes later Kate put on her coat and walked out the door into the brilliant sunshine. She turned the corner onto her street, then stopped short when she saw a flash of blue. Ian's car was parked at the curb, and he was leaning up against it, smiling.

Her Sunday had just gotten a whole lot more interesting.

She walked up to him. "Are you ever not smiling?"

"Why wouldn't I be smiling? It's awesome being me."

"Been waiting long?"

"About an hour. I'd almost given up on you."

"I was at brunch with the girls."

He checked her out, not bothering to hide the way his gaze traveled slowly from her head to her feet. "You look amazing. I am fascinated by those boots."

Kate unbelted her trench coat. "What about my sweater? A friend bought several of them for me."

"It's very nice, and that is an excellent color on you. What else did this friend buy you?"

"He bought me some pajamas. I love them."

"He thought you might. Was there anything else?"

"There was a black babydoll nightie."

"Did it fit?"

"It fit perfectly. I'm going to save it for a special evening should there be one in my future."

"Oh there will be, Katie. He'll make sure of it." He opened the passenger door. "I was wondering if you have plans for the rest of the day."

Kate got in, and after Ian closed the door, he walked around to the driver's side and slid behind the wheel.

"That depends," she said. "What did you have in mind?"

He started the car. "You'll see."

What Ian had in mind was drinking champagne in the park under a canopy of trees before they lost the last of their fall leaves. It was a perfect day to be outside. The fifty-degree temperature was slightly above normal for that time of year, and their coats would keep them warm enough to enjoy one last hurrah before the sleet and snow arrived. Winter was coming, but on that day they could almost convince themselves otherwise.

Before he'd locked the car, Ian had reached into the small trunk and retrieved a shopping bag. Now he led Kate off the park's walking path to a grassy area and took a blanket out of the bag. After he shook it out, he and Kate sat down. Then Ian pulled out a bottle of champagne and expertly popped the cork.

"You do realize that if you keep plying me with alcohol, I may develop an *actual* drinking problem?"

Ian sighed. "The health of your liver is definitely a concern of mine."

"I'm sure it is."

He reached in for two flutes, filled one, and handed it to Kate.

She leaned toward him. "What else do you have in that bag of tricks?"

"Chocolate-dipped strawberries." He took out the container of strawberries and fed one to her, tossing the stem over his shoulder after she bit down.

"While I appreciate your being the polar opposite of Kent, I'm afraid I'm not very hungry."

"I wish I'd known about brunch. Not having access to your computer means I have no idea what you're up to these days. However, I want this to count as an actual date—our second, I might add—and not just a quick outing in the park."

She laughed. "I suppose that will be okay. I wouldn't want to throw off your schedule."

He took a drink of his champagne. "How has your weekend been so far?"

"Good."

"Do anything fun?"

"I met some friends for happy hour on Friday, and then I had a date on Saturday."

"You had a date?"

"You sound so surprised. A man actually messaged me on my dating account, despite my less-than-attractive profile picture. He read my bio and asked me out. I had to say yes. He did seem a bit confused when I showed up."

"That's because he'd just hit the online dating jackpot. Where did you go?"

"Lunch and a matinee."

"And?"

"I had a good time. He was very nice." That much was true. Justin had been courteous, funny, and kind. He was also Stuart 2.0, and Kate had felt nothing. Not one single spark. She let him down gently with a handshake at the end of their date.

"I bet he wasn't as charming as me."

"Do you know who else was supposedly very charming? Ted Bundy."

"I may be a thief, but I would never harm you, Katie." He said it so softly and sincerely that the quip she'd been about to make about Ted Bundy promising the same thing died on her lips.

"No," she said. "He was not as charming as you."

When Kate's glass was empty, he took it, and Kate thought he meant to refill it. But he set down the empty flutes, caught her chin between his thumb and index finger, and tilted her face up to his for a champagne-flavored kiss, closing his eyes right before their lips met. Though they were in a clearing off the main path, it was still a public place where anyone could come upon them. Kate didn't care. She kissed him back and ran her fingers through his hair because she'd wanted to do that since the day she met him. It felt soft and luxurious.

"You really know how to turn an average Sunday into a great day, don't you?" Kate said when they came up for air.

Ian reached for the champagne bottle and refilled their glasses. "Are you having a great day?"

"I am. When I was at brunch, the girls were complaining about having to spend the rest of the afternoon cooped up inside working, the same way I used to. But instead of working, I get to stroll the sunlit paths of a magical urban forest and drink champagne with a charismatic, green-eyed man."

Ian smiled. "And to think I had to convince you to give me a chance."

"Astonishing, I know."

"And now?" He paused in front of Kate's mouth with another strawberry.

"You're growing on me," she said and opened her mouth.

Kate insisted on feeding Ian a strawberry every time he fed her one until finally they were gone. There was more kissing and even fewer inhibitions on Kate's part when the flutes were empty again. Ian was currently giving Kate a kiss that she'd labeled the number three because it resembled the third kiss he'd given her at the end of their first date. It was a little more demanding than the others, but still slightly restrained. It hinted at what his kisses might be like if he were to stop exerting control over them. That thought made Kate's stomach explode with butterflies.

Drowsy from the champagne, Ian lay down on the blanket and coaxed Kate into lying down beside him and using his arm for a pillow, which she did. The sun was bright and Kate hadn't brought her sunglasses, so she closed her eyes. She wished she could take a nap right there on the blanket with Ian.

"I'm so comfortable," she announced.

"My arm is asleep," Ian said.

Kate immediately tried to move, but Ian laughed and encircled her with his other arm so that he was spooning her. "I'm just messing with you."

"Stop spooning me," Kate said, rolling over to face him. "This is a public park."

"How is this any more appropriate?" Ian asked, pulling her closer so they were pressed up against each other.

"It really isn't," Kate admitted.

"Kiss me."

Kate obliged willingly and then tucked her head against his neck. "You sure seem to enjoy kissing."

"What's not to like?"

"Nothing. I love kissing. I'm just not used to it. Stuart wasn't really a kisser. It was mostly a means to an end for him."

"Stuart is nuts."

Kate looked into his eyes. "Are you ever going to tell me your last name?"

"No," he said. His tone was quite serious. Then he kissed her again.

Around four o'clock, when the temperature had started to drop a little and the sun went behind the clouds and stayed there, Kate started to shiver. Her hands were getting cold, and they decided to call it a day.

"Ready?" Ian said.

He held out his arm and Kate took it.

When Ian pulled up in front of Kate's building, he turned off the car, and she waited for him to come around and open her door.

"Would you like to come in?" Kate asked.

"I have to. It's our second date. You can give me the grand tour since you barely let me inside last time. And don't worry, I won't overstay my welcome. A project I'm working on for one of my clients has monopolized my entire weekend, and I'm still not done."

Once they were inside, Kate showed Ian around. Her one-bedroom apartment was tiny in comparison to the pricier, two-bedroom apartment she'd lived in for three years with Stuart, but she loved it. She'd picked out the furniture by herself, purchasing a couch that had an attached chaise, a soft oversized chair, and a plush, brightly colored fake-fur rug that gave her living room a funky, comfortable feel.

"Very nice," Ian said.

They sat down on the couch.

"You know, this refusal to tell me your last name is making things awkward for me," Kate said. "At brunch I had to refer to you as Ian Smith."

"Smith?" he said with mock indignation. "Is that the best you could come up with? Why not just call me Ian Doe?"

"You were almost Ian Spoon because that's what I happened to be holding in my hand when the question came up. The girls probably think I've resorted to inventing imaginary suitors to help me get past my breakup with Stuart."

"Could an imaginary suitor do this?" Ian asked, giving Kate what she decided to dub the number six, which was deep, openmouthed kissing with tongue while cradling her face after he'd pulled her onto his lap.

"Good God, your eyes are crossed," Ian said when it was over.

She held her finger to his lips. "Shhhh… no one likes a braggart."

He smiled and bit it gently. Kate liked being held on Ian's lap, so she stayed where she was. Ian, no slouch in the proximity-awareness department, leaned in again. This time he brushed aside the tendrils of hair that had escaped her French twist and gave her a series of soft kisses that started below her ear and continued down her neck. Kate leaned her head back against the couch to give him better access, which he took full advantage of by turning the kissing into the most erotic nibbling. If she wasn't careful, Ian might try to kiss her right into bed, and she wasn't ready for that yet. Reluctantly, she climbed off his lap.

"Where are you going?"

"No one likes a braggart, but no one likes a tease either."

Ian grudgingly announced that he needed to go. "I would rather stay and kiss you some more and then take you to dinner, but I really must get back to my project."

"That's okay. I'm still stuffed full of strawberries." She walked him to the door.

"Are you free Friday night? Around six thirty? I'd like for us to go on our third date. And you know what that means."

"I do happen to be available, and I'm well aware of what *sometimes* happens on the third date. But for your information, we're not quite there yet."

"We're not?"

"No."

"Are you sure? Because I feel like we could be."

Kate pretended to think about it. "Positive."

"That's okay. I'll be happy as long as I can still kiss you. I'm really very patient, Katie." He kissed her again—deep, lingering—as if to show her just how much he enjoyed it.

Before he turned to go he said, "So are you?"

"Am I what?"

"Past your breakup with Stuart?"

Kate knew she was more than likely just something for Ian to play with. A girl to rile up, an interesting diversion at best. By his own admission, he didn't stick around in any city for very long. But she was glad he'd asked, because it was the first indication he'd given her that he possessed any vulnerability at all. Very few men wanted to get involved with a woman only to watch her return to her old boyfriend because she still harbored feelings for him.

"Yes, Ian Smith. I can assure you that I am."

CHAPTER EIGHT

SOMEONE WAS BANGING ON THE door. Kate buried her head under the pile of blankets on the couch and prayed they'd go away. She'd started feeling sick after she got home from the food pantry on Thursday and had spent the rest of the afternoon and evening on the couch coughing. Things had taken a decidedly worse turn overnight, and she'd been awake—and miserable—since around three that morning. In an attempt to ease the tightness in her lungs, she'd taken a long, steamy shower at four, but it hadn't helped much.

The knocking became banging. Slowly she made her way toward the door, zigzagging dizzily across the room. "What?" she croaked.

"It's Ian. Open up."

She managed to get the door open but felt light-headed and reached for the doorjamb to steady herself. She missed it completely and pitched forward into the hallway. Ian caught her with a soft oomph, swung her up in his arms, and kicked the door shut with his foot. She laid her cheek against his chest.

"You're sizzling, sweetness. I can feel the heat through my shirt. When's the last time you took something for that fever?" He laid her down gently on the couch.

"What time is it?"

"A little after nine."

"Five maybe? I've been counting the minutes until I could take more Motrin. I think I can have another dose now."

She started to sit up, but Ian gently eased her back down. "I'll get it. You stay here."

That sounded like a fabulous idea to Kate. Horizontal felt marginally less wretched than vertical. "It's on the kitchen counter."

Ian returned with a tall glass of ice water and some Motrin. Kate was suddenly thirstier than she could remember being in a very long time. Ian put his arm behind her shoulders and helped her rise to a sitting position. After she swallowed the pills, she drained the glass and said, "I'm a level-five biohazard. You should get out now while you still can."

"That's ridiculous," he said. "I'm impervious to germs. I rarely get sick."

"No kissing," she said as she fired off three giant sneezes that made her eyes water and her nose run. "I'm a mess, and I do not feel pretty."

He plucked a Kleenex from the box on the coffee table and handed it to her. "Fair enough."

"Why are you here? Our date wasn't until this evening." Because she had no way to get ahold of him, she'd planned on canceling when he showed up at her door and witnessed for himself the condition she was in.

"I went to the food pantry to make sure we were still on for tonight, and Helena told me you called in sick."

"If we communicated by phone like normal people, you could have saved yourself a trip," she said and then became engulfed by a coughing attack so violent it sent daggers of pain shooting through her chest and head.

"This is not a wasted trip. Tell me what you need."

In addition to the pile of blankets she'd wrapped herself in, Kate was wearing the flannel pajamas Ian had bought her and a pair of slippers, but she still couldn't get warm. "I'm freezing. Can you get the comforter from my bed?"

Ian retrieved the comforter and tucked it around her shoulders and under her legs. Then he sat down next to her. "Lay your head in my lap."

Kate did as he said. She didn't care that she wasn't wearing makeup or that her hair was still damp from her shower and drying in a mess of tangles. She was more miserable than she could remember being in a long time.

She closed her eyes as Ian lightly stroked her head. "That feels good."

When the Motrin kicked in, her shivering subsided, but she felt weary clear down to her bones.

"Sleep, Katie," Ian said, and there was nothing Kate wanted to do more.

When she woke up three hours later, he was still there. There was a fire burning in the fireplace, and he was sitting on the chaise end of the couch, typing on a laptop. She poked him with her foot.

He stopped typing, looked over, and smiled. "How's my patient?"

Kate still felt awful, but she said, "Okay."

"You don't sound okay," he said. "You sound miserable."

"I feel a little better than when you arrived. I think the nap helped." Kate's voice was so raspy Ian had to lean in to hear her. "Did you leave?"

"Only for a short while. I ran home to get my laptop. I figured I could work and keep an eye on you at the same time."

"Do you live far from here?"

"I live downtown. I also dropped by the pharmacy because you were almost out of Motrin and the only other medicine I found in your kitchen was a half-empty bottle of NyQuil that expired two years ago. I wasn't exactly sure what you needed. Usually I turn to the Internet for answers, but in this case I decided a pharmacist would be my best bet."

"You spoke to a pharmacist?"

"Yes. He said you're more than likely suffering from a viral upper respiratory illness but warned me that I should take you to the doctor if your condition worsens or you have trouble breathing. Are you having trouble breathing?"

"Not at the moment."

"Good. He also hooked me up with everything you could possibly need. It looks like a Walgreens exploded in your kitchen."

Ian was wearing a sweatshirt and well-worn jeans, and he'd kicked off his shoes. She liked the way he looked stretched out on the chaise: comfortable, like he planned on staying a while.

"You're really great, you know," she said.

"Are you just now noticing? I'm hurt, Katie. Really." But he smiled when he said it, and Kate had to admit that for all Ian's faults—faults he made no excuses for and that Kate realized he had no intention of ever working on—he was more than willing to compensate in other ways.

She told herself she could do a lot worse.

Ian ordered a pizza for lunch and tried to get Kate to eat some off his plate, but the thought of food repulsed her. "If you're not going to eat, then you need to drink," he said. "And don't get excited, because wine is not one of the options."

He went into the kitchen and returned with two glasses, one filled with orange juice and one with ice water. He set them down on the coffee table next to an assortment of medicine, a new box of Kleenex, and an ear thermometer.

"You seriously bought an ear thermometer?"

"Yes, and I've been dying to try it out. Come closer."

Kate leaned over and Ian stuck the thermometer in her ear until it beeped.

"Just under a hundred. Could be better, but I'll take it."

Kate picked up the orange juice and took a sip. "You play doctor very well."

"For the record, I play doctor a lot differently than this. If you let me rub Vicks VapoRub on your chest or give you a sponge bath, I could show you what I mean. It would be win-win, Katie."

"Thanks, but I'll hold off on both for now."

"I'll be sure to ask again later."

Kate glanced over at his laptop. All she could see were lines of code, which made no sense to her at all. "What are you working on?"

"World domination, obviously." He looked over at Kate and grinned. "When I'm done with that, maybe I'll swing by Victoria's Secret and buy you another pair of pajamas."

Kate took another drink of her orange juice, set the glass on the coffee table, and curled up next to Ian with the blankets wrapped tightly around her. "I probably wouldn't hate that."

They spent the rest of the afternoon and evening that way, with Ian working and Kate not feeling well enough to do much of anything but watch daytime TV. He checked Kate's temperature around dinnertime and discovered it had risen to one hundred and three. He gave her more Motrin, and she snuggled on the couch next to him while his fingers tapped on the keyboard. He was wearing his glasses, and Kate decided it was definitely a look she preferred. A while later someone knocked on the door.

"I ordered Thai online," Ian said, setting his laptop on the coffee table. "Do you think you can eat something?"

She shook her head and then burrowed back into the blankets. Around ten, Ian convinced Kate to go to bed. He picked up the box of Kleenex and followed her to the bedroom, setting it down on the nightstand while she crawled underneath the covers. She ached, her head was throbbing, her chest hurt from coughing, and she could hardly hold her eyes open.

"I'll be right back," he said.

When he returned, he had Kate's comforter and he covered her and made sure it was tucked in tight. The last thing she thought of was hoping Ian would turn everything off on his way out.

She slept until almost nine the next morning and awakened feeling a little better than when Ian had put her to bed, which meant she probably wasn't going to get any worse. He'd left a glass of water and two pills on her nightstand with a note that said "Take these as soon as you wake up." She swallowed them, aware that the ache in her body was still present but that it had lessened considerably. A hot bath would do wonders for alleviating some of the remaining pain.

In the bathroom, she poured in a generous amount of bubble bath and brushed her teeth while the tub filled. *I don't look too horrible*, she thought as she pulled her hair into a high ponytail. Her face wasn't quite as pale, and the hot water would pink up her cheeks a little more.

She undressed and lowered herself into a cloud of bubbles. After she soaped herself, she leaned back and sighed. Ian crept into her thoughts and she smiled. It had been a long time since a man had taken care of her like that. Stuart had hated being sick, so Kate usually quarantined herself in their spare bedroom until she got over the worst of whatever illness she'd come down with. The way Ian had swept into her apartment and taken charge, and the genuine concern he'd shown, made Kate pine for him in a way she knew was dangerous. He wasn't the kind of man who stayed in one place too long, and she doubted any woman would ever be enough to make him want to settle down.

Kate closed her eyes and allowed herself a daydream in which she and Ian were a couple. He would walk in the door at the end of the day and kiss her senseless. Then he'd undress her right in the kitchen and carry her off to the bedroom for a round of hot, steamy sex. Afterward he'd pour them a drink and they'd eat dinner in front of the fireplace. They would cuddle and have round two on the living room floor. She felt certain Ian would be an excellent lover: Confident but not selfish. Tender but not boring. As she pictured his large, capable hands stroking her breasts, her fingers drifted toward her chest. She was still awfully worn out, but she wondered if she might possibly find the energy to touch herself while pretending it was him pleasuring her.

Ian shattered her reverie when he walked through the door of the bathroom. "Your couch is incredibly comfortable. I was sleeping so deeply I didn't even hear you run the bath. You took the pills, I see. That's good. You need to stay one step ahead of the fever."

Speechless, her mouth hung open. *I am naked, and Ian is in my bathroom. I was contemplating touching my own breasts.*

"I know you've alluded to my boundary issues," he said, sitting down on the edge of the tub. "And this is probably a shining example, but I wanted to make sure you were okay. Passing out in the bathtub or shower is one of the leading causes of death while bathing. And I can't see anything because of all the bubbles. Actually, that's a blatant lie because I can pretty much make out your entire left nipple. The suds are a little disparate in that area."

Frantically, Kate raked the biggest mound of bubbles—which were down by her feet and doing her no good at all—toward her chest. "Get out! Get out, get out, get out!"

He smiled and said, "I'm going. Now that I know you're okay, I'll just start the coffee. Please do carry on with whatever it was you were about to do."

Once Kate had dried off and dressed in her comfiest sweats, she stomped into the living room and stood in front of Ian, who was sitting on the couch drinking coffee and typing on his laptop.

"Repeat after me: I, Ian."

"I, Ian."

"Will never ever, ever, ever, ever, ever, ever, ever, ever walk in on Kate in the bathroom again unless specifically invited to do so."

"Will never ever, ever—how many evers was that?"

"Ever, infinity."

"Ever, infinity, walk in on Katie in the bathroom again unless specifically invited to do so." Ian took a drink of his coffee. "I feel like that last part means the possibility of a future invitation exists, which is encouraging."

He handed Kate a mug of steaming dark roast, and she sat down beside him.

When he started to speak, she held up her hand. "I have not had enough coffee to deal with you yet."

Ian turned his attention back to his laptop and waited until Kate took the last drink from her mug.

"You know that saying, 'Act now, apologize later?' I'm pretty much the poster boy."

Kate looked at Ian. "You think?"

"I'm truly sorry. Is there anything I can do to make us even?"

"Well, I'd threaten to walk in on you in the shower, but we both know how that would turn out." Kate handed her empty mug to Ian, who wisely returned to the kitchen to refill it.

When he came back with her coffee, she said, "I thought you left after you put me to bed."

"First of all, I can't lock your door from the outside without a key, and there's no way I'd let you sleep in an unsecured apartment. Second, what kind of man would leave a woman alone when she was in such rough shape? I was worried. I even checked on you in the middle of the night. You were a hot, snoring, drooling mess, but other than that you seemed okay."

"I did tell you yesterday that I wasn't feeling especially pretty."

"Even when you're sick, you're a solid eight point five."

"How very sweet in a completely sexist way."

"When you're not sick you're an eleven."

She took a drink of her coffee to hide her smile. Ian walked over to the fireplace, crouched down, and began stacking logs. When the fire crackled to life, Kate wished her nose wasn't so stuffy because the wood-burning fireplace was one of the things she loved most about her apartment. The fireplace in her and Stuart's apartment had been gas, but in Kate's opinion nothing compared to the real thing.

Ian stood up and brushed his hands together. "Who were you thinking about in the bathtub, Katie?" he asked, coming over to stand in front of her.

"How can you be so sure I was thinking of someone?"

"Your left nipple was noticeably erect, the image of which is now burned into my brain. Therefore I deduced there might have been a man on your mind."

Her body temperature spiked suddenly, and it had nothing to do with a fever. "A girl needs to be able to keep some secrets from you."

"Well, he's a lucky man, whoever he is." He leaned down and kissed her on the forehead.

"I said no kissing!"

"Oh, relax. I'm going home to shower and pick up some food. Don't get off this couch." He jingled his car keys, threw on his coat, and said, "Back soon."

He returned an hour later, hair damp, wearing sweatpants and a long-sleeve T-shirt, which made him look especially cuddly to Kate. He was holding two large carryout bags. The sky had darkened even though it was only half past noon, and large white flakes were swirling through the air.

"First snowfall," Kate said. "We're supposed to get six inches."

"I heard," he said. "It's getting slick already. I have *got* to get the Shelby into storage." He set the bags on the kitchen counter. "Hungry?"

It had been over twenty-four hours since she'd eaten anything, and her stomach had started to rumble, which she took as a positive sign. "Yes."

Ian threw another log on the fire and gave it a poke before disappearing back into the kitchen. The clinking of silverware and dishes followed, and he returned with two plates on which sat a grilled cheese sandwich and a cup of chicken noodle soup.

"This is perfect," Kate said, taking one of the plates from him. "It's actually the only thing that sounds good to me."

"I thought it might. There's plenty more to heat up for dinner later. I brought a few other things too, in case you want something different. And just so you know, it's not exactly what I'd envisioned, but I'm still going to consider this our third date." He ducked back into the kitchen for a glass of orange juice for Kate and a Coke for himself.

"What did you have planned for us?" she asked.

"I'd made three reservations: seafood, steakhouse, Mexican. When I went to the food pantry yesterday morning, I was going to ask what you preferred. Then after dinner we were going to see a movie—one of those romantic comedies you like so much. On our way home we'd stop for drinks or dessert—your choice. Naturally you'd choose drinks, and I'd ply you with chardonnay in a halfhearted attempt to convince you to change your mind about what might happen at the end of our third date."

"I wouldn't have changed my mind, but that sounds like a great date. I'm sad it didn't happen."

"That's okay. We'll go as soon as you're feeling better."

The gently falling snow and the fire's glow made the room feel extra cozy. Kate sighed with pleasure. When they were done eating, she looked over at Ian and smiled. "You really are a superhero," she said. "I feel much better."

He pressed the back of his hand to her forehead. "I don't need that fancy ear thermometer to know your fever's gone, at least for now." He took their plates into the kitchen. When he returned, he had a phone in his hand.

"I brought you something."

Confused, Kate took the phone from Ian's outstretched hand. "I already have a cell."

"I only want you to call me from this one. My number is already programmed in."

"Will this ping the Batcave?" She kept her tone light, but she knew this signified a turning point in their relationship.

He smiled. "It will ping me, and I will always answer you."

Kate examined the phone. It looked like a smartphone, but it was stripped-down and very basic with no noticeable bells and whistles.

"It's got data and a halfway-decent camera," Ian said. "I can track it and wipe it remotely if you lose it or it gets stolen."

"It's disposable, isn't it?"

His smile faded and his expression turned serious. "Only because I'm overly cautious."

"It's okay."

"It's just that if you're sick or you need anything, I want you to be able to get ahold of me."

Kate nodded. "Ian, I understand." She had come to the realization that being with Ian meant accepting him on his terms, and for now she was willing to do that. She was starting to suspect there might come a day when she'd have to reevaluate and make a choice.

"You were right. If I wanted to reach you, I could have called. Next time I will."

She slid the phone into the pocket of her sweatpants and motioned toward the window. "Looks like it's really coming down out there. You should stay here again tonight. I'd hate for you to be out driving in this. The kissing ban is still firmly in place though."

"You don't know how much I'm looking forward to that being lifted."

"Me too, Ian. Me too."

Kate's fever came back that night, shortly after they finished eating dinner. She'd started shivering and her head throbbed. Ian watched as she reached for the bottle of Motrin on the coffee table, and as soon as she swallowed the pills, he pulled her toward him and stuck the thermometer in her ear.

"One hundred and two," he said. "At least it's not as high as yesterday." After wrapping her in a blanket, he pulled her head into his lap, stroking it the way he had the day before. His large, warm palm skimmed softly across her temple and she sighed.

He held the remote in his other hand, and he flipped through the channels, stopping on *Bridget Jones's Diary*. Pulling the blanket tighter around her, he draped his arm across her chest in a way that made her feel content. She'd never met a man who could be so infuriatingly intrusive yet so caring and tender.

When the movie ended, Kate slipped into the bedroom to get ready for bed. She also put on fresh sheets, and Ian appeared in the doorway as she was pulling on the last pillowcase.

"Comfortable as it may be, does this mean I'm not sleeping on the couch?"

"It's up to you. If I haven't gotten you sick already, sharing a bed with me will probably increase your chances of coming down with it. But if you do, I assure you I'll be happy to assume the role of doctor."

"Actually, I'd prefer you assume the role of nurse, in a low-cut uniform, of course. And I'm definitely signing up for the Vicks rubdown and the sponge bath."

"I never doubted that for a single minute."

"However, I show no sign of any symptoms, which I find somewhat disappointing because that means you may not need to attend to me. Shame."

"Damn your luck," Kate said, crawling underneath the covers. Being upright had tired her, and she was ready to return to a horizontal position.

After Ian locked up and shut off the lights and TV, he returned to the bedroom and stripped off his T-shirt but left his sweatpants on. He turned off the lamp on Kate's nightstand and climbed into bed. Nudging her onto her side, he spooned her, tucking an arm underneath her breasts. Kate might not have been feeling her best, but she wasn't dead, and the sensation of Ian's body pressed up against hers was more than a little arousing.

"Looks like I'm sleeping with you on the third date after all," he said.

"You got me," she said, laughing softly.

"If someone else messages you through that dating site and asks you out, are you going to say yes?"

Kate smiled in the darkness. "Maybe. But probably not." She pulled his arm in tighter and said, "Night, Ian."

When she woke up the next morning, he was gone. She hadn't felt him get out of bed, but she'd slept better than she had the previous two nights. Whether that was because she was finally on the mend or because he'd been next to her, she wasn't sure.

She padded into the kitchen to start the coffee. The phone he'd given her was sitting on the counter where she'd left it the night before. He'd sent her a text at 8:03 a.m.

Ian: *Felt your forehead before I left, and you were cool. I've got some work to do, but call me if you need anything. The streets are a mess, so don't leave the house. I'll know if you do. Just kidding. Not really.*

CHAPTER NINE

KATE AND HELENA WERE BUSY running through the checklist for Thanksgiving. "I feel bad abandoning you," Kate said, although she knew Helena was more than capable of running things on her own as she'd recently demonstrated when Kate was sick.

"Your family wants to see you," Helena said. "Go home and enjoy the holiday with them."

Kate's last visit home had been at Christmastime, and it had been almost six months since her mom and dad visited Kate in Minneapolis. She had a good relationship with her parents, and she missed them as much as they missed her. Though Kate was reluctant to leave the food pantry before a major holiday, they'd reached a compromise where Kate promised to come home for Thanksgiving if her parents would fly to Minneapolis for Christmas. Kate was leaving tomorrow, and she and Helena had a lot to get through before then.

Kate's clients needed so many things at this time of year. In addition to their regular food needs, they also sought out warm clothes, boots, and coats for their children. Kate had been holding clothing drives since early fall, and now that Minneapolis had received its first snowfall, she and Helena had begun outfitting people in winter gear at a steady rate.

A little boy pushed open the door and made a beeline for Kate. He was two years old and his name was Georgie. He was followed by his mother, Samantha, and two older sisters, seven-year-old Alex and nine-year-old Emily.

Samantha had been a regular of Kate's since she'd opened the food pantry. She was raising her kids alone after divorcing an abusive husband who had never paid a penny of child support. Even though Samantha worked as many hours as she could at her waitressing job, it was never enough to carry the four of them through to the end of the month. Kate was always there to make up the difference.

Because Kate had gotten to know the family well, she knew their sizes and had begun setting things aside as she received them. Fortunately, Georgie already had a winter coat, but Kate had held back a Curious George stocking cap with ear flaps and a pair of gently used navy snow boots.

She crouched down and slid the hat onto Georgie's head. "This monkey has your name!" Georgie laughed as Kate swapped his worn-out tennis shoes for the boots. "You look adorable." Georgie didn't talk much, but he hugged Kate, took off his hat, and hugged that too.

For the older girls, Kate had managed to snag two parkas, one pink and one blue. They both had fur around the hood and were in excellent condition. Kate had gloves for both of them, and she'd also thrown some lip gloss into her cart the last time she'd shopped at Target.

The girls squealed in delight as Kate presented the items. "Thank you, Kate!"

Next to Samantha, Kate knew the family's circumstances were hardest on nine-year-old Emily who was old enough to understand what was going on.

While Samantha and the girls filled their box with food, Kate pulled Georgie onto her lap and unwrapped a Hershey's Kiss for him. He crammed it into his mouth.

"Someone likes chocolate," Kate said, giving him a little squeeze.

He held out his hand for another.

"One more," Kate said.

When Samantha was ready to go, she thanked Kate and told her good-bye. Georgie scooted off her lap and joined his mother and sisters.

"I'll see you soon," Kate called after him.

When she looked up, Ian was standing in the doorway. Now that he'd given her the phone, he texted her throughout the day, but the last time she'd seen him was two nights ago when he'd fallen asleep in her bed. Kate stood as Ian approached her desk.

"Hi," he said.

She smiled. "Hi."

Helena sidled up to them. Kate had shared quite a few details about the dates she'd gone on with Ian and how he'd taken care of her when she was sick. She might have forgotten to mention the hacking and that she didn't know Ian's last name, but Helena didn't need to know everything.

"Hello," Helena said. "We spoke briefly once before."

"Helena Sadowski, please meet Ian Smith," Kate said, emphasizing *Smith*.

"It's nice to meet you." Ian shook her hand.

Helena appeared ready to swoon. "It's nice to meet you too," she said. "Kate can't stop talking about you."

Ian looked at Kate and grinned. "Is that right?"

"Oh, yes. She goes on and on."

Kate made a mental note to talk to Helena about the importance of keeping certain things to herself.

"Katie? A moment alone, please," Ian said.

"I'll be in the back for a second, Helena."

Ian followed Kate into the back room and waited until she closed the door behind them.

"What is it?" she asked when she turned around. He looked so serious, and she wondered if he was going to tell her he'd decided to leave Minneapolis in favor of the next city. She was surprised by how much that thought bothered her.

He put his arms around her and pulled her close. "Now that you appear to be back to your former, healthy self, I trust that the kissing ban has been lifted?"

She tried her best to look as serious as he did. "I suppose since I haven't sneezed at all today and my cough is intermittent at best, it would be okay for you to kiss me now."

"Good. I need to get you out of my system so I can get some work done. For some reason, I'm having trouble concentrating."

Ian backed her up against the door and tangled his hands in her hair. He kissed her lightly at first and then let his teeth graze Kate's lower lip. He kissed her again and then tugged down lightly on her lip before pulling it into his mouth. He switched back and forth, nibbling gently and then kissing her more aggressively. It made Kate feel as though she'd fallen into some kind of kissing-induced trance. She wrapped her arms tightly around his waist and pulled him closer, delighting in his groan as he kissed her harder. If she and Ian were alone and had access to a bed, she'd gladly spend the rest of the day lying on it with him with their mouths attached.

"There. Is that better?" Kate asked when they stopped to take a breath.

He shook his head in frustration. "No. Not at all."

"So this romantic interlude has not had the effect you desired?"

"Quite the opposite actually."

"That's too bad. Is there anything I can do?"

"I don't suppose you can take the rest of the day off?" he asked.

"I wish I could, but Helena and I have a lot of work to get done before I leave tomorrow, so I'll need to stay here."

"Damn."

"What about later?"

"Unfortunately, I'm dealing with a cyberattack that will require monitoring throughout the evening and possibly overnight."

Kate took a step back. "An attack? Are you serious? What does that even mean?"

He pulled her in again. "Nothing you need to worry about. Mostly it's annoying. They're very persistent."

"Who?"

"The hackers."

"So they're like you?"

"I'm one of a kind, sweetness," he said, deftly sidestepping her question.

Kate knew that getting information out of Ian wouldn't be easy, but it wasn't in her nature to remain in the dark forever. If their relationship were to progress to a certain stage—and Kate thought she should probably have her head examined for even contemplating such a thing—Ian would have to start opening up to her. But she didn't need to worry about that right now because she didn't have strong feelings for him yet.

At least that's what she told herself.

"Sometimes I just want to crawl inside your head and poke around," Kate said. "I imagine it would be fascinating."

"How… unsettling. Although to be fair, I too think about being inside you and poking around." He rocked his hips forward, thrusting gently. "Poking, poking, poking, poking a little faster. There's a rhythm I've got going, Katie, can you feel it?"

Kate felt something all right, and that something was pressing against her hip. "You're incorrigible."

"I believe you started it."

Kate was the one who rocked her hips forward this time, and Ian groaned.

"Stop sexually harassing me, or I'll contact your board of directors and tell them about the pervy way this food pantry treats its clients."

"Then it's a good thing you're not a client," Kate said, giving his perfect ass a little squeeze.

"I feel violated. I'm going now."

"You will never get me out of your system, you know."

"I do believe that's true, Katie Long Legs. Because now I only want you more."

CHAPTER TEN

IAN HAD OFFERED TO DRIVE Kate to the airport, and she'd accepted. When they got down to the bottom of the steps in front of her apartment, she looked around, confused. "Where's your car?"

"It's right in front of you," he said as he walked toward a shiny black Escalade, opened the back, and put her suitcase inside.

It shouldn't have surprised her, and the luxury vehicle seemed like a perfect match for him, but sometimes she forgot about his money. Kate could only hope he'd been telling her the truth when he said he earned it via legitimate means. He opened Kate's door and turned on the seat warmer for her.

"The Shelby's in storage until spring, which probably won't arrive until June, and that's only if we're lucky. I'm not sure why I ever thought moving to such a cold place would be a good idea."

All she heard was that he'd be staying until June.

"Thanks again for the package," Kate said. Another shipment from Victoria's Secret had arrived on her doorstep yesterday. This time, in addition to a pair of two-piece jersey pajamas in a rich, deep red, which were the softest pajamas Kate had ever slept in, Ian had sent a short black cashmere sweaterdress that crisscrossed in the back, and a pair of black lace-top thigh-high stockings that made her blush when she thought about wearing them. She'd already thanked him by text but felt it was the kind of gift that required another mention, and possibly a striptease.

"You're welcome. The dress and stockings are mostly for me."

Kate laughed. "Yes, I got that."

When they arrived at the airport, Kate said, "I'm flying American." She expected him to drop her off curbside, but he followed the signs for short-term parking and took a ticket. When the gate rose, he pulled into the ramp and found a spot on the second level.

"We're a little early," he said. "Maybe we can think of something to do."

"What are your plans for Thanksgiving?" Kate asked.

"Was I too vague? I meant steaming up the windows of this car."

"Humor me for a minute."

"I'll be working on Thanksgiving."

"You're not going home to Texas?" she asked.

"No."

"What about your family?"

His expression remained neutral when he said, "I don't really have any family to speak of."

How could he not have any family? Everyone had a family, didn't they?

"So you'll be alone?"

"I don't mind. Holidays have never really been my thing."

"Is there anyone in Minneapolis? Friends or maybe business acquaintances?"

"I tend to keep to myself."

"But don't you—"

Before she could finish, Ian leaned over and kissed her. Maybe that was why he was so good at it. Kate presumed there'd been other women, possibly more than a few, whose questions he'd silenced with his mouth. She put her arms around him, and he pulled her as close as the console would allow. When he slipped his hand up the back of her shirt, Kate nearly melted from the feel of his warm palm on her bare skin.

Ian pushed the button to run his seat back as far as it would go. "Come over here."

"Hold on. There's a family getting out of the car next to us. I don't want to traumatize the kids. Aw, they're wearing Mickey Mouse ears."

"Are they gone?"

"Almost." Kate waited until they shut their trunk and started to walk away before she scaled the console and sat sideways in Ian's lap.

"Much better," he said, kissing her deeply. He smelled so good, and she fit in his lap perfectly. She settled in and let herself get lost in his kisses, which was becoming easier and easier to do.

"Your upper lip has the most adorable curve right here on either side," she said, touching it with her finger. "It makes you look like you always have a secret."

"You have many curves that I like." He ran his hand along the side of her breast, down to her waist, and along her hip.

"You are one gorgeous man," Kate said, looking into his eyes.

"I thought you said you didn't find me all that handsome."

She kissed him. "Lies, nothing but lies."

He slid his hand up the front of her shirt and rubbed his thumb back and forth across the cup of her bra while he kissed her. Her nipple hardened immediately.

"Admit that I'm the one you were thinking about in the bathtub."

"Of course it was you."

"Is this what you were imagining?" He slipped his hand inside her bra and caught her nipple between two fingers, tugging gently on it.

"Yes," she said, whimpering into his mouth. Kate didn't want him to stop. She was so turned on she didn't care that they were making out in a parking garage like a couple of teenagers and that the windows had, in fact, started to steam up a little.

She nibbled his earlobe and then kissed her way down his neck. She sucked the tender skin into her mouth, and he responded with a low, deep groan.

"You have no idea how much I want you," he said, and he was breathing every bit as fast as she was by then.

"I might have an idea." Her voice sounded ragged, and she could not seem to move her mouth away from his neck. "But I don't think our first time should be in a parking garage."

"All I took away from that is that we're going to have a first time. And as skilled as I am, it would still be nearly impossible to reach my optimum performance in the front seat of an SUV."

"Your confidence never fails to astound me. I'll be expecting big things when I return."

He smiled. "I've got one big thing I can promise you."

"Yes, I know," Kate said, giving him one last kiss. "I've already seen it."

Ian stayed with Kate until they reached the security checkpoint; the line stretched clear around the corner.

"I should go," she said. "It'll take a while to get through that." She stood on her tiptoes and gave him a quick kiss goodbye. "Thanks for driving me."

As she turned to leave, he grabbed her wrist and pulled her back. "Kate." He slid his hands underneath her jaw and kissed her tenderly.

Nothing was going to rush him.

Not Kate's flight.

Not the line for security.

Not the crowd milling around them.

Nothing.

When it was over and she opened her eyes, he was looking at her in a way he never had before. His usual smile had been replaced by an expression of longing and vulnerability. Kate wanted him to look at her like that all the time.

"You better get going," he said.

Kate's head was in the clouds as she waited her turn to pass through security. She hadn't even left yet, but already she wanted to be back. She remembered how mad she'd been that day at the café when Ian had sat down across from her and admitted he'd hacked her credit card information, how exasperated she'd felt upon discovering he knew so many things about her, how exposed she'd felt when he'd walked in on her while she was in the bathtub.

My how things had changed, because now every time she turned around she was kissing him. And worse than that, she didn't want to *stop* kissing him. She wanted to do *more* than kiss him.

Lots more.

All of this with a man she knew very little about.

For the first time ever, he'd called her Kate.

And that had not escaped her notice at all. Not one little bit.

Kate took a seat at the bar, which was conveniently located near her gate. She ordered a glass of wine and pulled out her phone. Ian had already sent a text.

Ian: *Did you make it through security okay?*

Kate: *Not without a thorough pat-down, but what else is new?*

Ian: *They know a golden opportunity when they see one.*

Kate: *My lips are swollen and my cheeks have stubble burn.*

Ian: *Did the TSA take you into that little room alone? Jesus, tell them someone has to accompany you next time.*

Kate: *LOL. You did it to me.*

Ian: *Then I've done my job. And you gave me a slight hickey, so we're even.*

Kate: *Oops. Pretty sure I haven't done that since high school. Sorry!*

Ian: *I never said I didn't like it.*

Kate: *Why does chardonnay taste so much better in an airport bar?*

Ian: *I can't imagine there's anyplace chardonnay doesn't taste good to you.*

Kate: *That question was rhetorical. When I land in Chicago, I'm going to have another glass. And Cinnabon!*

Ian: *I do hope you'll share more of these intimate details with me while you're gone.*

Kate: *I plan to. And I'll be expecting the same from you. Sharing is caring.* ☺

Ian: *Don't expect emoticons. And I will not be LOL'ing either.*

Kate: *You just did.* ☺

Ian: *That was only for the purpose of explaining that I won't be doing it.*

Kate: *Time to head to the gate. They just called my flight.*

Ian: *My fingers are crossed that your seatmate smells as good as you do.*

Kate: *LOL!* ☺

CHAPTER ELEVEN

KATE AND HER MOTHER DIANE were in the kitchen with Chad's fiancée, Kristin. They'd spent the better part of the day preparing for tomorrow's Thanksgiving meal and were ready to take a break. Chad, who was two years older than Kate, had proposed to Kristin right around the time Kate and Stuart's relationship had imploded, which had put a slight damper on their announcement. Kate had felt bad about that. She liked Kristin, and since she didn't have a sister of her own, a sister-in-law was the next best thing.

"How is Stuart?" Diane asked. Next to Stuart, Kate's mom had taken the news of their breakup the hardest.

Kate pulled a bottle of wine out of the refrigerator. "You do remember he's not my boyfriend anymore, right? You didn't forget the part where I turned down his proposal because I didn't think I could spend the rest of my life with him and then rented my own apartment."

"Of course I didn't forget. And if that's the way you felt, you made the right decision. I just feel bad for him. It's his first major holiday without you."

Kate thought of Ian, who didn't have anyone to spend the holiday with, not that he seemed to mind. But Kate did. Ian might have claimed not to care about the holidays, but Kate had decided that if he was willing, she would include him in all her Christmas plans.

Kate poured a glass of wine for each of them, and they sat down at the kitchen table. "I met someone," Kate said. "I'll introduce you to him when you come for Christmas."

"Who is he?" Diane asked.

"His name is Ian."

"How did you meet him?" Kristin asked.

"He made several donations to the food pantry."

"He sounds very generous," Diane said.

"You have no idea."

Chad wandered into the kitchen. He and their dad had been parked in front of the TV since noon.

"Are you coming in to help?" Kristin asked, teasing him. "Because all the work is done."

"More than likely, he's in search of another beer," Kate said.

"My sister knows me too well," Chad said, reaching into the refrigerator for a Heineken. He pulled out a chair and sat down beside Kristin.

"Please make sure that's your last one because Kristin and I need you to drive us to the bar later," Kate said. "It's the least you can do to pay us back for the delicious meal we've been prepping all day, which you'll inhale tomorrow in seven minutes flat."

Chad looked adoringly at Kristin. "I'll be happy to be your designated driver."

"That reminds me. Guess what I drove, Chad? A Shelby."

"No way," he said as he uncapped the Heineken.

"Really I did."

He took a long drink. "A Shelby? Are you sure?"

"Well, obviously it was a replica, but yes."

Chad looked at her skeptically.

Kate pulled out her phone and texted Ian.

Kate: *Chad doesn't believe I drove your car. Clearly he's jealous (and delusional).*

Ian responded moments later with a picture of Kate behind the wheel, one hand on the gearshift and a smile on her face.

Kate: *I had no idea you took my picture.*

Ian: *You were too busy driving. It's hot. I made it my lock-screen picture.*

Kate handed her phone to Chad. "Look."

Chad studied the dashboard in the picture. "That is definitely one of the most authentic replicas I've ever seen, at least from an interior standpoint." He turned her phone over, looking at it from several angles. "What kind of phone is this?"

Kate grabbed it back from him. "It's a special new phone."

"Who owns the Shelby?" Chad asked.

"A friend of mine."

Chad laughed. "Not ready to tell your big brother about your new man yet?"

"How do you know I have a new man?"

"Because the only girl a guy is going to let drive his Shelby is one he's interested in. I hope you didn't squander the opportunity."

Kate mouthed the words *one hundred and ten.* Chad whistled.

"What was that all about?" Diane asked.

Kate and Chad smiled and said, "Nothing."

Few things were as entertaining as visiting a favorite bar the night before Thanksgiving. It was like a mini class reunion, and Kate looked forward to it every year. Chad handed her and Kristin a beer, and Kate made the rounds, chatting with her friends from high school. Her phone vibrated in her back pocket.

Ian: *You are apparently at some sort of honky-tonk in Indianapolis.*

Kate: *Oh hi, stalker!*

Ian: *Turn around.*

Oh God.

She spun in a circle, heart pounding, eyes searching as she looked for him.

Ian: *If I were AT THE BAR, I'd be a stalker. But I'm at my apartment. I'm just taking a break and wondered what you were up to.*

Kate: *I knew you weren't really here.*

Ian: *Sure you did. Are you enjoying yourself?*

Kate: *I'm having a blast.*

Ian: *I bet there are peanut shells on the floor and men wearing Western shirts.*

Kate: *You forgot cowboy boots and buckets of beer.*

Ian: *Please be mindful of your liver.*

Kate took a picture of herself drinking from a longneck bottle of Coors Light and sent it to Ian.

Ian: *Who's the man standing behind you?*

Kate clicked over to her photos. Her photobomber had his arms in the air and his tongue extended toward her. *Ewwww.*

Kate: *His name is Russ. We went to high school together.*

Ian: *He looks completely hammered.*

Kate: *He said he's been here since noon.*

Ian: *Maybe you should move away from him.*

Kate: *I already did because Kristin and I are about to join the line dancers.*

Ian: *It's like a giant hoedown, isn't it?*

Kate: *Yee-haw!*

Ian: *Who's driving home?*

Kate: *Chad. He agreed to be the designated driver because he was planted in front of the TV all day while the womenfolk slaved away in the kitchen.*

Ian: *Sounds like a fair trade.*

Kate: *I have to go. Two words: Electric Slide.*

Ian: *Bust a move, tiny dancer. I miss you.*

Kate stared down at her phone and smiled.

"Come on, Kate." Kristin yanked on her arm. "Let's go."

"I'll be right there," she said.

Kate: *I miss you too. xoxo*

CHAPTER TWELVE

THE WATTS FAMILY THANKSGIVING CELEBRATION commenced in a flurry of final dinner preparations followed by the immediate arrival of grandparents, aunts, uncles, and assorted cousins. Kate had already answered the inevitable questions about her career change at last year's dinner, and this year she fielded multiple follow-up queries about how the food pantry was doing. Unfortunately, she also had to deal with a considerable amount of nosy fallout over her breakup with Stuart.

Kate couldn't wait for dinner to be over.

When the last relative had departed, Kate cut two pieces of pumpkin pie and transferred them to dessert plates, heaping whipped cream on one of them. Chad and Kristin were getting ready to leave for a visit with Kristin's grandmother, and Diane was doing the last of the dishes. Kate found her dad on the couch in the living room watching TV.

"I sure hope that pie is for me, Katydid," he said.

"With extra whipped cream. Just the way you like it."

Kate and her dad had a tradition where they would skip dessert and eat their pie together later after everyone had gone home. She handed him the plate and sat down beside him.

"Sure is nice to have you home," he said, taking a bite of his pie. "Your mom and I have missed you."

"I won't stay away for so long next time."

He smiled. "I'm going to hold you to that."

Though they'd both tried their hardest to pretend nothing had changed, Kate's relationship with her dad had been a bit strained during the past year and a half. Steve Watts had spent thirty years practicing law and was now one of the most respected justices on Indiana's Supreme Court, and while he'd never pushed either of his children to follow in his footsteps, he'd been incredibly happy and proud when they had. Chad had already been practicing law for two years at a large firm in Indianapolis when Kate passed the bar. In law school, she'd focused on public interest with the intention of pursuing a legal career in community outreach. But upon graduation, when she found those openings in incredibly short supply, she accepted a position as a corporate attorney at the same type of large downtown firm where Paige and Audrey worked. It had been the biggest mistake she'd ever made.

Her dad had started calling her "Katydid" when she was two because he said she was cute as a bug, but over the years he told her the nickname had come to mean something more. Kate *did* things. While Chad had always needed outside validation, whether it was in his schoolwork or sports or career, Kate's drive had come from within, and she needed very little support. She'd once overheard her dad say that his money was on Kate if he had to choose which of his children had what it took to follow him all the way to the Supreme Court. Telling her dad she was giving up her law career to open a small food pantry was one of the hardest conversations she'd ever had with him. Unlike Diane, Steve could easily handle the loss of Stuart. But watching Kate give up everything she'd worked so hard for, even for something she was fiercely passionate about, had been a tougher pill to swallow. All things considered, he'd taken the news as well as any father could.

"How are things going with the food pantry?" her dad asked.

"They're going okay. It's been more difficult than I thought it would be, especially at this time of year," Kate admitted. If Ian hadn't intervened, she wasn't sure she'd have been able to remain open through the winter. She couldn't rely on Ian to bail her out every time things got tight, so she told herself she'd have to work even harder.

"Times are tough for a lot of people. What you're doing is commendable, so you keep getting it done, okay?"

"I will." Kate's eyes filled with tears, and she pretended to be very interested in her pie. It was the first time she and her dad had ever really discussed the food pantry. Maybe he thought if he didn't mention it she'd eventually come to her senses, but now she wondered if he'd finally accepted it. When they were done eating, Kate took their empty plates into the kitchen.

"More?" Diane asked. She looked exhausted.

"I'll do them," Kate said. "You go sit down."

"I opened a bottle of wine. Why don't you pour a glass and join me?"

Kate nodded. "Be out in a bit."

Her phone pinged while she was drying the plates.

Ian: *Happy Thanksgiving.*

Kate: *Happy Thanksgiving to you too.* She went into her bedroom, closed the door, and stretched out on her childhood bed.

Kate: *What are you doing?*

Ian: *Eating dinner.*

Kate: *Turkey?*

Ian: *Thai carryout.*

Kate: ☹

Ian: *I'm a rebel. And I like Thai.*

Kate: *Are you at least having pie for dessert?*

Ian: *I'm having bourbon, which is way better than pie.*

Kate: *What have you been doing today?*

Ian: *Hack, hack, hack, hack, hack, hack.*

Kate: *All work and no play...*

Ian: *There are no holidays in cyberspace.*

Kate: *I bet they can't hear you scream there, either.*

Ian: *You are such a clever girl.*

Kate: *Did that make you LOL?*

Ian: *I will admit to a chuckle. Nothing more.*

Kate: *Tough crowd.* ☺

Ian: *What are your plans for the rest of the evening?*

Kate: *My mom and I are going to do a little mother-daughter bonding over a glass or two of wine.*

Ian: *The apple didn't fall far from the tree, did it?*

Kate: *Clearly it did not.*

Ian: *I'm ready for you to come home. I haven't kissed anyone in days.*

Kate: *I'll be sure to give you lots of extra kisses to make up for it.*

Ian: *Now there's something to be thankful for.*

Kate: *I'll text you my flight information on Saturday morning.*

Ian: *Seriously?*

Kate: *You're not supposed to be in my computer!*

Ian: *I'm not. I hacked American Airlines. Their site is not at all secure.*

Kate: *Oh. SORRY.*

Ian: *I'm no longer tempted by the thought of accessing your personal information. If there's something I want to know, I'll ask you.*

Kate: *WHO IS THIS IMPOSTER? IF YOU HAVE IAN LOCKED UP SOMEWHERE, LET HIM OUT RIGHT NOW!*

Ian: *You're adorable. I'm working on my SHORTCOMINGS.*

Kate: *You've made real progress.*

Ian: *I'm still going to access your Victoria's Secret account, but I can just hack into the website.*

Kate: *Yes!*

Kate: *I mean, if you must.*

Ian: *Maybe I'll drink my bourbon and put some things in your shopping cart later.*

Kate: *You're the best.*

Ian: *Go drink your wine. I will be waiting for you inside the airport on Saturday.*

Kate: *Can't wait.*

Ian: ☺

Kate: *OMG, an emoticon! I bet LOL will be next.*

Ian: *Look what you've done to me.*

Kate: *Malleable.*

Ian: *NEVER.*

Ian: *Maybe occasionally, but only because I like you so much. Saturday I will have you.*

Kate read the text twice. The message aroused her. If he could do that to her with his words, she couldn't wait to see what would happen when they were in the same room together.

Kate: *We'll see.* ☺

Ian: *That only encourages me. I do love a good challenge.*

Kate: *Then I'll make sure you have your work cut out for you.*

Ian: *I can hardly wait. Good night, sweetness.*

CHAPTER THIRTEEN

KATE THUMBED THROUGH A MAGAZINE while she waited for her connecting flight from Chicago to Minneapolis.

The man sitting across from her was talking loudly on his phone, complaining about the vomiting and diarrhea that had ruined his holiday and left him severely dehydrated. "I swear to God, I didn't think there was anything left in me, but I barely made it through security before I had to find a bathroom."

Kate gagged. She did not wish to be privy to this information, not to mention the complete lack of consideration he was showing his fellow travelers by plunking himself right down in the middle of everyone. She got up from her seat and moved as far away as she could. Having been illness-free for only a short time, she was in no mood to get sick again and wondered if there was any place in the airport where she could buy a surgical mask. Her phone vibrated, alerting her to an incoming text.

Ian: *What's up, buttercup?*

Kate: *Killing time at the gate. I'm going to need a decontamination shower when I get home. The guy who was sitting across from me is trying to bring cholera back. Seriously, it's like the Black Death up in here. Ten bucks says he's my seatmate on the plane.*

Ian: *Please tell me he didn't breathe on you.*

Kate: *Not directly, but he's already clouded the whole area with his death mist. I moved as far away as I could. Knock wood, baby.*

She was trying to gauge whether she had enough time to dash to Cinnabon when her phone vibrated again.

Ian: *Your flight has been canceled.*

Kate: *Wait. What?*

Kate looked at the three airline employees. They had moved into the classic huddle, which meant they were discussing damage control.

No.

No, no, no, no, no.

Ian: *Stand by.*

Kate listened to the announcement that the flight had been canceled due to a mechanical problem and started to panic. She wanted to get home to Ian more than anything, so she opened the browser on her phone to see if there were any other flights available. Before she could get very far, her phone rang.

When she answered, Ian said, "Okay, Katie, time to see what those long legs can do. There's only one more flight heading to Minneapolis tonight that isn't full, and I've got you a seat on it. It's leaving soon, so make your way quickly to concourse F, gate 14. That's in terminal 2. As soon as we hang up, I'll text you your new boarding pass."

"I'll never make it," Kate said. "I'm in terminal 3 right now."

"It's a bit of a trek, and while I do want you to get to the gate as soon as you can, that plane isn't going anywhere until you're on it. I guarantee you'll be home tonight."

"I'll text you when I reach the gate," Kate said, ending the call and quickening her step.

After a jostling ride on an overcrowded tram, she arrived at terminal 2. F14 was clear down at the end, so she started to run, dodging people. A quick glance at the ticket information Ian had texted showed the flight departure as 7:45 p.m. Kate checked the time. It was 7:42. Disappointment washed over her. The aircraft doors were surely closed by now. In addition to not being reunited with Ian, she'd probably have to spend the night in the airport or venture out to find a hotel.

She expected the gate area to be empty, but to her surprise it was packed. The sign above the flight number said DELAYED. Kate had never been so happy to see that sign in her life, and she exhaled. Maybe she'd make it home after all.

Kate: *Made it to the gate. They haven't started boarding yet. The flight is delayed.*

Ian: *Every flight out of O'Hare is delayed right now.*

Kate: *Did you "appropriate" this ticket?*

Ian: *I paid for it, but I chose not to go through the "usual" channels to obtain it. Not enough time. My way is much faster.*

When they opened the door fifteen minutes later and started boarding passengers, Kate smiled and shook her head when she realized Ian had put her in first class. She made her way to her seat and accepted the offer of a glass of wine from the flight attendant.

As Kate stowed her purse under the seat, the captain made an announcement. "Good evening, folks. Air traffic control is currently experiencing technical difficulties that are delaying all departures. We'll keep you posted."

She groaned and pulled out her phone.

Kate: *Just sat down. Thank you for the ticket. First class was not necessary. I would have been perfectly fine in coach.*

Ian: *Nothing but the best for you. Chardonnay?*

Kate: *In hand.*

Ian: *Seat belt on?*

Kate: *Yes, but the pilot said there's a problem with air traffic control. Technical difficulties, blah, blah, blah.*

Ian: *Then I'd better unfuck air traffic control so the pilot can get your plane in the air.*

Kate: *Oh my God. You did NOT.*

Ian: *You say that to me a lot. I am LAUGHING OUT LOUD.*

Five minutes later, the pilot announced that the problem with air traffic control had been solved and they were third in line for departure.

Kate: *WHAT KIND OF HACKER ARE YOU?*

Ian: *How many times do I have to tell you, sweetness? I'm the best.*

CHAPTER FOURTEEN

HE WAS WAITING FOR HER at the bottom of the escalator. Kate spotted him standing off to the side, and when she walked up to him, his face lit up.

That smile, the one that was just for her, made her heart skip a beat.

He pulled her into his arms and lifted her clear off the floor.

Kate grinned. "You're unbelievable."

The look of longing that had been on his face the last time she saw him was back. "I couldn't wait another day, Kate. I just couldn't."

She put her arms around his waist and kissed him. His mouth was soft and warm, and it was all she could do to keep from devouring him right there in the airport.

"I'm glad you're back," he whispered, their foreheads touching.

"Me too."

"Unfortunately your suitcase did not make it home. I've already spoken to someone, and they'll deliver it tomorrow."

"You think of everything, don't you?"

"Always."

As they started to walk, he reached for her hand and interlocked their fingers. The hand-holding seemed more significant than any of the kisses they'd shared. It was intimate, possessive.

Like he'd claimed her in some way. He didn't let go of her hand until they reached the car and he opened the passenger door. Kate was fairly certain Ian would be staying the night, and her hunch was confirmed when he parked the Escalade in the lot behind her building and reached into the back seat for his laptop and a small overnight bag. Kate was already filled with anticipation and couldn't wait to feel Ian's arms around her.

"I'm going to take a quick shower," Kate said after she unlocked the door and set her purse on the coffee table. "There's beer in the fridge if you'd like one."

"Do you want anything?"

"No thanks. I had two glasses of wine on the plane. They took excellent care of me in first class."

"As they should," Ian said.

He went into the kitchen to get the beer, and Kate headed for the bathroom. After piling her hair on top of her head, she ducked under the spray and soaped herself quickly. Then she dried off, brushed her teeth, dressed, and wrapped herself in her robe.

She couldn't wait to kiss Ian.

She couldn't wait to touch Ian.

She couldn't wait to do *everything* with Ian.

When she came out of the bathroom, he was lying on her bed with his shoes off, drinking the beer. The only light in the room came from the small lamp on Kate's nightstand.

"I made myself comfortable."

Kate smiled. "You always do."

She walked over to the bed, and Ian sat up and swung his legs over the side so that Kate was standing between them. He grabbed the sash of her robe and pulled her closer. Kate thought he might ease her down onto the bed or kiss her, but what he did instead was untie her robe and remove it. His expression was one of raw desire as he stared at Kate in the black babydoll nightie. It had a flyaway front that exposed most of her torso, and Ian leaned forward and kissed her right below the center tie that held it together, pressing his palms flat against the expanse of bare skin.

"You look stunning in it," he said, his voice low. "I knew you would." He slowly untied the nightie as if Kate were a present he was unwrapping. Then he slipped the straps off her shoulders so that she was standing in front of him in only the thong.

He seemed in no hurry to pull her down onto the bed, maybe because he was at eye level with her breasts. Her suspicions were confirmed when he stroked her nipples with his thumbs. When he put his hands on her waist to bring her closer so that he could circle her nipples with his tongue, Kate's legs got wobbly. She rested her hands on his shoulders and watched him, sighing when he began to suck.

Kate pulled off his sweater and T-shirt. She wanted them to be skin-to-skin, and Ian pulled her down onto the bed as if he'd read her mind, holding Kate close as he kissed her. His hands were everywhere: in her hair, on her hips, and moving lightly up and down her back. He slipped his fingers under the elastic of her thong and slowly pulled it off, his fingers trailing down her legs from her thighs to her feet.

"Your legs are every bit as incredible as I thought they'd be," he said before spreading them.

Silently he drank in the sight of her naked before him, and she ached for him to touch her. Her breathing quickened when he finally began to stroke her, starting near the top of her thigh and then moving slowly inward until he reached her center.

"Oh," Kate said, letting out a moan. "Look at you, finding that spot on your first try."

Ian circled it with his thumb. "I don't understand how anyone can have trouble finding it. It's right *here*."

Kate squirmed under his fingers because even though Ian knew exactly where it was, he was skating around it, not quite touching it, which was driving her insane in the most wonderful way. He dragged his finger downward and slipped it inside her, then dragged it back up again and repeated the circular torture. He did this slowly, continually, until Kate couldn't remember her own name. Her apartment would have to be on fire for them to stop, because there was nothing she would rather be doing at that moment than letting Ian explore her body with his magic hands.

Until he started exploring her with his tongue.

He kissed his way down her body until his head was between her legs, and Kate found the feel of his scruff scraping her inner thigh incredibly arousing. Holding her open, he resumed the same movements with his tongue that he'd been doing with his fingers. As wonderful as that had felt to Kate, this was even better.

She was so close, but he kept her on the brink, slowing down his movements before speeding back up again. "Ian," she said, shamelessly holding on to his hair and trying to keep him in place. "Please, I'm begging you."

He slipped a finger inside her and then flicked his tongue right where she wanted it most. When the flicking turned into light sucking, Kate came harder than she ever had in her life, and the pulsing waves of her orgasm seemed to go on forever.

"Did that feel good?" he asked.

Kate's sigh, and her incoherent response, made him laugh softly. As soon as she came back down to earth and caught her breath, she straddled Ian's thighs, unbuttoned his jeans, and pulled his zipper down slowly.

"How did this possibly fit inside here?" she asked, sliding her hand down the front of his jeans and palming him.

"It was a tight squeeze," he said, groaning.

"It's even bigger than I remember."

"That's because I am very, very hard."

Kate took off the rest of his clothes, thankful for the weak glow coming from the bedside lamp. Ian's body was long and lean and strong and hard, and this time instead of just looking at it, she could touch him anywhere she wanted. Twisting her fingers in his hair, she kissed him and then nibbled on his ear and sucked gently on his neck. There was something about the smell of his skin that made her want to explore every inch of him with her face. She licked and nipped her way from his shoulder down to his chest. Then she brought her hand lower, skimming over his hardness and cupping him from underneath. Slowly she teased and tortured him, the way he'd teased and tortured her. But it was the sweetest, most erotic kind of torture, and Kate didn't think he minded at all.

When she switched from her hands and fingers and started exploring him with her mouth, he was the one who twisted his fingers in her hair as he groaned. One by one, she followed the steps she'd learned from reading the article about oral pleasure. That information was clearly golden as evidenced by the fact that Ian seemed in danger of losing his ever-loving mind. His breathing sounded out of control, and his whispered praise would have put a smile on Kate's face had her mouth not been otherwise engaged.

It surprised her when he stopped her. "As incredible as this feels—and I should mention that the time you spent online was time very well spent—when I come, I want it to be when I'm inside you." He sat up. "Where are my jeans? I brought condoms."

Kate found his jeans on the floor, reached into the front pocket, and handed him a condom. She expected him to hurry, to only be thinking about himself, but he leaned over, kissed her, and began to stroke her the way he had when he'd first started exploring her. His touch was so light, so teasing, that she became aroused again almost immediately, and she arched into his hand, wanting more. When he put on the condom and covered her with his body, she welcomed the solid weight of him pressing her into the mattress.

Wedged between her legs, not yet inside her, *but oh so close*, he hesitated. "Do you know what I'm about to do to you, sweetness?"

"What?" she asked breathlessly. "Of course I do."

"What's it called?" he asked, and there was no mistaking his cocky tone.

When she realized why he'd asked, all she could do was laugh. "You are about to penetrate me, Ian."

He laughed too. "I am. I'm about to go as deep as I can until I'm as far inside as you'll let me go. I promise you'll like it. I am *really* good at it."

"Then stop talking and show me."

Ian made the most delicious sound when he entered her, somewhere between a groan and a sigh. He pulled out almost all the way and slowly pushed back in, eliciting a similar sound from her.

Though she absolutely wanted to be with Ian and was definitely turned on, she didn't have high hopes that he'd be able to bring her to orgasm again. In the five years she'd been with Stuart, Kate had rarely found her release from penetration alone. This was more than likely due to Stuart's tendency to skimp on foreplay and the fact that he never varied his rhythm and preferred a speed and intensity that was too hard and too fast for her no matter how much she tried to slow him down. He was always good about circling back around to help her out afterward, but because she knew he'd rather roll over and pass out, she felt like a burden and often told him not to worry about it, especially toward the end of their relationship.

So when Ian pulled back out again, she braced herself for the rapid onslaught that was certainly about to start.

But that didn't happen.

His pace was slow, rocking more than thrusting, which put the perfect amount of pressure right where she needed it most.

"Oh, keep doing that," Kate murmured, and he did.

She locked her ankles behind his back and tilted her hips up to meet him. The pleasure started to build as he matched his thrusts to the rhythm she set until she was the one who wanted, needed, him to go faster. Unlike sex with Stuart, it was different when she was the one who increased the speed. Sex with Ian was so much better than she'd ever imagined it could be with anyone, and when she came, she wasn't shy about letting him know how good it felt.

He joined her moments later, shuddering and shaking, breathing heavily and groaning out her name. Not Katie, but Kate. His pulsing movements slowed and came to a stop, and he pulled out of her and shifted his weight so that he was lying on his side, holding her in his arms. They kissed lazily as Ian stroked her cheek with his thumb. He left briefly to go into the bathroom, and when he returned, he wrapped his arms around her and pulled her head down onto his chest.

You let that mysterious hacker right into your bed. You let him do all those wonderful things to you, and you don't even know his last name.

"I'm not sure how this happened," she said.

"Well, first I undressed you, and then you undressed me. Then you let me penetrate you. You seemed to really enjoy it," he said mildly.

"It was absolutely incredible, and enjoy doesn't even begin to describe how good it felt. I meant how did we make it this far? I didn't even *like* you three weeks ago."

"Maybe you finally realized I'm actually a good guy. And maybe I was right about what you were looking for."

"Which is?"

"Someone who stimulates your body *and* your mind. You haven't completely figured me out yet, but you want to."

She propped herself up on her elbow and looked down at him. "You're right. I do." When he slid his hand behind her head to pull her mouth down to his, she had to admit, if only to herself, that she was more than a little turned on by that.

CHAPTER FIFTEEN

IT WAS NEARLY TEN BEFORE she opened her eyes the next morning, and sunlight was seeping through the cracks in the blinds. Ian was spooning her, which was apparently his default sleeping position. She listened to him breathing softly, feeling content and pleasantly sore in all the right places.

Slipping carefully out of his arms, she scooped her robe off the floor and headed for the bathroom. After she relieved herself and brushed her teeth and hair, she quietly made her way to the kitchen to start the coffee. As she waited for it to brew, she heard the water running in the bathroom, and Ian walked into the kitchen a minute or two later wearing only his underwear. His hair looked as if a woman had been running her hands through it all night, which wasn't far from the truth. She'd never known a man whose bedhead only made him more attractive.

He kissed her, tasting of toothpaste. "Good morning."

"Good morning. Are you hungry?"

"Starving."

Kate opened the refrigerator and found it empty. She wasn't much of a cook, but she could have made them an omelet or some toast if she'd had any eggs, cheese, or bread. "Unfortunately, I decided not to go grocery shopping before I left."

"No need for groceries. I say we shower and go out for breakfast after we finish our coffee," Ian said. "You can wear one of those new sweaters I bought you. It looks cold out there."

They carried their coffee into the living room and sat down on the couch.

Kate threw a blanket over them. "Did you sleep well?"

"I always sleep well when I have a naked woman's body to wrap myself around."

"You do like to spoon."

"What's not to like? Your skin is very soft and your hair smells good. Plus my hands can reach all kinds of places."

Kate had felt those hands wandering in the middle of the night. He'd kissed the back of her neck and then skimmed his palm down her chest and stomach, reaching between her legs and stroking her until she'd awakened fully, which had led to a rather prolonged and delightfully satisfying round two.

She smiled. "They certainly can. I have fond memories of those hands."

"I should hope so."

Kate took a drink of her coffee. "I'm surprised you don't have that laptop open yet."

"Cyberspace will just have to get along without me for a while." He put his arm around Kate and kissed her forehead, drinking his coffee as if nothing was more important than being with her.

She snuggled closer, thinking about how long it had been since she'd felt this happy.

Kate grabbed a couple of towels and set them on the counter in the bathroom. She hung her robe on its hook on the back of the door and turned on the shower to let the water warm up. Ian had disappeared.

She found him in her bed, lounging among the twisted sheets like he didn't have a care in the world. She stood naked in the bedroom doorway and said, "I thought we were getting in the shower?"

Ian beamed. "I am *loving* this revelation that you're not modest either."

"Well, not *now*," Kate said. "What are you doing? I'm so hungry I'm about to gnaw my own arm off."

"I, Ian, will never, ever infinity, walk in on Katie in the bathroom again unless specifically invited to do so."

Kate's eyes widened in disbelief. "After everything we've done and all the places your hands have been, you've suddenly discovered boundaries?"

"Don't forget my tongue," he said, as if she could.

Kate walked over to the bed and looked down at him. "Ian, would you like to join me in the shower?"

He pulled her down onto the bed and tickled her.

Kate squealed with laughter. "Stop that! Very ticklish!" She tried to get away and almost made it before he grabbed her ankle and pulled her back.

He was laughing as hard as she was, but then the laughing turned into kissing, and the kissing turned into touching.

"If we don't get in there, we're going to run out of hot water and then we'll both be sorry," she said. "Come with me. I promise to wash every inch of you."

Ian followed her into the bathroom, stripped off his underwear, and pulled her into the shower with him. "I'm an incredibly filthy man, Katie."

"Tell me something I don't know," she said, laughing. "Like your last name."

They walked to Wilde Roast Café. Ian had pulled off her glove and shoved it in his pocket so he could hold her hand. Despite the single-digit temperature, Kate was toasty warm in her parka and jeans and the white cable-knit sweater he'd bought her.

"Here we are again," Ian said after they'd been seated and ordered coffee. "What was it I said to you the day I tracked you here by your credit card activity?"

"You should be trying to make me forget you ever did that."

"Water under the bridge. I believe what I said was that I'd win you over eventually. Considering I've now been *inside you*, my prediction was quite accurate." His smile got even bigger, as if he couldn't be more delighted about the way things had turned out.

Ian was always happy. Forget moody. Forget brooding. An air of amusement surrounded him at all times, as if the world he lived in was just so infinitely entertaining and—in his case—there for the taking.

"You're quite pleased with yourself, aren't you?" she said, smiling back at him.

"Incredibly so." He opened his menu. "How was your visit home?"

"It was good. I could have done without all the 'poor Kate' comments from my assorted relatives. You know, because I'm no longer making the big bucks and Stuart and I broke up. The worst part was they all acted like I got dumped."

"But you broke up with Stuart."

"Exactly!" Kate said, pointing at herself. "I broke up with him. Ugh, I sound like I'm in middle school."

"You should have told them about your new boyfriend."

She smiled. "Boyfriend?"

He groaned. "Now we're both in middle school. I need to say something very manly *right now*."

"Trust me," she whispered. "You are *the* man. A six-foot-four-inch, gorgeous, strapping man with muscles everywhere and a big you-know-what."

He winked. "Don't you forget it, sweetness."

The waitress brought their coffee. "Are you ready to order?"

"Kate?" Ian said.

"Crème brûlée french toast please."

"And for you?" she asked, looking at Ian.

"Classic Benedict."

She gathered their menus. "Coming right up."

"So the rest of the visit was okay?" Ian said, taking a drink of his coffee.

"Yes. Things seem to be back on track with my dad."

"Had they been off track?"

"He had a hard time when I stopped practicing law. He began his law career as an attorney. My brother is an attorney. I'm no longer an attorney."

"What does your dad do now?"

"He's a justice on Indiana's Supreme Court. Have I not mentioned that?"

"You have not."

"Worried?"

"Not at all. Parents always find me especially charming."

"They'll be in Minneapolis for Christmas. Knock yourself out. Anyway, for the first time ever, my dad asked how the food pantry was doing. We'd never really talked about it before, so I guess we're making progress. I felt conflicted when I answered him though. If it wasn't for you and your donations, the report I gave him would have been dismal."

"Speaking of that," Ian said.

"No," Kate said firmly.

He looked surprised. "You're not even willing to discuss it? Christmas is coming. What about your clients? What about the *babies*?"

She didn't want to admit how much she'd already been worrying about Christmas. Kate's food pantry was teaming up with two other organizations to provide a Christmas Eve dinner that was quite ambitious in scope when it came to the number of people they hoped to feed. Not only that, but Kate wanted to give one unwrapped toy to each child who came through the line. Whether or not they would achieve their goal would depend on the dollar amount they raised and the number of toy donations they were able to bring in.

"I have to do this on my own, Ian. It's what I set out to do. If I can't make this work, then I threw away my law career for nothing."

"Don't be so hard on yourself. I'm sure all nonprofit organizations have their ups and downs. Maybe you can't help everyone, but you've helped a lot of people, and that counts for something."

"I know it does," Kate said. "It's just that once I help them, I feel like I'm letting them down if I can't keep doing it."

The waitress brought their meals and they dug in.

"Then let me help you," he said.

"You've already been way too generous. I can't accept any more."

"I really haven't given you that much."

"You've given me three thousand dollars, which is a small fortune considering I can feed eight people for six dollars and twenty-one cents. It isn't your responsibility to keep the food pantry afloat. I'll just work harder."

"Is it because I"—he made air quotes—"*appropriated* the money?"

"That's part of it, I guess."

"What if I give you some of my own money? I have plenty."

Kate shook her head. "I can't." Maybe she was being stubborn and ungrateful, but how could she feel like she was accomplishing her goals if Ian swooped in every month with a bag of cash, stolen or otherwise?

"Don't you think your clients are deserving of the assistance they receive, regardless of where the money comes from?" Ian asked.

"Of course I think they're deserving."

"Well, if you won't take money from me personally, then we're back to me playing Robin Hood."

She exhaled, torn between her decision not to accept his help and her desire to see her clients with the things they needed.

"Think of it this way," he said. "Wouldn't you rather see your clients benefit from the money instead of the thieves who stole it from people whose Christmases will probably be shitty this year because of it?"

"You make a valid argument."

He pointed his fork at her. "Exactly."

"Well, maybe I wouldn't struggle with it as much if you told me more about it."

"What do you want to know?"

"How does it work? When I asked you if there was a difference between hackers and cyberthieves, you said there was. What did you mean by that?"

"There are two kinds of hackers—white hat and black hat. The white hats are hackers who hack for good—like me. We hack into things, but our goal is to figure out how to keep everyone else out. The cyberthieves, or black hats, hack for malice or greed. They're the ones who introduce the malware that causes harm and launch attacks that cripple websites. They hack into Home Depot and Target, and they help themselves to your credit card information when all you were trying to do was buy a drill or paper towels and laundry detergent."

"Clearly you don't know how to shop at Target. There are way cooler things to be found there than paper towels and laundry detergent."

He laughed. "Duly noted."

Kate poured more syrup on her french toast. "When I asked you why you didn't return the money to the people it had been stolen from, you said it wasn't that easy. Why not?"

"Once the credit card numbers are stolen, they're bundled and sold to people called carders. The carders then use the numbers to make new cards to buy merchandise that will be returned to the store for a refund or sold, possibly overseas. At that point, there's no way to recover the merchandise or the cash. Most people—after canceling their cards—will hopefully receive compensation from their credit card company or get the charges reversed. But sometimes it takes a while to get everything sorted out, and for those who need the available credit to get them through to the next payday, or to buy food or put gas in their car, it can cause real hardship."

"So where do you go to steal the money back?"

"Right into the carders' bank accounts usually. Some of the more prolific thieves have hundreds of thousands of dollars sitting in them. I don't take a large enough amount at one time to raise any red flags, but even if they noticed the money was missing, they're not going to do anything about it—other than be very pissed—because they don't want to draw attention to their own illegal activities."

Kate was dumbfounded. "Hundreds of thousands?"

"It's not uncommon. Even a black hat who only dabbles is likely to have more cash than he could ever hope for."

Kate was silent for a moment.

"What is it?" he said.

"I'm sorry, I just… I got a visual of you all sitting around in front of your computers wearing little hats."

"That's very cute."

"So what color is your hat when you take the money from black hat hackers? Is it gray?"

"Yes. Gray hat hacking is typically done in the name of goodwill even though it's often illegal. My hat is gray whenever it suits me."

"I had no idea this whole culture even existed."

"People wouldn't sleep as well at night if they knew what hackers were capable of."

"Then I guess I'll sleep extra soundly when the best hacker of them all is in my bed."

"In case you weren't already aware, I'll be in your bed on a regular basis from now on."

"Lucky me," Kate said, smiling. "As for the 'appropriating,' your arguments are very persuasive. But it still goes against everything I believe in when it comes to the law. We don't get to mete out vigilante justice no matter how defensible it seems."

"It's an ethical quandary for sure, but not one I happen to struggle with. I have no trouble playing Robin Hood. I don't keep any of the money for myself. I don't want it, and I certainly don't need it. I do it because taking the money from thieves and giving it to those who are more deserving makes me feel like I'm playing an active part in offsetting the wrongdoing."

"I can understand that," Kate said.

"You know, the babies don't really understand Christmas. As long as they have enough to eat, they're in good shape. But the younger kids…"

"Don't you dare," Kate said.

"What? Mention that little boy I saw you holding on your lap? The one with the Curious George hat you were feeding chocolate to? And he has, what? Two sisters?"

When Ian said he missed nothing, he really meant it.

"I see that you've identified—and are now exploiting—my weakness so that I'll let you fix it, regardless of what it might cost me in integrity."

"I'm a hacker, Katie. It's what I do."

If Kate let Ian help her, she could feed her clients and give their children some semblance of a real Christmas. Sure, there were more important things than presents, but to a homeless child or one whose family lived far below the poverty line, a hot meal and a toy could make all the difference. "I'm resisting this with every part of my being."

"Given your education and professional background, I'd be more worried if you didn't have a problem with it. Just think about it, okay?"

"Okay."

When Ian took out his credit card to pay, Kate craned her neck in an attempt to read the name on it. Ian handed the card to her.

"Privasa?" she said.

"It's the name of my company," Ian said. "Everything I own is registered to it."

"Very fitting for a man who likes his privacy." She handed the card back to him. "But you're going to tell me your last name now, right? After all those things we did?" Kate had always been a good judge of character, and she didn't get the sense Ian was trying to pull anything over on her. At thirty-two, he'd undoubtedly had more than a few serious relationships, and she was fairly certain that at some point he revealed his last name to the women he dated because no woman in her right mind would be okay with a man withholding that kind of information indefinitely.

"No. I've already told you more than I ever thought I would. See? It's your beauty at work again. And your legs." He lowered his voice to a whisper. "And Jesus, your *mouth*. You have so many weapons in your arsenal now."

As they walked home hand in hand, Ian said, "I feel like taking a nap. And by nap I mean move in and out of your naked body at whatever speed you prefer."

"And they say men don't know how to communicate."

"Well, that's where they're *wrong*. I was crystal clear."

"You're going to kill me, Ian. And I mean that in the most wonderfully satisfying way."

CHAPTER SIXTEEN

IAN ARRIVED AT KATE'S APARTMENT around six. True to his word, he'd been spending a lot of time not only in her bed but with her in general. They'd meet at Kate's place after work, walk to a nearby restaurant for dinner, and then Ian would stay over. But sometimes they'd order in because rolling around on Kate's bed as soon as Ian walked in the door sounded a lot more enticing to both of them than venturing out into the cold for something to eat. Ian had followed through on his Thanksgiving Day promise of shopping at Victoria's Secret while drinking his after-dinner bourbon, and Kate was now the owner of several new push-up bras and matching panties. She'd modeled them for him, and that was one of the nights they definitely hadn't made it out of her apartment for dinner.

"Hey, sweetness," Ian said, tossing his keys onto the counter. He was wearing his glasses. "How was your day?"

Kate's day had sucked. There were so many people utilizing the food pantry that she was barely keeping up with the regular needs of her clients. She had no idea how she was going to pull off the Christmas Eve dinner, not to mention the unwrapped toys. Christmas was a little over two weeks away, and she'd only collected about a third of what she'd hoped to have by then.

"It was long. Yours must have been too. You're wearing your glasses."

"My eyes were burning."

He sat down on the couch, and after he took off his glasses and set them on the coffee table, he pulled her onto his lap and gave her the kind of kiss that made her want to order in.

"Ah, the number six," Kate said, sighing. "I love that one."

He looked at her curiously. "What are you talking about?"

"I assigned identification numbers to your kisses."

"Oh really," he said, laughing.

"That was the number six. It's a little different from the number five because not only do you give me a deep open-mouthed kiss with tongue, you also hold me on your lap while cradling my face in your hands. It's one of my favorites."

"Tell me the rest."

"The number one is the first kiss you gave me at the end of our first date. And the number two is the second kiss, and so on. Then there's the six. The number six knocks my socks off."

"Which one knocks your clothes off?"

"Pretty much all of them."

"Are there any more?"

"There's a seven."

"And?"

She smiled as if she were picturing it in her mind.

"Oh, Katie." His voice sounded like a purr. "It must be really good."

"The number seven is when you kiss me when you're inside me. It feels incredible."

"Do you know what sounds really good for dinner?" he asked, nibbling her ear.

"A number seven with a side of let's order in?"

"You're so quick," he said, easing her off his lap and pulling her toward the bedroom. "I really like that about you."

"Don't you mean devastatingly beautiful?"

"That too."

Ian ordered Chinese while they were still in bed, and when it arrived they ate dinner in front of a roaring fire.

"What do you want for Christmas?" Kate asked.

"I want you to accept my offer of another charitable donation," he said, taking a bite of his egg roll.

"How is that a gift for you?"

"Giving makes me feel good and so does helping you. Therefore, if you let me give you money, which will benefit those in need, I'll be happy. It's the only thing I want. Are you really going to deny me this request on our first Christmas together?"

"How about a nice sweater?"

"I have plenty of sweaters. I'd freeze to death if I didn't."

"I'm still wrestling with the idea," she said.

"Let me know when you've decided. But don't wait too long."

Kate was sitting at her desk organizing client files when Ian breezed through the front door of the food pantry to take her to lunch.

"Hi, Helena," he said, pausing in front of her desk on his way to Kate's.

"Hello, Ian," she said. "How are you?"

"Fine, thanks. How are you?"

"Busy. Christmas will be here before we know it."

He glanced over at Kate. "I keep telling Kate the same thing."

"I'm so happy to hear that the two of you are officially dating."

"So Kate told you?" He leaned against the edge of Helena's desk and crossed his arms.

"Oh yes. She tells me everything. The other day she spent fifteen minutes telling me about all the underthings you've bought her."

Kate wanted the ground to open up and swallow her.

"It sounds like you're quite sweet on our Kate," Helena added.

"Oh, I am. I am very sweet on our Kate. I mean, just look at her."

Kate's face was on fire, and her expression was somewhere between uncomfortable and mortified.

"Ready?" Ian asked brightly.

She put on her coat and grabbed her purse. "We talked about this," she hissed on her way past Helena's desk. Helena smiled and pretended she hadn't heard her.

Ian held open the door, and they stepped outside. "Bet this frigid air feels good on those flaming cheeks."

"Oh, be quiet," Kate said as he laughed and reached for her hand.

"Does Helena know what an excellent lover I am?" he asked as they walked down the street. "You did tell her about the underthings."

"I might have mentioned your Victoria's Secret shopping habit, but I do not share intimate details with her even though she'd probably enjoy hearing them. She's a very curious person. When I told her you were taking me to lunch, she wanted to know where you worked. I think she was worried you didn't have a job. I showed her your website."

After Ian told her the name of his company, Kate had googled Privasa but hadn't learned much about it. There were no rates listed or testimonials given. No explanation of services. On the contact page she'd found only a simple form to request more information. It reminded Kate of those nightclubs that were so exclusive they didn't need a sign. If you were allowed entrance, you'd know where to find it.

"Your website is quite stark," she said once they'd arrived at Mattie's on Main and been seated.

"That's because my clients come to me by referral. I used to advertise when I started out ten years ago, but now I don't need to. My reputation is legendary."

"As a hacker and a lover," she teased.

He winked at her and she melted. "I did struggle for a few years. I'm referring to getting the company off the ground, not my bedroom skills."

"Well, you did start honing them at fourteen."

"How old were you?"

"Seventeen. Prom night my junior year. He threw up on me later."

He grimaced. "I promise I will never do that, sweetness."

"So were you one of those computer geniuses who started their company in a dorm room?"

"Not exactly. In college I was all about seeing what I could hack into for my own amusement, regardless of how risky or stupid it was. But I knew before I graduated that the corporate track wouldn't be a good fit, so I came up with a way to channel my superior hacking skills into a revenue stream. It took hard work and some extremely long hours, but I have a one hundred percent success rate in penetrating any system I attempt to hack into. If a company needs a white-hat security firm, my name is always at the top of the list."

"And what name would that be?" she asked, leaning toward him with interest.

"Ian Merrick."

"Your last name is Merrick?" Well, that was easy.

"No. But Ian Merrick is the name I use for my business. I got tired of trying to convince clients they didn't need to know my full name. So I made one up."

"Oh." She looked down at her menu, flipping through the pages to hide the disappointment on her face.

He reached across the table for her hand. "It's not that I'm not telling *you* my last name. I don't tell anyone."

"It's okay," she said. There was obviously a reason behind his reluctance to share his last name, but considering they'd been together for such a short time, it was no surprise he wasn't quite ready to divulge it.

"Are you sure?" He gave her hand a squeeze.

She squeezed back and smiled. "Positive." It wasn't that she had doubts about Ian as a boyfriend, or even a person. Once they'd put their rocky start behind them, he'd been nothing but kind and generous. A true gentleman. But if one of her girlfriends had announced she'd met a great guy but he wouldn't tell her his last name, Kate would have told her to *run*. She'd give Ian some more time, but if he didn't eventually open up to her, she'd take her own advice. She only hoped it would happen before her heart got too involved.

Thankfully their waitress interrupted any further discussion when she appeared to take their order. They asked for bowls of wild rice soup to go along with their sandwiches.

"It's definitely soup weather," the waitress said. "It's supposed to get down to ten below with the windchill tonight."

"That is way too cold for my thin Texas blood," Ian said when she walked away.

"You went to college in Massachusetts. Are you telling me you failed to acclimate to single-digit temps, ice, and snow?"

He shook his head. "There's a reason I don't live there anymore."

"Tell me again how you ended up in Minneapolis. You said you were just passing through."

"I'd spent the summer in Winnipeg and was making my way south when the Shelby broke down on I-94 right outside the Twin Cities."

"Canada is awfully far north for an Amarillo boy," Kate said.

"I have a friend from college who lives there now. He talked me into coming. Said the fishing was great."

"You like to fish?"

"You sound so surprised."

"It's very outdoorsy."

"I'm outdoorsy. Do you not remember our afternoon in the park?"

"I stand corrected. You are very outdoorsy."

"I like to fish if they're biting, and they definitely were, along with the giant mosquitoes that also live in Canada. I spent three months being eaten alive. Anyway, the Shelby is not a car that is quickly repaired. It took a week to get the necessary parts and get her back on the road. In the meantime, I explored the area and decided it was as good a place as any to hang out for a while. It was August, so the cold wasn't a factor. The city was big enough, and I figured I'd be gone by the time the snow arrived. Then this beautiful woman crashed into me on the sidewalk on Halloween. I stuck around."

"Aw," she said. "That's very sweet. If you hadn't broken down, where were you planning on heading?"

"I hadn't really decided other than I wanted it to be some-place warmer."

"I feel compelled to point out that it's only going to get colder here."

He sighed. "So I've heard. I guess we'll have to spend our time inside. I sure hope I can think of something for us to do."

"Something tells me you won't have any problem."

CHAPTER SEVENTEEN

THE SUN HADN'T YET RISEN when Ian woke Kate up to tell her one of his clients had a problem that required his urgent attention. His phone had been on the nightstand, and she'd groggily remembered the call coming in and a few minutes later him kissing her good-bye and tucking the covers tightly around her. When her alarm went off at eight, she got out of bed, took a hot shower, and bundled up against the arctic air that seemed destined to stay until spring.

She sent the first text at nine, shortly after she arrived at the food pantry.

Kate: *I missed you in the shower this morning. I actually had to wash myself, which is not nearly as fun as when you do it.*

Half an hour later, she was still waiting on a response.

Kate: *Really? You're usually lightning fast regarding messages that contain even the slightest mention of my body parts.*

She'd sent a final text around eleven.

Kate: *Wow, they're not letting you come up for air at all.*

Although he often worked for hours without a break, his silence was unusual. It wasn't like him not to check in with her throughout the day, and he'd never gone this long without responding. She ignored the slight prickle of unease and continued on with her day.

Her phone finally chimed an hour later.

Ian: *Had to fly to DC. Not sure when I'll be back in town. Probably won't be able to call or respond to messages. Miss you already.*

Kate had been under the assumption that Ian's hacking was confined to the private sector. But if he'd flown to Washington, did that mean he was also hacking for the government?

Which he'd never mentioned.

Kate: *Must be very important. Don't worry about calling or texting. I'll see you when you get back. Miss you too.*

Kate had gone to Pilates after work. Now it was almost six and there'd been no more texts from him. The refrigerator held their restaurant leftovers from the night before, and Kate ate the rest of her pasta while sitting on the couch, her phone beside her.

So he had to travel unexpectedly for work. It's not a big deal.

But Kate wondered what kind of work required flying to DC with such little notice? And when would he return?

She spent the evening watching a movie. Finally at eleven she turned off the TV, locked up, and got ready for bed. In the bathroom she took off her makeup and brushed her teeth. On the nights Ian stayed over, they would shower together in the morning, and then he'd go home when it was time for her to head to the food pantry. He'd recently left a few duplicate items at Kate's so he wouldn't have to bring them every time, and though she'd tried to play it cool, she liked seeing another toothbrush in the holder next to hers and his shampoo in the shower.

After changing into her pajamas, she reached for a book but set it back down on the nightstand five minutes later and turned out the lamp. She'd skimmed the same page three times before deciding she wasn't in the mood to read. She tossed and turned, and it took her a while to get comfortable because her bed felt too big without Ian in it.

A few days ago, she'd had a breakfast meeting with her board of directors. Ian had been lounging on her couch, working on his laptop and drinking coffee, when it was time for her to go.

"Here," she'd said, handing him her spare key. "I have to go in early today. Lock up when you leave."

The last time she'd encountered these dating milestones had been with Stuart, and she'd forgotten how awkward they could be. She'd been pleased when Ian hadn't dropped the key like it was on fire or leaped from the couch to go with her so she could lock up as usual.

Instead, he'd closed his fingers around it, kissed her, and said, "Sure, Katie Brown Eyes. Have a good day."

She'd smiled all the way to work.

If Ian got back late and decided to come to her place instead of his, he'd be able to let himself in. He'd kiss her awake and snuggle in behind her, explaining what he'd been doing in Washington.

But that's not what happened. What happened was that Kate woke up Saturday morning alone.

By eleven she'd cleaned the apartment and done her laundry. At noon, when the walls started to close in, she decided to have lunch at Brasa Rotisserie, which was a fifteen-minute walk. The cold didn't bother her and neither did the snow falling from the sky in giant flakes. But walking made her think of Ian, especially the way he always pulled off her glove and shoved it in his pocket so he could hold her hand.

When she reached Brasa Rotisserie, she ordered a curried chicken bowl and took her time eating it. Her phone chimed, but the sound hadn't come from the special phone he'd given her. Carrying two phones was a bit of a hassle, but keeping them both meant she hadn't needed to let everyone know she had a new number. After pulling out the correct phone, she glanced at the text display.

Paige: *We're heading to Kieran's tonight for a few drinks. Bring your man!*

Kate: *Ian's out of town, but I'll meet you for a drink or two.*

Paige: *Great! 7:00?*

Kate: *Sure. See you then.* ☺

When she was done eating, she left the restaurant and walked for another half hour, her boots making crunching sounds in the snow. Eventually she made her way home. Because she hadn't slept the greatest the night before, she attempted to take a nap on the couch. But sleep wouldn't come, and she eventually gave up.

It felt odd not to be in contact with Ian after spending so much time with him. Even when they weren't together, they kept up a steady conversation via text, and his messages never failed to brighten her day. Lately she'd sensed a deepening of his feelings, had noticed the adoring look on his face when he showed up at her door and the way his gaze lingered when she walked into the room. She pulled out her phone.

Kate: *I know you're busy so no need to write back. I just wanted you to know I was thinking about you and I miss you. xoxo*

Meeting her friends was exactly the distraction Kate needed, and when she arrived at Kieran's that night, she was glad she'd ventured out. The Irish pub was decorated for the holidays, and the Christmas lights, the music, and the gently falling snow visible from her seat near the window put Kate in a festive mood.

She returned home a little before ten. Shivering, she pulled on the flannel snowflake pajamas Ian had given her. She wrapped herself in a blanket and sat down in the comfy, oversized chair near the window, looking down at the empty street below as the snow continued to fall.

At first she thought it was a dream. She heard a scraping noise, but in her half-asleep state, she was unable to process what was making the sound. She'd fallen asleep in the chair, and as she awakened further, she realized someone was trying to put a key in the lock. A quick glance at her phone showed the time as 5:53 a.m. Approximately forty-eight hours after he'd kissed her good-bye, it seemed that Ian was back. Kate sprang from the chair.

He'd managed to get the door open, and she flinched when she saw his condition. His hair looked as if he hadn't run anything but his fingers through it since he'd left, and his skin was pale, bordering on gray. The whites of his eyes were streaked with clusters of red. How long had he been staring at a computer screen? Had he slept at all? He wasn't wearing a coat, and his shirt was untucked and wrinkled.

He reached for her, his expression weary and unfocused. "I'm sorry I didn't text back."

"It's okay," she said, gently taking the key ring from his freezing hand and easing the laptop-bag strap from his shoulder and setting it down on her kitchen table. Hoping he hadn't driven, she led him by the hand into the bedroom.

He sat down heavily on the bed, reaching for the buttons on his shirt. His fingers wouldn't cooperate, and if it hadn't been for the complete lack of the smell of alcohol, Kate would have sworn he was drunk.

"Here, let me do it," Kate said, brushing his hands away.

"I'm sorry," he said again.

She gave him a quick kiss. "I know. We'll talk about it later." She took off his glasses and set them on the nightstand.

He seemed to fall asleep as she was undressing him, but then his eyes opened suddenly and he looked disoriented, as if he wasn't sure where he was.

"Don't worry. You're home," Kate said soothingly. When she had him down to his underwear, she pulled back the covers on his side of the bed and managed to slide him underneath, which was difficult because he was deadweight and almost incapable of helping her.

"My phone..." He was fading fast, the words trailing off.

Kate stroked his head. "I'll take care of your phone. You go to sleep." It was as if she'd flicked a switch. One moment he was with her, and the next he was out.

She found a few crumpled twenties, his company credit card, and his phone and charger in the front pocket of his jeans. The phone was exactly like hers and down to two percent battery. She plugged in the phone and placed it on the nightstand. Then she went into the kitchen and returned with a glass of water in case he woke up and needed a drink.

He was so still. She thought about sliding in next to him, wanting to put her arms around him and hold him, but she was wide-awake. She pressed a kiss to his lips, closed the bedroom door, and went into the kitchen to make coffee.

He woke up fourteen hours later. She was on her way to Ginger Hop to pick up an order of pad Thai and General Tsing's chicken when she received his text.

Ian: *I'm awake. I don't remember coming home.*

Kate: *You were pretty out of it. You must be starving. I'll be back soon with dinner.*

Ian: *Starving and still tired. I'm going to take a shower. I missed you.*

Kate: *I missed you too.*

When she walked in the door, he took the carryout bag from her, set it down on the floor, and slid his hand under her hair, gripping her by the back of her neck and pressing her face to his chest.

"Thanks for taking such good care of me," he said, raising her chin for a kiss. He tightened his hold on her, and she hugged him back.

"Anytime."

His eyes were still red, but they weren't nearly the road map they'd been when he'd come home.

"Please tell me you didn't drive here."

"I took a cab from the airport."

"Good."

"You're probably wondering what I was doing."

"I have a few questions, but let's have dinner first. We'll talk after."

He nodded. "Okay."

They dished up the food and brought their plates into the living room. Ian ate ravenously, finishing his meal and polishing off the rest of hers too. She waited until he set his empty plate on the coffee table before she asked her first question.

"Do you work for the FBI?" Kate had read everything she could get her hands on about hacking after Ian explained the difference between white and black hats. The subject fascinated her, and they'd had several in-depth follow-up discussions about certain aspects of the culture. She remembered from her reading that the FBI had a number of task forces dedicated to fighting cybercrime. If Ian was as good as he said he was, it made sense that he might be involved in something like that.

"I work *with* the FBI. But they have priority over my other clients. Always."

"Do they often whisk you away on airplanes without notice?"

"Only when absolutely necessary, and only if it's something that can't be handled out of the field office."

"What exactly are you involved in?"

"Remember that day at breakfast when I told you about the cyberthieves who steal credit card numbers and then sell them to people called carders?"

"You said they make new cards and use them to buy things. Then they return the merchandise for cash or sell it."

He nodded. "The credit card information is traded on a forum. It's basically an online black market for cyberthieves. Attacks against retailers and consumers have increased, which means more of this information is being bought and sold now than ever before. The FBI created a team whose sole purpose is to dismantle one of the biggest carding rings."

"The FBI hired you to help them with this?"

"It's not uncommon. They simply don't have the technical skills to do it themselves. Sometimes it takes a hacker to catch a hacker."

"So you're an informant?"

"More like a special consultant."

"Does the FBI have something against letting you sleep?"

"No, but one of the team members logged on to the forum from his government IP address, which prompted accusations that it had been infiltrated by the FBI. Most cybercrime rings have been, so the paranoia is rampant and, in this case, justified. The leader of the task force summoned the team to headquarters to do damage control. My phone started blowing up after I got the call, and the plane was already waiting for me on the tarmac when I arrived. They brought in food, and we could take a quick break to stand under a cold shower in the locker room, but no one slept. We've spent over two years earning the trust of the forum's key members, and we stayed online around the clock until we'd convinced them it had been a false alarm and they had nothing to worry about. Then I got back on the plane and came home."

It wasn't that Kate didn't know the FBI utilized civilian assistance because she did. And she could understand how anyone working in that capacity would need to maintain a certain amount of anonymity. But it was a little disconcerting to discover that the man she was falling for actually *was* a superhero who spent at least part of his time fighting cybercrime and that she'd had no idea.

"You ask me about my day, and I tell you about the people I've helped. But when I ask you about your day not once have you ever said, 'The team and I made some good progress toward bringing down a ring of cyberthieves.'"

"I wasn't intentionally withholding it. When things are running smoothly I don't think much about it. The FBI is just another one of my clients, and I sometimes forget it's a bit out of the ordinary for most people."

"How long have they been one of your clients?"

"A little over ten years."

"What kinds of things have you worked on with them?"

"High-tech crime, exploitation, cyberterrorism, fraud. Some assignments are short. Some, like the carding ring, are much longer."

"Is that the reason you move so much?" He could downplay it all he wanted, but if relocation was necessary, it meant that the duplicitous nature of his work carried a certain amount of risk.

"Yes. The days of simply tracking an IP address are over, and there are dozens of ways to remain anonymous online. But if someone is patient, if they're technically savvy, which these hackers are, there are ways to obtain my personal information, including my identity and location."

"And they're trying to do that to you?"

"Hopefully not at the moment, but they'd like to. Hackers protect their identities at all costs, so doxing one—especially if he's working with any kind of law-enforcement agency—is considered a badge of honor. We're trying to gather enough evidence to send these people to prison. That's a pretty big motivator for them to try to find me."

Occasionally I find myself in a bit of hot water, which I prefer to keep other people out of.

"What would happen if they found you?"

"There would be threats, highly disturbing but mostly empty. It wouldn't matter, because I'd be long gone before anyone knocked on my door."

Kate was silent. She'd chalked up his frequent changes of address to wanderlust and the fact that he could live anywhere he chose for as long as he wanted before moving on to the next city. But wanting to stay and needing to leave were two very different things.

Her expression was apprehensive. "Would you tell me before you left?"

"Kate." He looked hurt, as if he couldn't believe she'd ask such a thing. "Of course I would tell you."

How had she let things get this far? She seemed to have forgotten the promise she'd made to herself: that if she reached the point where she had strong feelings for Ian—and the feelings she had for him were growing stronger by the day—he would have to start opening up to her.

"I wasn't sure. You know everything about me, but there's so much I don't know about you. I've never been to your place. You could have a wife and kids stashed there, and I wouldn't have a clue. You know where I am—all the time—because of that phone. But I still don't know your last name."

"I don't have a wife and kids. My last name is Bradshaw."

It took her a moment to process what he'd said. "You said you were never going to tell me."

"I was always going to tell you. I'm just very protective of my last name because someday when I actually *have* a wife and kids, I want to share it with them. But if it's out there or if it's ever linked to my work, I might not be able to. I had a girlfriend once who didn't understand my need for discretion, and she talked about what I did and gave my name to anyone who would listen, which caused me nothing but stress. It's made me a bit gun-shy, and I'm more cautious about when I tell someone than I used to be."

"I would never say anything, Ian."

"I know you wouldn't because I know I can trust you." He picked up his phone from the coffee table and started typing. When he finished, he said, "Give me your phone."

She pulled the phone he'd given her from her pocket, unlocked it, and gave it to him.

He started typing, and a few minutes later he handed it back to her. "The only reason I track your phone is so I can wipe it if it gets lost or stolen. I didn't know it bothered you."

"It doesn't bother me. Stuart and I used to track each other if one of us wasn't answering our phone or was late. But it's not reciprocal with us."

"If you open the app and select Ian's Phone it will give you my location. I should have done it from the beginning. I'm sorry."

She glanced down at the unnamed plain blue icon. "Special app for a special phone?"

"Developed for my own private use."

Kate could only guess the functions it was capable of, but she was glad he hadn't hesitated to make the change. "I'm going to start stalking you now."

He smiled gently. "I'm afraid you'll find it very boring. If I'm not at my place, I'm probably here."

"There's nothing boring about that at all, at least not to me." She set the phone on the coffee table. "I really like you, Ian. I think about you all the time, and when you're not here I miss you. But the longer we're together, the higher the chances are that you'll have to leave—maybe without much notice—

and I don't want to get hurt. I'm sure there are things you can't tell me, but I need to know about anything that might increase your chances of leaving. If you can't promise me that, I can't do this."

A flicker of something crossed his face—surprise, concern, fear?—and then it disappeared.

He reached for her hands and squeezed them. "I promise. I don't want to lose you. You're far too special to me."

"All right," she said softly. She'd told him what she needed, and he'd promised to give it to her.

"Come here," he said, pulling her onto his lap.

He kissed her, held her, told her how much he'd missed her.

He promised.

CHAPTER EIGHTEEN

THE NEXT NIGHT, WHEN they returned to Kate's apartment after dinner, Ian said, "Why don't you pack a bag? We can stay at my place tonight, and I'll drive you to work in the morning."

She knew where he lived because they'd driven by his building several times and he'd pointed it out.

"The only reason I haven't taken you there before now is because I prefer your place. Mine is just where I work."

Kate packed a bag.

Ian lived across the river in a high-rise apartment downtown. When they arrived, he pushed a button on a key fob that he held up to a sensor and then pulled into a marked stall in the underground parking garage.

"Where do you store the Shelby?"

"At a private storage facility in Bloomington. I miss her. I might have to drop by and take her for a spin every now and then."

They rode the elevator to the twentieth floor, and she followed Ian down the hallway and into his apartment, waiting as he switched on the lights.

"No wife, no kids," he said gently.

"I didn't really think that."

The luxury unit was pristine but stark. An oversized sectional and coffee table faced a large, wall-mounted flat-screen

TV that hung over the fireplace. There were no other chairs or tables. A massive L-shaped desk sat adjacent to the sectional. On it sat two desktop monitors, an open laptop, and four cell phones.

"I'm guessing electronics won't be showing up on your Christmas list anytime soon."

He smiled. "Probably not."

There were no personal touches. No art on the walls. No lingering cooking smells or pile of shoes by the door. He had blinds for privacy but no decorative window treatments surrounding them. The room needed color and warmth; lamps and rugs and throw pillows. It wasn't remotely a home, not that Kate thought he was trying to make it one. No wonder he preferred her place.

She looked out the floor-to-ceiling windows of the living area. The lights of downtown Minneapolis twinkled in the darkness. "It's a beautiful space," Kate said, turning back around. "When do you finish moving in?"

"Don't let the cars fool you. I'm not a man who needs a lot of material things."

"That's not what I meant. This is a place you could move on from quickly if you had to."

He must have heard the unease in her voice because he turned toward her and said, "Just because I can doesn't mean I will."

He showed her the bedroom next. In addition to the king-size bed, there was a dresser and nightstand with a lamp. The sunken tub in the attached bathroom dwarfed the one in Kate's apartment, and the large walk-in shower had two showerheads. Those two rooms were also devoid of anything not meant for function.

Lastly, he showed her the kitchen. She ran her hand along the granite countertop, upon which sat a high-end coffeemaker, and admired the shiny stainless steel appliances.

"The Batcave is gorgeous, if a little unfinished."

"Most everything I rent ends up looking like this. I never take the time to do much to the apartments. I work, sleep, use the gym, and order in."

Kate looked at the glass-front cupboards. Other than a few coffee cups, they were empty. She opened a drawer, but instead of silverware she found the plastic-wrapped forks and spoons that accompanied a takeout order. There was no knife block or fruit bowl or toaster to be found.

"All you have in your kitchen is a coffeemaker." She hopped up on the counter.

"Well, now I have a coffeemaker and a beautiful woman. What more do I need?"

He stood between her legs, and she wrapped them around him. Looking into his eyes, she kissed him softly. Then she rubbed her cheek against his scruff, which was long enough not to hurt but short enough to provide the most arousing friction, especially when he dragged it along her inner thigh. "I love the way this feels on my skin."

"Bet I know where you love it the most."

"Bet you're right."

After pulling off his sweatshirt, she ran her hands along his shoulders and then leaned forward, kissing and nibbling and sucking her way down the side of his neck.

"I do so enjoy it when a woman makes the first move."

"I'll keep that in mind. However, you seldom allow me enough time to make one before you swoop in with one of your own."

"It's because I find you so irresistible."

"Aren't you a charmer?"

He leaned forward to catch her earlobe between his teeth and whispered, "You know it."

She shrieked when he put his hands on her lower back and pulled her forward, sliding her off the counter. "Don't drop me," she said, tightening her arms and legs around him.

He laughed, and with his hands underneath her, he boosted her higher and headed for the bedroom. "I'm not going to drop you."

Maybe he didn't drop her in the kitchen or while walking down the hallway, but when he reached the bedroom, he leaned over his bed and let go. Kate landed on her back with a bounce. He took off his jeans. The room was dark except for the light coming in from the hallway. It was the perfect amount, romantic but not too bright.

"Oh yes," Kate said. She propped herself up on her elbows and let out a wolf whistle. "Look at you. Bravo. *Bravo*."

"And I'm not even done yet."

"Take it all off, you gorgeous man."

While he was removing his underwear, Kate inched her way to the edge of the bed so that she was right in front of Ian.

Deliciously naked Ian.

And his very impressive erection.

Which Kate decided she simply had to put in her mouth.

"Oh, Jesus," Ian said. He plunged his hands into Kate's hair.

When she flicked her gaze upward a few minutes later, his eyes were wide open and he was watching her every movement. His groans and his ragged breathing made her never want to stop doing this to him.

A few minutes after that, he put his hands on her head to still her. "Kate."

"Are you sure?" she asked, pausing to look up at him.

"Rain check. Very, very soon," he said, pulling her shirt over her head and reaching around to unhook her bra.

Kate lay back on the bed, and Ian tugged off her jeans, socks, and underwear. He kissed her hungrily, his mouth moving from her lips to her neck to her breasts, and when he put his hand between her legs, she moaned.

Turning onto his back, he pulled her into a sitting position on top of him. They had explored many positions in the days since they'd first slept together, and she'd discovered this was one of Ian's favorites.

He held on to her so she wouldn't topple off, and he reached over to get a condom from the nightstand. "I really hate these things. I'll take whatever test you want me to take if we can stop using them."

"Deal," she said. Kate was already on the pill, and if he was willing to jump through a few hoops in order to ditch the condoms, so was she.

After he rolled it on, she took him in hand and prepared to guide him into her.

"Not yet, sweetness." He lay back and put his hands on her hips, lifting and pulling her forward until she was hovering over him.

Oh.

Oh.

He tucked his arms under her thighs and brought her down onto his face.

"Ahhhhh." She balanced on her knees, gripping the headboard as his tongue probed and swirled.

He pressed her tighter to his mouth, and it felt so good that she let go of her inhibitions and stopped worrying about whether he could breathe. It was easily the most erotic thing she'd ever experienced, and his enthusiasm only made it better.

Gripping the headboard tighter, she murmured a series of encouraging sounds to let him know how close she was. She cried out his name a moment later, and she was still riding the endless waves of her orgasm when he grabbed her roughly by the hips and moved her down his body, frantic in his need. She sank down onto him, and now she understood why he'd put the condom on first. He looked directly into her eyes, and when she held his gaze they shared a moment that was more intense than anything she'd ever felt with him. It made her want to give him things he hadn't asked for yet.

Cupping her breasts, he began to stroke her nipples with his thumbs, which shot an electric current directly between her legs. She moved faster, grinding against him as he held her hips tight.

"God, Kate. Yes."

Their rhythm and his roaming hands felt incredible, and she came for the second time—passionately, breathlessly. Not long after that, so did he. She collapsed onto his chest, her heart beating fast, feeling him pulsing inside her.

"How can it be this good every single time?" She'd wondered if the fireworks she'd experienced when they slept together the first time had been a fluke, but she'd discovered that sex with Ian had only gotten better. They were gasoline and fire, and he made her feel uninhibited in a way Stuart never had.

He smoothed the hair back from her damp temple and kissed her. "Maybe it's us."

Us.

"Maybe it is," she said, trying to catch her breath. Whatever the reason, she never wanted it to stop.

Ian ducked into the bathroom, and when he slipped back into bed, he held her tight, her head on his chest and his arms wrapped around her, their legs entwined. Ian spooned her when they slept, but this was the way he held her after sex. She could feel his heart beating under her cheek, and at that moment she thought she could easily spend the rest of her life in his arms.

"How many cities have you lived in?" she asked.

"Too many to count."

"A girl in every port, right?"

"There have been women in some ports. But never more than one at a time. And now only you."

"And when it's time to go, you move on? From the town and from them?"

"In the past ten years, I've asked two of them to come with me. They both declined. My lifestyle is not for everyone."

Kate remained silent. If he were to ask, would she be willing to follow him wherever it was he wanted her to go?

"It doesn't mean I love any less fiercely," he said.

Her heart fluttered at the mention of love. How would it feel to be loved by Ian? To hear him utter those words to her?

"You said you didn't really have any family to speak of. What happened to them?"

"I don't have a lot of contact with my mom. She's not really interested in my whereabouts and doesn't know much about my adult life. She's always been somewhat distant. I'm an only child, so I guess she never really took to parenting."

"What about your dad?"

"My dad was wonderful. He was as warm as she was cold. He worked long hours at an office job so my mom could stay home with me, but she left me to my own devices most of the time, and once I started school she disengaged even more. She never showed up for things a parent was supposed to show up for, but my dad always did. He'd take off work and would be sitting right in the front row of my school program or award ceremony. When I got a little older and started playing sports, he never missed a game."

Kate's heart broke for him. Her parents had always been there for her and Chad, cheering on their accomplishments and showing their support. Her mother had taken things one step further, acting as homeroom mother several years in a row for both her and Chad. Diane was the kind of parent who volunteered to bake five dozen cupcakes for the bake sale or sew costumes for the school play.

"My dad's the one who introduced me to computers. He was fairly technical and had always been interested in programming. He had an old Commodore computer in the basement, and he used a textbook to show me how to write programs for it. I was only twelve, but it didn't take long before I'd surpassed everything he taught me, and he was amazed at what I could make that computer do. I was fourteen when we started accessing the Internet from home via dial-up, and my dad and I spent hours online. It was like a whole new world had opened up for me. For him too, although in a vastly different way."

Ian seemed lost in thought for a moment. "As I got older, I realized he hated his job and that the thing he wanted most was to be independently wealthy. My mom rode him pretty hard—nothing he did was ever good enough—and it was no secret that he didn't like his boss. He wanted desperately to be a self-made man, but he could never figure out how to make it happen. Though he should have been, he wasn't suspicious about the financial opportunities he found on the Internet, and he fell victim to an online pyramid scheme. It was fairly sophisticated and nearly impossible to identify it as a scam, and he lost everything he had. But worse than that was the blow to his pride. I remember hearing my parents fight, massive screaming arguments, my mom yelling about how foolish he'd been. They argued all the time after that, especially about money. About six months later, when I was at school and my mom was out, he came home from work and left the car running when he shut the garage door."

Kate's eyes filled with tears. "I don't know what to say, Ian. I'm so sorry. It sounds like he was a wonderful person."

"It's okay, sweetness," he said soothingly. "The story ends well, I promise. After my dad died, my mom had to get a job and she was just so angry all the time. She couldn't stand the sight of me on that computer, so I moved it into my bedroom and the two of us went our separate ways even though we lived under the same roof. I was lucky though, because I had an advisor in high school who'd picked up on the fact that I didn't have any parental involvement when it came to planning for college. She's the one I credit for helping me gain admission to MIT, which is not an easy thing to achieve even when you're a 4.0 student like I was. I'd always shown a strong aptitude for math and science, so she made sure that everything I did from tenth grade on would benefit me during the admission process, whether it was encouraging me to sign up for extracurricular activities or asking my teachers for letters of recommendation. She knew I had no money for college but assured me that MIT had a great financial-aid program and that if I got in, she'd help me with the paperwork. I took every AP class available and several at the local community college so I could start earning credit while I was still in high school. When it came time to write my admissions essay, I made sure it would pull on the heartstrings of every person who read it. I spared no detail about my dad because I'd already figured out that playing upon the sympathies of the admissions board was just another way of identifying their weakness and using it to my advantage. No one was more excited when I got into MIT than my advisor."

"Do you stay in touch?"

"I send her an e-mail every now and then. I wonder sometimes if she's ever figured out where the extra money in her bank account comes from."

"You put money in her bank account?" Kate loved that.

"I can tell by her average balance that she needs it, so a few times a year I make a deposit and make sure it can't be traced back to me."

"Your dad would be so proud of who you've become and the things you've accomplished."

"I think he would," Ian said, stroking her hair. "After I graduated and left for college, I never looked back. MIT was a perfect fit for me. It's where I came alive, Kate. I met other students who were every bit as driven as I was, and it was like being reborn. To everyone else, I was this computer whiz kid from Amarillo who was desperately trying to lose his accent, but I knew I could be anyone I wanted to be. They knew nothing about my history, and I spent my first year of college trying my best to forget where I'd come from. One day I realized I could use my growing skills to go anyplace I wanted. I hung around with other computer science majors, and we spent hours in our dorm rooms trying to one-up each other, competing to see what systems we could hack into. It took me a while to track down the man who'd cheated my dad, but I'm very patient and eventually I found him. Then I made his life a living hell by crippling every single scam website he attempted to launch and corrupting every computer he ever tried to use. Eventually I learned how to steal from people like him."

"What about your mom? Do you ever talk to her?"

"She's remarried now. I keep track of her, out of curiosity more than anything. I call and leave a message once or twice a year. She doesn't call back. I don't give her money. I would if she asked for it, but she can't be bothered to learn enough about me to know I have it. So I give it to others, people who are more deserving. It makes me feel good."

He grew quiet then. Kate shifted her body so she was lying on top of him. She pressed her lips tenderly to his and said, "I think you're amazing."

She kissed him again, slowly, softly, gently. His body stirred underneath her, and she responded with her touch because at that moment there was nothing she wanted more than to share that closeness with him again.

Maybe she didn't know how it would feel to be loved by Ian, but she knew how it would feel to love him because that night, in his bed after hearing his story, Kate's heart felt like it would burst and she fell hard.

The next morning when she awakened wrapped in Ian's arms, he nuzzled his face in her hair and asked if she'd accept his donation.

"Yes," she said. She could no sooner deny his request than she could the hungry people who walked into her food pantry, and he probably knew it. "But I'd like it to be my Christmas gift from you, and I'd rather it came from you personally. I don't care that you take money from cyberthieves, but there's no justifiable reason for you to do it on my behalf."

"Whatever you want," he said, and both of them were happy.

A few days later, she and Ian met at Target after work. If he was going to donate the money, she wanted him to see what he was paying for. They worked from the list Kate had brought, making sure to buy toys in a variety of age ranges that any child would enjoy, regardless if it was a boy or a girl. By the time they were done, neither of their SUVs could hold anything more. Because Ian was providing the toys, the organizations she was partnering with were able to put the money they'd raised toward the holiday meal, and everything was set for Christmas Eve.

Afterward, Kate insisted on taking Ian out for dinner and to Nicollet Mall where they walked hand in hand, looking at lights and checking out the Christmas Market. Then, when they were sipping mulled wine and watching the winter fireworks, he squeezed her hand and said, "I am falling so hard for you."

She smiled up at him because his words filled her with joy. Kate wanted to tell him she'd already fallen. She wanted to tell him that when she woke up in his arms she wondered what it would be like to wake up in them for the rest of her life. She wanted to tell him that *his* babies were the ones she'd been thinking about lately. But she worried it was too early to say any of those things, so she squeezed back and said, "Me too."

CHAPTER NINETEEN

IAN WAS SITTING ON KATE'S couch with his laptop. When she walked into the room, he set the computer on the coffee table, took off his glasses, and said, "C'mere, sweetness. I've got a number six for you."

"I *love* the number six." She sat down on his lap, and he cupped her face and pulled her in for a kiss.

"When do you need to leave?" he asked, sliding his hands under her sweater so that his warm palms rested on her bare skin.

Kate was meeting some friends from college for a Timberwolves game. She wasn't a huge basketball fan, but the group had been going once or twice a season for years and used the outings as a way to stay in touch.

"Soon."

"You don't sound very excited."

"It's hard to get excited when it's so cold outside and so warm and cozy in here." Though Kate enjoyed getting together with her old friends, she was tired and really didn't feel like venturing out on such a bitterly cold night right before Christmas. But the tickets had already been purchased, so she was going.

"I know a little something about hard and excited," Ian said, a devilish smile on his face.

She smiled back. "Do you ever." Kate gave him a long, warm, soft kiss, relishing the way it made him groan. "Will you stay? Wait here for me until I get back?" Though she couldn't remember the last time he'd slept at his place, Kate didn't want Ian to think he had to go home just because she was leaving. She wanted him to still be on her couch when she returned from the game.

"Of course."

"Good." Reluctantly she lifted herself off his lap. "I'll be home as soon as I can. Keep your fingers crossed that the game doesn't go into overtime."

The Target Center was packed when Kate arrived. She and her friends spent a lively fifteen minutes talking and having a drink in the concession area. There were seven of them in the group, four women and three men. A man named Derek smiled when he spotted Kate. She'd known him since her senior year of college and had once been very interested in dating him. It had never worked out between them because they never seemed to be single at the same time. Derek was attractive, smart and confident, but over the past few years Kate had noticed a bitterness creeping in as the glory days of college gave way to the not-so-glory days of a lackluster career in middle management.

When it was time to take their seats, Derek followed closely behind Kate, sloshing beer down the back of her sweater when she stopped to let someone pass by.

"Sorry," Derek said, pawing at her with a napkin once they sat down. The area where Ian's warm hands had been was now cold and wet.

"That's okay," she said, brushing his hands away. "It was an accident."

"You're looking good, Kate."

"Thanks." She glanced down the row, wishing she was sitting closer to the other women. Lisa was sitting on the other side of Derek, but Brooke and Julie were clear at the other end.

"Heard you and Stuart broke up."

"Yes."

"You were together a long time."

"Five years," Kate said.

"That's rough."

Kate didn't appreciate Derek's pitying expression. "Well, I broke up with him."

"How are you holding up?"

"I'm doing fine. Really."

Further conversation was cut short when the announcers began the pregame show and the players took to the court. Derek rested his arm across the back of Kate's seat, but since he wasn't actually touching her, she thought it would seem petty if she asked him to move it. During a break in the action, she tried to lean around Derek to talk to Lisa. Unfortunately, this caused Kate's body to press up against Derek's spread legs, and he did nothing to move them out of the way. She settled back into her seat, having forgotten about Derek's arm, which now rested lower on the back of her seat. She scooted forward slightly to avoid his touch.

"I'm going to get another beer. Want one?" Derek asked.

Kate held up her nearly full beer. "No thanks." She was finally able to talk to Lisa while Derek was gone.

When he returned, he settled into his seat and put his arm around her again. "Remember how we were never single at the same time? Now that we are, we should go out sometime."

"Actually, I'm seeing someone."

He whistled. "Didn't waste much time, did you?" His voice carried an edge she hadn't noticed before, and Kate wondered how many beers he'd had at home before he joined them. "Guess the early bird gets the Kate. I'll remember that next time."

"It's been over six months since Stuart and I broke up," she pointed out.

"So where is this guy?"

Derek knew as well as she did that significant others had never been a part of these outings, which was something that had always bothered Stuart. "He's waiting for me at home."

"How long have you been seeing him?"

Kate didn't really want to give Derek any ammunition by admitting she'd been dating Ian for such a short time, but she didn't need to prove anything to him either. She knew what she had with Ian was more than a fling. "November."

He stopped short of rolling his eyes, but the look on his face told Kate he'd already dismissed Ian. "Sounds like early days to me."

She smiled sweetly. "And sometimes you just *know*."

"Let's go to dinner next week. We can catch up."

"I can't. I'll be having dinner with my boyfriend."

"I'm sure he'll understand if you save one night for me."

"Thanks, but I'll pass," Kate said firmly.

"Come on, you can have dinner with an old friend. Bring him along." He grinned at Kate. "Tell him I'm willing to share if he is."

Kate laughed dryly. "I'm not yours to share, buddy. Seriously, how many beers have you had?" Had Derek always been an asshole and she hadn't noticed, or was this the alcohol talking?

He should have paid more attention to her incredulous—and irritated—expression, but instead he smiled and held up his empty glass. "Not nearly enough."

Kate wished she hadn't come and was glad when Derek left to go to the bathroom at the start of halftime. Her phone buzzed.

Ian: *Having fun?*

Kate: *No. I'm irritated, wet, uncomfortable, and cold.*

Ian: *I'm confused by your words considering you're at an indoor basketball game with friends.*

Kate: *I'm trapped at the end of the row so I can't talk to anyone, and Derek spilled beer down my back.*

Ian: *Derek?*

Kate: *The token drunk guy in our group, or at least he will be by the end of the evening if he doesn't slow down. He's being an ass.*

Derek came back, holding a giant beer. He scowled when he noticed Kate typing on her phone. That didn't stop him from putting his arm on the back of her chair *again*.

Ian: *Is he bothering you?*

Kate: *It's nothing I can't handle. But if you're watching the game on TV and they happen to flash a picture of us on the Jumbotron, it was not my idea for him to rest his arm across the back of my chair. Also, he's miffed that you scooped me up when I was single. How dare you!*

Ian: *Please elaborate.*

Kate: *I told him about you, but he's still acting like he has a shot with me. He said he's willing to share if you are.*

Kate was surprised when there wasn't an immediate response from Ian. He didn't strike her as the jealous type, but his extreme confidence made her think he might have something to say about Derek's behavior.

She was looking right at the Jumbotron when the first message appeared on the screen.

KATE IS MINE

She sat bolt upright and looked around to see if anyone else had noticed, watching as Derek took a big drink of his beer and squinted at the screen. Turning away from him slightly, she pulled out her phone.

Kate: *Oh my God. You did NOT hack the Jumbotron.*

Ian: *You know, I believe I did.*

BEAUTIFUL KATE BELONGS TO ME

People in the crowd had begun to point at the Jumbotron.

Lisa leaned toward Kate. "Didn't you say your new boyfriend's name was Ian?"

"Well, yes," Kate said, noticing that Derek was listening in. "But those are both pretty common names."

"You can pay to have a message put on the Jumbotron," Lisa said. "I read something about it in the program."

Kate shook her head. "Trust me, it's not him."

Kate: *I'm never leaving you at home without a sitter again.*

COME HOME KATE I MISS YOU

The announcers joined in on the fun. "I don't know who Kate is, but she's a lucky girl."

More pointing, more cheering.

Heads turned as people tried to pinpoint "Kate's" location.

"Kate, if you're in the stands," the announcer said, "stand up and wave your arms so we can get a shot of you." A cameraman panned the crowd, and a live video feed of the fans was now appearing on the Jumbotron.

"Are you sure, Kate?" Lisa asked again. "Maybe he did it to surprise you?"

"Bit of a lame surprise, if you ask me," Derek said. Which no one had.

Kate: *Derek just said the messages were "lame." And he still has his arm around the back of my chair.*

STOP TOUCHING KATE
THIS MEANS YOU DEREK
ESPECIALLY YOU
AND I DON'T SHARE
EVER

"Look!" Lisa said, pointing at the screen. The crowd was no longer paying any attention to the halftime show. They were too busy watching the Jumbotron to see what would happen next.

Kate stifled her laughter, sinking lower in her seat and trying to appear as unobtrusive as possible so as not to attract the attention of the cameraman filming the crowd.

She wished Lisa would *sit down.*

"What the fuck?" Derek said, looking warily at Kate and *finally* removing his damn arm.

Kate stared back at him, an innocent smile on her face. "What an absolutely bizarre coincidence."

Kate: *OMG. I'm dying.*

Ian: *Do you think he got the message? Or do I need to continue?*

Kate: *He's very confused. And fairly drunk. But he moved his arm!*

Ian: *VICTORY IS MINE.*

Kate: *I'm coming home.*

When she arrived at her apartment fifteen minutes later, he met her at the door. After removing her coat, he backed her up against the wall, sliding his hands into her hair and crashing his mouth onto hers. His kisses were rough, demanding, and he didn't stop until they were both gasping for air.

"You sure know how to make a statement," she said, breathing heavily.

He pressed his body against hers and sucked his way down the length of her neck. "Just staking my claim, sweetness."

He lifted her sweater over her head and took off her push-up bra. He yanked on the button of her jeans, unzipped them, and pushed them down. "Step out," he said when they'd cleared her hips and landed at her ankles. Then he pulled a condom from the front pocket of his jeans, ripped it open with his teeth, and spit out the narrow strip of foil. She looked at him questioningly as he unzipped his jeans and freed himself enough to put on the condom.

He smirked, desire blazing in his eyes as he pulled down her underwear. Then he lifted her and pinned her against the wall, and all she could do was press her shoulders into it and grab his biceps as he entered her.

Stuart had *never* done anything like that.

There was something so powerful about Ian holding her that way because she was confined and yet completely exposed. And because of the way they were lined up, with her slightly below him, there was an amazing kind of friction occurring with each thrust. Powerless to do anything but enjoy how good it felt, Kate pulled his mouth to her neck by grabbing him roughly by his hair. She closed her eyes and moaned softly as he sucked on her skin.

"I meant it," Ian said as he moved inside her. "I don't share. Not ever."

Kate wasn't surprised. Ian would not be good at sharing. He was too used to getting his own way, too used to ignoring the rules and breaking them to get what he wanted.

"Here's something you should know," she said finding it hard to get the words out because it felt so good and she was almost there. "I don't either."

The next morning while sipping coffee in bed next to Ian, Kate read with interest the article in the newspaper about the mysterious hacking of the Jumbotron that had occurred the night before at the Timberwolves game.

"Listen to this part," she said. "The sophisticated attack was undoubtedly carried out by a highly skilled team of hackers."

Ian snorted. "No, just me, and I did it from my *phone*."

"They also mention that it was"—she made air quotes—"*illegal*."

"Does that bother you?"

"It should, but somehow it doesn't." Now that she knew him better, it was hard for Kate to think of Ian as anything but good, even when he broke the law. She threw a pillow at him. "You're such a rebel."

"I'm a hacker. We're all rebels." He tucked the pillow behind his head and grabbed Kate's wrists when she tried to take it back. "Harmless halftime fun. I was watching it on TV. The crowd seemed to really enjoy it."

He pulled her close, and she rested her head on his shoulder and continued reading. "It says that 'steps are being taken to strengthen the integrity of the Target Center's computer systems.'"

"That's hilarious," Ian said. "I'm tempted to demonstrate how futile their efforts are by doing it again."

Kate laughed. "That'll show 'em."

"Never a dull moment, right Katie?" He trailed his fingertips along her shoulder, took the newspaper out of her hands, and covered her body with his.

"There is nothing dull about you, Ian. And I wouldn't have it any other way."

Later that day, she received a text from Lisa.

Lisa: Everyone was talking about the Jumbotron messages after you left last night. Did you see that article in the paper? Those names were an awfully strange coincidence. Your new boyfriend's not a hacker is he? Come on, you can tell me. ☺

Kate: *Hahaha. No. My boyfriend is definitely not a hacker.*

Lisa: Is it weird that I think it would be kind of cool if he was? Those messages were awesome.

Kate: *Yeah, I thought so too.* ☺

CHAPTER TWENTY

WHEN IAN WALKED THROUGH THE door of Kate's apartment on the afternoon of Christmas Eve, she gasped. "What have you *done*?"

He laughed. "I knew you were going to say that."

He'd cut his hair, and not just a trim either. It was short, above the ears, and not one single strand was out of place. He still looked breathtaking. In fact, Kate might have been able to argue that the haircut made him look breathtaking in a completely *different* way than before, but she'd loved the length of his hair, especially the way it felt under her fingers when she ran her hands through it.

"If I were meeting my daughter's boyfriend for the first time, he would make a much better impression on me if he were a neatly trimmed business owner and not a scruffy hacker whose hair always looked like a woman had been running her hands through it in bed." He set a gift-wrapped box on the table. "Nothing's open tomorrow, so I had to do it today."

"What am I supposed to grab on to now?"

"My ears?" He bent down to kiss her.

She put her arms around him. "I think it's wonderful that you want to make a good impression. And you look superhot."

"I do, don't I?"

She grinned. "Humble as always." She turned her attention to the box he'd set on the kitchen table. "Who's the present for?"

"You, of course."

"But we weren't going to buy presents for each other. That was our deal."

"Santa dropped it off. I had nothing to do with it."

"When do I get to open it?" She picked it up and shook it.

"Not until we get home," he said, taking it from her and crossing the room to place it under the tree.

Kate had been delighted to learn that Ian wanted to help serve meals with her. "Did you actually think I was going to spend Christmas Eve somewhere else?" he'd asked. "Besides, it will be nice to see the kids with their toys."

Kate glanced at her watch.

"What time do we need to leave?"

"Not for another hour or so. I told Helena we'd be there by four to help set up."

He smiled at her. "Maybe we can think of something to do until then."

"Maybe we can."

A steady stream of Kate's clients came through the line while Kate and Ian were serving meals. There was Mike, a young man in his twenties whose girlfriend had broken up with him and kicked him out of her apartment. He'd been laid off three months before the breakup and had already gone through what little savings he had. He'd admitted to Kate how frantic he'd been when he'd scraped together enough to pay his bills and a deposit and first and last month's rent on a new apartment only to realize there was nothing left to feed him.

There was a family of three who'd moved to Minneapolis from California for jobs that later fell through. When the mother had come into the food pantry—desperate, cold, hungry—the only thing she'd begged for had been formula for her nine-month-old daughter. Kate had soothed her, given her the formula, and filled a box with food. She'd been coming back ever since, often with her husband and baby in tow.

Rose, a sixty-year-old woman who looked a decade older, came through the line with her daughter and three young grandchildren. Her son-in-law had died two years ago, and Rose had been trying to help her daughter pick up the pieces ever since. Some months were better than others.

None of them had been able to resist giving Kate a hug or her hand a quick squeeze. She was their savior, and at that moment Kate didn't care that she herself had needed Ian's help in order to assist them. All that mattered was that they were warm and fed and wearing hopeful smiles despite their circumstances.

Kate had confirmed that Samantha would be attending the dinner, and when Kate spotted her in line with the girls and Georgie, she waved at them. When they reached her, Kate leaned across the table and said, "Santa gave me your present for safekeeping, Georgie. I'll deliver it as soon as I'm done, okay?"

He nodded excitedly as Samantha ushered them along.

Helena's husband Bert had dressed up as Santa, and when the children finished eating, they climbed onto his lap and told him what they'd wished for. Then Helena handed a present to them, and none of the children seemed to mind if the gift wasn't exactly what they'd told Santa they wanted. Kate got choked up on more than one occasion as she observed their smiling faces.

Two volunteers took over for Kate and Ian twenty minutes later. Kate retrieved Georgie's gift and found him playing alongside the other children a few feet from Bert and Helena. She sat cross-legged on the floor next to him, the gift in her hands. He smiled when he saw Kate and climbed into her lap. She pulled the Hershey's Kiss from her pocket and watched as he unwrapped it and crammed it into his mouth. Next she handed him the Curious George stuffed animal she'd picked out at Target. Grinning widely, he examined it and then hugged it close.

Kate squeezed him tight. "Do you like it?"

Georgie nodded. "Mine."

"Yes. It belongs to you. Merry Christmas, sweetie." She kissed his temple. "Go play."

Ian had been standing nearby, watching. Kate wiped her eyes as she walked up to him.

"You made that child's night," she said. "You made everyone's night."

He put his arm around her. "So did you."

When they got home, Kate kicked off her shoes and Ian built a fire. He reached under the tree and pulled out the present he'd brought, setting it between them on the couch.

"Go ahead," he said. "Open it."

Kate untied the gold ribbon, removed the wrapping paper, and lifted the lid. Nestled within the layers of tissue were the most gorgeous items she'd ever seen. There was a black ribbed bustier, its lace bodice shot through with glittering metallic threads and covered with tulle. It zipped up the side but also laced up the back with black ribbons. The matching black thong had bands of wide lace on the sides.

"It's La Perla," Kate said, her eyes growing wide when she noticed the tag. The Italian lingerie was a ridiculously indulgent gift, and she didn't want to know how much it had cost.

"Do you like it?"

"I love it. But I'm perfectly happy with Victoria's Secret."

"I know you are."

"Promise me you'll be careful when removing it from my body."

"I promise to *try*." He pointed at the box. "There's more."

The second item was a diaphanous ecru Chantilly lace babydoll nightie. The full skirt had chiffon inserts and a tea rose design. Kate didn't think she'd ever had a need for the word diaphanous before, but it described the lingerie perfectly. Accompanying the nightie was a tiny pair of lacy high-cut briefs.

"It's so delicate. And beautiful." She looked at Ian. "You seem quite partial to babydoll nighties."

"With good reason. There's a lot to like."

Using great care, Kate gently folded the lingerie and placed it back in the box. "Everything is gorgeous. Thank you." She kissed him, then took a present from under the tree and handed it to him.

"You weren't supposed to get me anything either."

"It's not from me. Santa must have dropped it off."

Ian unwrapped it, pulled out a bottle of Four Roses single barrel bourbon, and grinned. "Lingerie and liquor. The jolly fat guy sure knows how to party."

"There are glasses too," Kate said.

He pulled out one of the rocks glasses and then leaned over to kiss her. "Thank you. This is the perfect gift, and I think Santa would want me to start enjoying it right now."

He went into the kitchen and returned with the bourbon and a glass of wine for Kate. After throwing another log on the fire, he sat down next to her. Drinks in hand, they snuggled together on the couch.

"What are your mom and dad doing tonight?" Ian asked. Kate's parents had arrived that afternoon and were staying at a hotel downtown. Kate and Ian were going to join them for dinner on Christmas Day. Their relationship was still fairly new, and Kate didn't want Ian to feel pressured in any way. But when she'd extended the invitation, he'd said yes immediately and told her he was looking forward to meeting them.

"If he can't be in his own home on Christmas Eve, my dad would prefer to spend it in a steakhouse with my mother, sipping whiskey. I do not begrudge him that desire. They had a seven-o'clock reservation at Manny's."

"Well then, your dad and I have something in common already. We're both spending Christmas Eve with Watts women and whiskey." He took a drink and set the glass on the coffee table.

"How is it?"

"Excellent. You chose well." He kissed her, and Kate found the combination of his warm mouth and the smoky yet buttery flavor of the bourbon highly arousing.

When they'd finished their drinks, he went to the kitchen to refill them, and she slipped into the bedroom. She put on the bustier, zipping it up the side and admiring what it did for her cleavage. Kate thought she might be in danger of spilling out the top, but the ribbing kept everything in place. She stepped into the thong and then reached into her closet for her black stilettos. Her long limbs and full breasts were made for lingerie, and she felt sexy and bold.

Ian was going to combust.

She walked into the living room and watched his face as he took in the sight of her. He'd been in the process of raising his glass to take a drink, but he paused and stared. "Wow."

"I was dying to try it on."

"I'd say it fits perfectly."

She walked toward him, and he didn't stop looking at her even when he finally brought the glass to his lips.

"I need you to lace me up." She sat down on the couch and turned so that her back was to him. He ran his hands through her hair, gathered it, and laid it over her shoulder. She took another drink from her wineglass while he cinched the ribbons tight and placed a kiss on the back of her neck.

Leaning back on the couch, drink in hand, he watched closely as she made several trips across the room, chest out, hips swaying, one hand trailing along her neck and collarbone. Kate grinned when her back was to him because he appeared to be in some kind of trance. Men were so visual, and she had a hunch that while Ian took immense pleasure in seeing her naked, there was something about seeing her half-naked that really turned him on. She made a few more passes in front of the couch, reveling in the way he never took his eyes off her.

"What do you think?" she asked.

"I'm incapable of forming coherent thoughts because all the blood has rushed from my brain to a different part of my body. I've never seen anything so hot."

She sat down beside him and took a sip of her wine while he unlaced her. He reached around and cupped her breasts, squeezing them. Sighing, she leaned back and twisted her neck to kiss him. "Think you can handle the babydoll?" she asked with a mischievous smile.

"Only one way to find out."

She went into the bedroom and slipped into the babydoll nightie and the tiny briefs. It covered more of her than the bustier had, and the off-white color made the garment seem more demure, but if Ian looked closely he'd be able to see her entire body through the nearly transparent fabric. Her nipples were dark pink buds under the tea rose pattern.

When Kate returned, Ian was semi-reclined on the couch, holding the bourbon glass loosely in his hand. He stared, eyes half-lidded, lips parted. "Come closer."

Maybe it was the way he was looking at her or maybe it was the wine, because at that moment Kate suddenly found herself with very few inhibitions. Slowly she approached him and then turned in a circle so he could see her from every angle.

"Beautiful," he said, his voice heavy with desire. "Now take it off."

CHAPTER TWENTY-ONE

WHEN IAN CAME OUT OF the bathroom on Christmas Day, Kate did a double take and clutched her chest as if she were having a heart attack. "You're killing me. You know that, right?"

He grabbed her hand and dragged the back of it along his clean-shaven cheeks.

"No, no, no," she said. "Way too smooth."

"Respectable," he countered.

Kate watched as he pulled a suit out of her closet and got dressed. "One minute you're a free-spirited hacker, and the next you're suiting up to meet the parents," she said. "I never know what I'm going to get."

He tightened his tie. "That's because being with me is never boring. I believe I promised you that, Katie."

"That it would not be boring was a bit of an understatement. You might have downplayed a few things."

Kate stood in front of the dresser mirror and ran a brush through her long curls, loosening them slightly. Then she applied her lipstick and spritzed on some perfume.

"You look gorgeous," Ian said. He watched as she stepped into a modest pencil skirt and pulled on a sweater. "What about the dress I gave you?"

"That one's a bit short for Christmas Day." She paused. "And my dad. Plus I'm saving it for New Year's Eve. It's perfect for downtown." Paige had invited Kate and Ian to join her and her husband at a party at the W Hotel. Audrey and her fiancé would be there too. Kate stepped into her shoes, grabbed her purse, and said, "Okay. Let's go."

They were meeting Kate's parents for dinner at Nicollet Island Inn. She had no worries regarding any questions that might arise over dinner about Ian's occupation, but it had been a long time since she'd introduced them to someone new, and she took a deep breath to calm her nerves as they got out of the car.

Ian seemed relaxed, smiling at Kate and holding her hand as they walked into the restaurant. Diane and Steve were waiting for them by the door. Her mother looked elegant in a wrap dress and silver hoop earrings, her hair blown out in a sleek bob that reached her shoulders. Kate thought if she looked half as good at fifty-five as her mother did, she'd be very happy. Like Ian, her dad had worn a suit, and after seeing his face light up when he spotted her, Kate realized how happy she was to be seeing her parents again.

After she hugged them, she turned around. "Mom, Dad, this is Ian."

Ian shook her mother's hand and Diane held it warmly in hers. "It's nice to meet you, Ian."

Kate's dad and Ian shook hands. Steve smiled, but Kate knew he was going through the mental checklist he'd been using to measure Kate's boyfriends since she'd been old enough to have them.

"It's nice to meet you both," Ian said. "Kate speaks of you often."

Diane couldn't stop smiling at Ian, and it was adorable. Her mother had always been close to Stuart and had been genuinely fond of him, but Kate didn't think it would be long before Diane pledged her allegiance to Ian.

They placed their drink orders once they were seated in the dining room: wine for Diane and Kate and single malt whiskey for Steve and Ian. Kate felt herself relaxing as they made small talk and looked at their menus.

"Have you heard from Chad?" Kate asked. Her brother was spending Christmas with Kristin's family in Ohio.

"Yes," Diane said. "He called this morning to wish us Merry Christmas. He and Kristin are flying back tomorrow."

Kate had worried that her parents might ask Ian why he wasn't spending the holiday with his own family, so she'd told her mom about Ian's upbringing one day when they'd talked on the phone. She didn't go into detail, but she'd told Diane about Ian's dad and that he didn't have much contact with his mom.

"That's heartbreaking," Diane had said.

"I know. He and his dad were really close. But he's handled it well, and he's doing fine on his own. Honestly, I couldn't be more impressed by what he's accomplished. I just don't want you to say anything about his parents at dinner." Diane had promised that she wouldn't.

Their drinks arrived and Diane took a sip of her wine. "How did last night go?"

"We didn't have to turn anyone away, so I'd say it was a success," Kate said. "We served meals for about three hours. The kids were so excited to receive their presents."

"Were you there too?" Diane asked Ian.

"Yes. Kate did a wonderful job organizing everything."

"Ian's being very modest. His contribution helped bring it all together."

"Kate told me you two met when you made a donation to the food pantry," Diane said.

"Yes. I saw her on TV and wanted to help."

"Ian is very philanthropically inclined," Kate said.

He smiled at Kate. "It balances out my shortcomings."

"What shortcomings?" she said, smiling back.

Diane looked at the two of them and beamed.

Ian had once teased Kate that the apple hadn't fallen far from the tree when she'd mentioned having a glass of wine with her mother. But Kate thought the tree she'd fallen from was more likely her father's. He had the same need for excitement that Kate did, and he'd satisfied it in a courtroom. Maybe that was one of reasons Kate's defection from the practice of law had bewildered him so.

Steve had always been kind to Stuart, but during the five years they'd been together, she'd noticed a slight dismissal in the way her dad spoke to him, as if he knew as well as Kate that there wasn't much under Stuart's surface that needed excavating. Ian would be a more stimulating conversational partner for her father. She envisioned Ian sharing only what he wanted to and Steve always being aware that there was more.

"Kate tells me you went to MIT," Steve said.

"Yes."

"And I hear you own your own company."

"For about ten years now. I specialize in computer security."

Kate's dad asked several questions, and Ian gave him examples of the work he'd done for some of his clients. She was impressed when her dad seemed to grasp it so quickly. Steve Watts was a highly intelligent man, but he was definitely out of his comfort zone when it came to technology.

"Sounds like you're very good at what you do," Steve said.

"I genuinely enjoy it, which helps," Ian said.

"Do you think it's true what they say about the next terrorist attack being launched by computers?" Steve asked.

"Yes. We've only just begun to see the impact hackers will have on national security."

"What are the implications?"

"It's our infrastructure that's most vulnerable. Electricity, gas, oil, water. Bringing those to a standstill would cripple us."

Kate had never seen Ian look so serious.

Or so worried.

After they finished eating, Kate and Diane excused themselves to go to the restroom.

"He's wonderful, Kate," Diane said when they were washing their hands. "He looks at you like all he wants is to have you by his side."

Kate knew exactly what her mother was talking about. "I haven't told him yet, but I love him. And I love him in a way I never loved Stuart. I can't describe it."

Diane smiled and took Kate's hands in her own. "One of the things I admire most about you is that you follow your head *and* your heart. Keep trusting your instincts. This is your life. Make the choices that will bring you the most happiness."

Kate hugged her mom. "I will." She started to laugh. "You would not *believe* how much I didn't like him at first. Someday when we're alone and have time, I'll tell you the whole story."

When they sat back down at the table, they ordered dessert and coffee. Kate and Diane made plans to meet for brunch and to go shopping the next day, and then Kate would spend some more time with her parents before they headed home the day after that. Kate hoped that next year Ian could come home with her for Thanksgiving or Christmas. Kate wanted Chad and Kristin to meet him too.

When the check came, Ian didn't challenge Steve about who would pay it, and Kate was relieved. There was a clear hierarchy about who picked up the tab for the first dinner, and Steve held the top spot.

They walked to the door of the restaurant and said their good-byes. Kate hugged her parents and Ian shook their hands. Diane couldn't resist giving Ian a hug too.

"It was wonderful to meet you," Ian said. "Thank you for dinner."

"I'll see you tomorrow, Mom," Kate said, giving her mom another hug.

Kate's parents watched as Ian opened the passenger door for Kate, and she waved to them as they walked to their own car. Ian slid behind the wheel and pulled out of the parking lot.

"Well?" she asked.

"I think your mom approves. She didn't stop smiling at me the entire time. Your dad might enjoy cross-examining me under oath or administering a lie detector test, but I'm guessing that's standard operating procedure for any man you've ever introduced to him."

Kate nodded, laughing. "He'd love to do those things, but my mom won't let him."

"I liked them. I'm not just saying that either."

"I was a little nervous. I haven't introduced them to anyone since Stuart."

"I could tell. But I'm pretty sure I passed."

"After watching you use your impeccable manners to charm the pants off my parents—my mother's almost literally—I would have to agree."

Ian flipped on his turn signal. "When we get home, I'm going to build a fire and have some more of that bourbon Santa brought me. Then I'm going to take off all your clothes and lay you down on the rug in front of the fire. After that I'm going to make my way down your body until my face is between your legs. Then I'd like to hear what you think about my smooth cheeks."

Kate smiled and looked at him affectionately. "I was thinking just the other day about how I kind of miss that cocky, over the top, wildly inappropriate man I first met. But then you go and say something like that and I think, *Oh... there he is.*"

When they got home, Ian helped Kate off with her coat and built a fire. Then he poured the drinks, and when they'd finished them, he did exactly what he'd promised in the car.

And Kate decided his smooth cheeks felt very fine indeed.

CHAPTER TWENTY-TWO

LOUD ELECTRONIC BEEPING ROUSED KATE from a deep sleep. At first she thought it was her alarm clock, which was set to wake her at 8:00 a.m. But the bedroom was pitch-dark, and Ian would not have thrown back the covers and bolted out of bed if the noise had come from her alarm. A quick glance at the clock showed the time as 2:11.

He moved fast for someone who had only moments before been curled around Kate, asleep, and by the time she pulled on her robe and caught up to him, he was already sitting on the couch, fingers flying across the keyboard of his laptop. He'd silenced the alarm, which she now realized had come from the computer.

"Grab our phones and pull out the batteries as quickly as you can." He spoke calmly, but there was an undercurrent of urgency in his tone.

That woke Kate up in a hurry.

Trying not to panic, she went into the bedroom and retrieved his phone from the nightstand, already prying off the cover as she walked back into the room. She reached into her purse for the phone he'd given her and sat down beside him as they worked, each of them silently absorbed in their tasks.

When both batteries were lying on the coffee table, she said, "What about the SIM cards?" In a regular cell phone, the SIM card contained the identity of the mobile subscriber, but

Ian bought prepaid cards and when the minutes were up, he replaced them.

"I already wiped the phones, and I'll swap out the cards tomorrow." As he typed, he muttered a string of curse words, which did nothing to soothe her nerves or slow the galloping of her heart.

Kate went back into the bedroom and retrieved Ian's glasses from the nightstand. After cleaning the lenses, she sat down on the couch and handed them to him.

"There's that quickness I like so much," he said, putting them on with one hand and taking the other off the keyboard just long enough to give hers a brief squeeze. "Don't worry. I've got this. Go back to bed."

Kate didn't want to go back to bed. She was wide-awake and wanted to ask a stream of frantic questions about what had triggered the alarm and what it meant for him and for them. But Ian had entered a hyperfocused zone and he kept his eyes on the screen, pounding the keys and typing faster than she'd ever seen anyone type before.

Not wanting to impede whatever it was he was doing, she let him be and went back to bed.

But sleep would not come, and Kate stared at the clock, watching the minutes tick by as different scenarios played out in her head. An alarm had to be a bad thing, and an alarm that woke you in the middle of the night seemed even worse. And asking her to pull the batteries from their phones. Kate knew what that meant and half expected him to rush into the bedroom and start gathering up his things.

He'd said he'd tell her if he ever had to leave, but the promise did nothing to lessen the impact of how she'd feel if he actually did.

At 3:48, she got out of bed. Silently she stood in the doorway and watched him. He was still typing, but at a much slower speed. Then he took off his glasses, laid them on the coffee table, and rubbed his eyes. When he looked up and spotted her, he smiled, held out his hand, and beckoned her. She went to him, and he pulled her down onto his lap.

"Why aren't you sleeping?" He scanned her face, and his smile faded as he registered the worry etched in her expression.

"Will you have to leave? I'll understand if you do, but I don't want you to."

"I'm not going anywhere."

"No?" she asked, relieved.

"No." His voice was soft, soothing.

"Then what was that all about?"

"I've been monitoring the traffic moving over a network. I wrote an alarm into the code to alert me to any intrusion attempts, but I didn't really expect to get a hit. It's kind of like entering a building you thought was abandoned and walking around a corner and encountering someone."

Though she knew it didn't work that way, Kate couldn't help but picture Ian coming face-to-face with the intruder in a dark cyber hallway. "Then what happened?"

"Then I reconfigured the firewall to stop the attack and prevent him from hacking me."

"Did he try?"

"Yes, repeatedly. He was good, I'll give him that. But I was better."

The best, she thought.

"Does he know where you are?" Kate twisted the sash of her robe, and Ian reached for her hands, stilling them.

"I use a proxy server to conceal my IP address. We all do."

"Then why did you have me pull the batteries on our phones?"

"It's protocol anytime someone attempts to breach my firewall."

"I thought disposable phones couldn't be traced back to us."

"When it comes to hacking, nothing is impossible. There's always a vulnerability, a weakness, somewhere. But removing the batteries stops the flow of information."

"So everything's okay?"

He wrapped his arms around her tighter. "Everything's fine."

She exhaled, feeling some of the bottled-up tension leaving her body.

"Hey," he said pulling back to look at her. "Are you all right?"

"I'm just not used to being awakened in the middle of the night by a cyberattack. I didn't know what it meant."

He smiled and brushed the hair back from her face. "Welcome to the cyberwars, sweetness. Sometimes things get a little bumpy."

She could sense his exhilaration, almost feel the adrenaline coursing through him. When the alarm sounded and he'd leaped from bed, he'd been wearing only his underwear, but his back felt warm under her fingertips, as if what he'd been doing had invigorated him and kept him warm.

He loves this. He's a junkie and hacking is his drug, she thought.

He slipped his hands into her robe and kissed her.

"Tired?" Kate asked, kissing him back.

"Wired," he murmured against her lips. "Do you know what a cyberbattle does to me?"

"I can probably guess."

"What about you, Katie? Are you tired?"

"I'm not that tired," she said.

He took off her robe, and now they were both wearing only their underwear. He lay back on the couch and pulled her over on top of him.

"Don't worry about what happened tonight, okay?" he said, twisting a lock of her hair in his fingers.

"I just didn't want you to have to go."

"It would take a lot more than something like this to make me leave you."

"So it wasn't a big deal?"

"Pretty mild in the grand scheme of things. Remind me to tell you about the time I got into it with a hacker from the Russian mafia. Boy, did I piss him off. I did leave town after that. It seemed like the smart thing to do."

"Ian," she said, hoping he could hear the frustration in her voice. "That's not helping to ease my mind."

He grinned. "But it's such a good story."

She wedged her hand between their bodies and pinched the front of his thigh, hard.

"Ow," he said.

"You exasperate me."

"I don't mean to."

"Try to remember that your world is very strange and I'm not completely used to it."

"I'm sorry. I'll do better. Now let's kiss and make up."

"I've already kissed you."

He reached for her hand and held it, their fingers intertwined. "I think we should kiss some more." He kissed her hard. Then soft. Then hard again. "Still exasperated?"

She trailed a finger along his bottom lip. "Maybe a little less so."

"Ah, it's working." He kissed her again, and Kate's body relaxed.

Now that the threat of him leaving had been eliminated, she convinced herself there was nothing to worry about, and she lost herself in his kisses and his touch. He led her back to bed, but it was another hour before they slept. And when Kate's alarm clock went off at eight and she awakened with his arms around her, she was no longer quite so exasperated with him.

CHAPTER TWENTY-THREE

IAN WAS SITTING ON THE couch looking incredibly handsome in his dark jeans and sport coat when Kate walked into the living room on New Year's Eve. She was wearing the black cashmere sweater dress he'd bought her, and she'd paired it with her black over-the-knee high-heeled boots, the ones she'd been wearing the day they drank champagne in the park. The dress hugged her curves, and the short length made her legs appear as if they went on for miles. She'd styled her hair in the messy French twist again, which had required a multitude of hairpins and quite a bit of patience. She stood in front of him, and his eyes roamed up and down as he studied her.

"I see what you mean now," he said. "Not an outfit for Dad."

"Nooooo," she said.

Leaning forward, he lifted the hem of her dress, pulling it up until the lace of the thigh-high stockings became visible. He lowered it without saying anything. He already knew she was wearing the bustier because he'd laced her into it, but she hadn't put on the stockings until the last minute.

"You weren't supposed to see those yet," Kate said.

"Sometimes I have poor impulse control."

She grinned. "Sometimes?"

He pulled her down onto his lap, wrapped his arms tightly around her waist, and looked into her eyes. "I love you."

"You do?" She nuzzled her cheek against his newly restored scruff.

"I never say those words unless I mean them."

"I love you too."

He smiled, his eyes crinkling at the corners. Oh how she adored him when he smiled at her like that.

"I loved you first," she said. "I just hadn't told you yet."

"Someday I'll tell you exactly when I knew I loved you. Then we'll see who was first."

"Must you always have the upper hand?"

He cupped her face and kissed her. "Always, Katie."

After his declaration of love there was a part of Kate that wanted to stay home, to keep him all to herself. She pictured him lighting a fire and them sipping drinks and snuggling on the couch. But she was also excited to introduce Ian to her friends. Certainly no one would think he was imaginary after tonight, and they'd have plenty of time to be alone when they returned home.

Kate slipped her arms into an A-line black wool cape with a hood.

Ian whistled. "Holy smokes, a cape."

"A necessary purchase when you're dating a superhero. I bought it when my mom and I went shopping the day after Christmas. Do you like it?"

"Yes. You look like Little Red Riding Hood's beautiful—and more adventurous—big sister."

"I am definitely open to new experiences," she said, laughing.

What Ian didn't know was that he was the one who was making her that way. He was as free-spirited in bed as he was in everything else, and she'd gone along for the ride eagerly, willingly. She had no reason to say no when everything he did felt so good. He seemed to love taking her out of her comfort zone, which was a bit of a misnomer considering nothing he'd done to her so far was uncomfortable in the least. Stuart had simply not bothered to explore that side of Kate, which was something she hadn't fully realized until Ian had come along.

He grinned. "Would you be open to wearing the cape sometime without anything on underneath it?"

"Keep saying things like that and we're not even going to make it out the door. But yes, I would." Kate reached for her purse. "Okay. I think I'm ready." She turned back around, worry creasing her face. "Are you sure my dress isn't too short?"

"Sweetness, there's no such thing."

The New Year's Eve party was being held at the W Hotel in the Foshay Tower downtown. Ian pulled up in front, gave his key fob to the valet, and opened Kate's door, helping her out of the car.

"Paige made a bottle-service reservation," Kate said as they walked into the hotel. "We're supposed to meet everyone upstairs."

Ian held her hand as they made their way to the second floor. When Kate spotted Paige, she pointed and said, "They're over there."

Paige and her husband, Jason, were sitting at one end of a large, circular booth. Audrey and her fiancé, Clay, were sitting in the middle, and after Kate introduced Ian—Smith because Bradshaw was a name she wouldn't share with anyone—they slid in next to them.

"What'll you have, Kate?" Clay asked.

She eyed the array of bottles and mixers. "Stoli and cranberry, please." Clay poured the vodka, added cranberry juice and ice, and passed it to Kate.

"Ian?"

"Bourbon. Thanks."

After the drinks were poured, Kate and Ian fielded the obligatory round of questions: where was Ian from, what did he do for a living, where had he gone to college, etc. It was not the ideal venue for Kate's friends to get to know Ian because the DJ was already playing crowd favorites at an earsplitting decibel level, but Kate knew by their interested expressions and their smiles that they liked him.

It felt good to be out with her friends, and it was easy to get caught up in the pounding rhythm of the music and the excitement of the occasion. And Kate was flying high because Ian's "I love you" was still playing on an endless loop in her head.

"Let's dance," Paige said, tugging on Jason's sleeve.

"I'd much rather watch you girls," he said. Kate and her friends loved to dance, and they'd been tearing up dance floors for years. "You're in for a real show, Ian."

"Is that so?" Ian said, looking over at Kate and raising an eyebrow.

She laughed. "Club moves are even more fun than the Electric Slide."

"I don't think they're ready yet, though," Jason said. He topped off his wife's drink, and Kate's and Audrey's too.

"Not quite," Clay agreed. "But soon."

Forty-five minutes later when Paige couldn't wait any longer, she pulled Kate and Audrey onto the dance floor. They had to shout to hear each other over the music.

"Kate, your man is *gorgeous*," Audrey said. "And tall. What is he, six three?"

She smiled. "Four."

"Where did you find him?" Paige asked.

"Actually, he found me. He saw me on TV and made several donations to the food pantry."

"He must be doing pretty well," Paige said knowingly.

She shrugged. "I think he does okay."

Kate wasn't about to shed any light on Ian's situation, financial or otherwise. He might own nice cars and reside in a luxury apartment, but so did lots of people who lived in Minneapolis. He seemed most comfortable when he was sitting on Kate's couch wearing jeans and a sweatshirt or when he walked hand in hand with her to a nearby restaurant and they each ordered their favorite meal, even if it happened to be the least expensive item on the menu. She liked that about him. One of the things leaving the law firm had done was make her realize she didn't need as much money as she'd once thought. Seeing how little her clients were getting by on had been a real eye-opener.

"Are we going to talk or are we going to dance?" Audrey asked.

"We're going to dance," Paige said. "Just try to keep up, girls."

It wasn't long before they were in their element. Kate's dance moves were tempered a bit by her concern that her dress would ride up and expose the tops of her stockings if she raised her arms over her head. She made up for it by moving her hips in a way that had Ian smiling and clapping when she looked over at him. Jason held his finger in the air and moved it in a quick circle, urging the girls to give them a three-hundred-and-sixty-degree show, a request they happily obliged. When they finally returned to the table, they fanned themselves, ready to take a break and cool down. Clay refilled their drinks, and it wasn't long before they were back out on the floor. When the DJ played a slow song, the men joined them, claiming it was the only kind of dancing they knew how to do.

At midnight, they counted down and toasted each other with a bottle of champagne. Ian gave Kate an especially hot kiss, sliding his hand up her dress under the table until he reached the top of her stocking. Then Paige—who'd had a considerable amount to drink—leaned over and gave Kate a friendly peck on the mouth.

Jason, who was sitting between Kate and Paige, yelled, "Yes!"

"Seriously?" Kate said, laughing.

"I hope you enjoyed it, because it's the closest you're ever going to get to a threesome," Paige said, turning to her right to give Audrey a kiss too.

Kate looked at Ian.

He smiled and then leaned in to brush her ear with his lips. "I told you it was universal. But all I need is you."

Downstairs in the lobby, Ian helped her on with her cape. "Stay here while I give the ticket to the valet."

While she was waiting, she heard someone say, "Kate?" Glancing up, she spotted a man standing a few feet away, his brows knitted together in confusion, a woman by his side. He looked vaguely familiar, but it took her a few seconds to make the connection because she'd only seen his profile picture and had never met him in person.

Kent from online dating. Supposed lover of cooking, animals, and long hikes in the woods.

He approached her, eyes glassy, shirt untucked, hair mussed.

"Hello," she said coolly.

"So it is you."

"Yes."

"Wow. You look great. Weren't we supposed to go out once?" he asked.

"Yes, but you decided I was too fat and you canceled on me at the last minute."

Ian walked up then.

"Look," Kate said. "It's Kent."

Ian looked contemplative. "Speaking of threesomes."

"You're not fat," Kent said.

"Well, maybe not now, but I could blow up again at any moment."

"She really likes Cinnabon," Ian said.

Kent looked her up and down. "Maybe we could reschedule."

Ian folded his arms across his chest. "Never gonna happen."

Kent's date said, "I'm standing right here," and she did not sound pleased.

"Just so we're clear. Now that you know I'm not fat, you think we should go out?" Kate said.

"Sure. Why not?"

"Oh, sweetness," Ian said, "let him have it."

"You know, I thought I'd dodged a bullet by not going out with a guy who tapes himself having sex with unsuspecting women—"

Kent's panicked and guilty expression confirmed Ian's hunch, and if either of them had any lingering doubts about the tapes, the look on Kent's face had certainly removed them.

"—but now that I know you're not even bright enough to figure out when someone's profile picture has been Fat-Boothed, the bullet I dodged was twofold."

"You FatBoothed yourself?"

"My boyfriend did."

"Why would you be on a dating site if you already had a boyfriend?"

"He wasn't my boyfriend at the time."

"But I wanted to be her boyfriend, so you had to go." Ian made a motion with his hand like he was brushing away something unpleasant.

"What do you mean by taping himself having sex with unsuspecting women?" Kent's date asked.

"My boyfriend suspected Kent might be taping the women he sleeps with without their knowledge," Kate said.

"But I wasn't positive," Ian said. "More like erring on the side of caution."

"But we're more positive now," Kate said.

Ian nodded in agreement and looked at Kent's date. "But if you're cool with shooting some video, carry on."

"No judging," Kate said. "If the two of you decide *together* that you want to do that, you should definitely move forward."

Ian smiled. "Really?"

"I'm not speaking from experience," Kate said. "But sure. Why not? Although I'd probably lean toward photos instead of video. And they'd have to be stored securely, of course."

"Well, not in the damn *cloud*, that's for sure."

"Hey!" Kent said.

All three heads turned.

"Oh. Right. You," Ian said.

Kent's face was so red it was almost purple. "I don't know what the hell you two are talking about."

"I think you might know a *little bit* about it," Kate said.

Kent's date looked as angry as he did. "If you think I'm sleeping with you tonight, you're crazy." They watched as she turned on her heel and stomped away.

"I don't think she's cool with the video thing," Kate said.

Kent glared at Ian. "You're an asshole."

"Trust me, you have no *idea* how big an asshole I can be."

Kate slid her arm around Ian's waist. "He has a few boundary issues, that's all. He's actually quite wonderful."

"Watching my girl cockblock you was even more satisfying than when I did it myself." Ian pointed at Kent's date, who was halfway down the hall. "But maybe if you catch up with her and do some groveling, you can turn this around. Good luck."

Kent looked like he couldn't decide if he wanted to punch Ian or try to salvage what was left of the evening with his date. Considering he was several inches shorter than Ian and more than a little drunk, he made the wise choice to take off after her.

Ian turned to Kate. "We make a good team, don't we?" he said, lifting her hood.

She looked into his eyes. "The best."

Snow was falling hard when they walked outside. Ian held Kate's hand while they waited, and right before the valet pulled up with his car, he raised her hand to his mouth and kissed the back of it.

"I should probably delete my dating profile," Kate said as Ian drove carefully through the swirling snow. She'd long since turned off all notifications and had no idea if there'd been any activity—or what her current profile photo looked like.

"Keep it," Ian said, laughing. "I like it better this way."

"Ian Bradshaw, what have you done?"

She used her phone to log on to her account. He had changed her profile picture to the one he'd taken of her driving the Shelby.

"A nice, normal photo," she said. "How unexpected."

"I want them to know exactly what they can't have."

He'd changed her bio too. It was short and simple and made her laugh: *I like meat, driving fast, and Ian Smith.*

She leaned across the console and kissed his cheek. "What am I going to do with you?"

"Maybe we can figure that out when we get home."

Kate slipped off her boots, walked into the bedroom, and turned on the bedside lamp. She was standing in front of the dresser removing her jewelry when Ian joined her. He caught her eye in the mirror and began removing the pins from her hair, working patiently to find all of them. Once her hair was down, he ran his hands through it, massaging her head.

"That feels so good," she said, holding his gaze as she laid her head back on his chest. He slipped one arm around her in front but trailed the fingers of the opposite hand along the curve of her waist, the slope of her hip. He nibbled her ear and then placed kisses, whisper soft, down the length of her neck, making her shiver.

She turned around, desperate for his mouth on hers. He slid his hands underneath her jaw and lifted her face, his kisses alternating between teasing and urgent. He'd taken off his jacket as soon as they walked in the door, but Kate needed the feel of his skin under her lips and fingers. She unbuttoned his shirt and removed it, then stripped off the T-shirt he wore underneath. Lightly rubbing her face on his chest, she breathed in the spicy smell of his cologne and sighed as she reached around, seeking the hard muscles of his back.

He turned her so she was facing the mirror again. Without breaking eye contact, he raised the hem of her dress and slowly pulled it over her head. Her thighs were touching the edge of the dresser, and he pressed the full length of his body up against her. She could feel how hard he was, and she pushed back, making him groan. Slowly he unlaced the ribbons on the bustier.

"You promised to be careful," she reminded him.

Locking eyes with her in the mirror, he gave her a half smile and unzipped the lingerie, catching it before it could fall to the floor. He placed it gently on the dresser.

He cupped her breasts and squeezed. He sucked on her neck and pulled on her nipples, gently at first and then harder on both.

She couldn't think, couldn't breathe. "Ian."

"Keep watching," he said, his voice low and heavy. He slipped his hand into the front of her thong, stopping just above where she wanted his fingers the most.

She ached for him to touch her. "Please," she whispered, looking at his hand in the mirror with her eyes half-closed.

With agonizing slowness, he lowered his hand and stroked her, and nothing had ever felt so good. His fingers slid in and out of her with ease, and she gripped the edge of the dresser, almost panting with her need. Then he knelt behind her and pulled the thong down to her ankles, his palms skimming along her bare skin on the way. He ran his hands up the inside of her thighs. "Spread your legs a little wider."

Kate stepped out of the thong and did what he said. He left the stockings on.

"Don't move," he said, crossing the room to grab a condom from the nightstand. When he returned, the rasp of his zipper going down filled her ears, and there was something about that that set her on fire more than if he'd taken off his pants.

Was he going to bend her—

Yes.

She closed her eyes when he entered her. She had no choice. It was too much, too intense. The sensations were overpowering, but they were overpowering in the best possible way. He would watch though. She was sure about that.

He moved inside her, his hands gripping her hips tightly, and it was perfect. He took her to the edge repeatedly until finally neither of them could hold off any longer. After she cried out, after he added his own drawn-out groan, he pulled her upright so the back of her head rested on his rising and falling chest. "I love you." The words sounded ragged as he said them in her ear.

"I love you too," she said, trying to catch her breath.

I love you, I love you, I love you.

CHAPTER TWENTY-FOUR

IAN WAS SUMMONED TO WASHINGTON again at the end of January. He got the call early on a Sunday evening when he and Kate were walking home from dinner.

"Who reaches out to let you know when you're needed?" Kate asked.

They'd quickened their pace after Ian hung up and explained that he needed to leave right away.

"His name is Phillip Corcoran. He's head of the cyber task force. He wanted me to stay over last time, get some sleep. Good guy."

"Why didn't you?"

"Because I wanted to get home to you."

"So what's happening now?"

"A forum member posted details of an imminent cyberattack. Very big data breach. If they're successful, it's going to leave behind a mess. Phillip wants us all in the same place so we can communicate more efficiently."

"Cyberattack sounds so ominous."

"You have nothing to worry about. It's not an actual battle. It's all just keystrokes. Names on a screen. None of them real, of course."

"Of course not. How long do you think you'll be gone?"

"Not sure. But I'm going to show up with more than the clothes on my back this time, just in case."

"Make sure you take a warm coat. After your last visit to Washington, you showed up at my door practically hypothermic."

"I think I left my coat on the plane. I was so out of it."

"Maybe you could catch some sleep this time. If Phillip offers again, take him up on it, okay?"

"If I've been up for more than twenty-four hours, I will. I'm not eager to relive that experience. I'm pretty sure I hallucinated in the cab on the way home."

When they reached Kate's apartment, Ian grabbed a duffel bag and set it on the bed. Kate went into the bathroom and gathered up his toiletries.

"How many of these carders want to know who you are?" Kate asked. She placed the items in his bag, and Ian added a change of clothes.

"Too many to count."

"How many of them would like to see harm come to you?" It was something that had occurred to her belatedly. If one of the carders doxed Ian and showed up at his door before he could leave, what would they do?

"Not as many."

"But some?"

"My name more than likely appears on a few lists."

Though she knew he was in a hurry, she reached out and put her hand on his wrist. "Ian."

He took her hand and squeezed it. "Don't worry."

"How can I not?"

"I've done everything I can to mitigate the possibility of discovery. Everything I do, every hack I make, is done behind an alias and a proxy. Nothing is in my real name."

He spoke the truth because the morning after he'd told her his real name, Kate had reached for her phone while they were still in bed, laughing and telling Ian that he shouldn't have told her because now she could find out anything she ever wanted to know about him.

"You won't find me. I've erased Ian Bradshaw from every search engine, every online database and public record," he'd said. "I literally do not exist on the Internet."

She'd googled him anyway, and while she found plenty of men named Ian Bradshaw, none of them were him. After ten minutes of searching and coming up empty-handed, she'd admitted defeat.

Next she'd googled Ian Merrick. There was only one hit, and it was for his website. "Any other names?" she'd asked.

"No. You know everything about me, Kate. There is no more to discover."

But now as she watched him zip up the duffel, she wondered if there was anything he'd omitted because he thought the details would be too alarming for her to handle. "Let me drop you off."

"You don't have to do that."

"I don't mind, and it will make it easier if you decide to take a cab home again. Which you definitely should if you're tired."

"I'll take a cab home if I'm tired or it's late. I'm not dragging you out of bed in the cold and dark." He smiled, grabbed the duffel, and said, "All right. I'm ready."

The private airstrip was a fifteen-minute drive away. Ian pulled into a gravel parking lot surrounded by a chain-link fence. A small plane Kate estimated would hold six to eight passengers sat on the tarmac.

"It's a charter?" Kate asked.

"Yes," Ian said. "Contrary to popular belief, the FBI—and the people who work with them—aren't hustled into first class on private jets. If time allowed, they'd have put me on a commercial flight and I'd be sitting in coach. But a local charter works well in a pinch."

Ian reached into the backseat for his bag and they got out of the car. "Things are going to get very hectic once I arrive. I'll send you a text when I'm on my way back." He cupped her face and pulled her in close for a kiss. "I love you. Stay warm."

"I love you too." She got back in the car and waited until he'd walked up the short flight of steps and disappeared into the plane. Then she put his car in gear and drove home, hoping he wouldn't be gone too long.

It had been a little over twenty-nine hours when he texted her. It was almost midnight, and Kate had just turned off the light and rolled onto her side when her phone pinged.

Ian: *Boarding the plane. Caught a shower and a short nap earlier and will take a cab from the airport. Don't wait up. It will be close to 3 a.m. before I'm home. Love you.*

Kate: *I'll expect nothing less than a good spooning when you arrive.*

Ian: *Wish I could give you a good something else but will probably fall asleep the minute I crawl into bed. I'll make it up to you. Promise.*

Kate: *Love you. Safe travels.*

He pulled the covers back and slid in behind Kate a few hours later, wrapping his arms around her and whispering, "Katie, I'm home."

She mumbled a reply and thought she'd dreamt the whole thing until she woke up the next morning with his chest pressed up against her back and his arm across her breasts.

He didn't stir when she gently extricated herself to get ready for work and quietly left the apartment. He sent her a text at noon to tell her he was awake, and Kate went home, picking up lunch on the way. By the time she walked into her apartment, he'd showered and was drinking coffee on the couch. He stood and held open his arms, and Kate went to him, sighing as he enveloped her in a hug.

"My hacker is back." She kissed him, and he pulled her down onto the couch. "How did it go?"

"It got a little intense there for a while—I won't bore you with the technical stuff—but we were successful in blocking the attack. We saved a lot of consumers the giant headache of having their financial information compromised."

"You love it, don't you?"

"It's not the same kind of cybercrime my dad fell victim to, but it still feels good every time I stop it from happening."

"I think it's wonderful." She smiled and kissed him. "Ready for lunch?"

"Thai?" he asked with a wide, hopeful smile.

"Thai."

While they were eating, Kate said, "Can I talk to you about something?"

He looked a little worried. "Sure."

"It's nothing bad," she said. "I just have a favor to ask. Do you remember the little boy named Georgie? We bought that Curious George hat for him at Christmastime?"

"Yes, of course."

"When he came in with his mom and sisters to pick up their box of food last week, I could tell that Samantha was really upset about something. I pulled her aside, and after a little prodding she admitted how bad her financial situation has become. Georgie had been sick and needed two rounds of an expensive antibiotic, and the girls had outgrown their shoes. The budget billing on her gas and electric bill had increased by eighty dollars, and she told me she was trying to decide which bill she could put off. I felt horrible for her, but she said not to worry, that she'd figure something out. After she left I tried to come up with a way to help her, but I'm not equipped to provide for a family of four on an ongoing basis, and I don't want to create a potentially problematic situation down the road. I told myself when I started the food pantry that getting personally involved was a slippery slope."

"Do you want me to help her? Because I'd be happy to."

"Yes. But it needs to be anonymous. She's very proud, and it's hard enough for her to accept help from the food pantry. But I don't want you to give her any of your money."

She could tell by his surprised expression that he hadn't seen that coming. "You don't?"

"No. I want you to find the most obnoxious thief who's bragging the loudest and just take it. It's not fair. Samantha works hard and has three children who never asked to grow up this way. And yet there are people out there who steal and have more than they'll ever need."

"Write down her name for me and I'll take care of it."

Kate thought about how relieved Samantha would feel upon receiving the money. How the kids would pick up on the fact that their mother was no longer stressed out and afraid. "Something so wrong shouldn't feel this good."

"Ah, she understands me now."

"I always understood you, but now I can feel it for myself. Thank you for helping her. It means a lot to me."

Ian pulled her close and kissed her forehead. "Anytime, sweetness."

After lunch she put on her coat and got ready to walk back to the food pantry. Before she returned to the couch to say good-bye, she lingered near the entrance of the room and watched him as he tapped out a message on his phone. She admired the perfect angle of his nose, his well-defined cheekbones, the square line of his strong jaw, his mouth. Ian was gorgeous, there was no doubt about it, but it was the mischievous sparkle in his smile that gave him the extra edge.

He looked up suddenly, catching her in the act, and her cheeks flamed. "Did I just bust you staring adoringly at me, Katie?" He crossed the room, and when he reached her he leaned in for a closer look. "Aw, I've missed those blushing cheeks." He tickled her, and she pulled his hands away.

"Did you know that when you smile, your whole face lights up and there are little crinkles right here in the corners of your eyes?" Kate said, pressing lightly on them.

"I do now."

"You make me really happy."

He held her face tenderly in his hands and kissed her. "You make me really happy too."

CHAPTER TWENTY-FIVE

KATE DUCKED HER HEAD AGAINST the biting wind that was blowing straight out of the north as she and Ian walked to Dunn Brothers for breakfast one Saturday morning at the end of February. The smell of dark roast coffee beans and the sound of light jazz greeted them when they walked through the door.

"I've had about enough of the cold," Ian said, letting go of Kate's hand and stomping the snow from his boots.

Kate removed her hat. "Thank you for being willing to endure it anyway."

"There isn't much I wouldn't do for you," he said, dropping a kiss on her forehead.

Once they had their coffee and breakfast sandwiches, they sat down at a small table in the corner.

"I have to go back to my place after breakfast," Ian said. "There are some things I can't take care of from my laptop."

"Okay," she said.

"Come with me."

Usually whenever Ian needed to work at his apartment during the weekend, Kate occupied herself with a number of different activities: she called a friend to go shopping or to meet for lunch and a movie. She went to Pilates or ran errands or cleaned her apartment. But lately he seemed to want her near him all the time. And since there was no one else she wanted to spend her time with as much as she wanted to spend it with him, she smiled and said, "Sure."

When they arrived at Ian's, Kate made herself comfortable on his couch. She'd brought her laptop and busied herself sending e-mails and working on a few things for the food pantry. Ian settled in at his desk, and soon his fingers were furiously tapping the keyboard.

An hour later she walked over and stood behind him, massaging his shoulders.

He groaned. "Ah... that feels good."

Kate looked at the blinking cursor on one of the computer monitors. "Who's Phantomphreak?"

"Me."

"Seriously? That does *not* sound like you."

He let out a short laugh. "It wouldn't be my first choice for a screen name, but I needed something that would fit in. Phreak refers to a type of hacking using phone lines. Phantom is my own little inside joke."

"So this is the forum?"

"This is it."

"And you're monitoring their activity?"

"Yes. Gathering information, engaging when necessary."

"How did you get them to trust you?"

"A fabricated yet credible backstory that can be verified by a Google search goes a long way. That and patience."

Kate read the words appearing on the screen. The interactions seemed mostly an exchange of insults interspersed with racial epithets.

"Do they always speak to each other this way?"

"It's posturing, mostly. Everyone's a badass on the Internet."

"Is it tedious?"

"This part is. I greatly prefer the hacking end of it—plugging security holes and intercepting information—versus watching a bunch of low-life thugs brag about all the credit card numbers they just ripped off."

"So they're all thieves?" Kate asked pointing to the user names running down the length of the screen.

"Pretty much."

Kate used her thumbs to gently knead the tight muscle on the back of Ian's neck.

"Oh yeah, right there," he said.

"What will happen next?"

"Once we have enough evidence, we'll round up the worst offenders. Many of them will see jail time. If they're smart, the ones that are left will scatter."

He turned his chair around and pulled Kate onto his lap, which was one of her favorite places. His long legs were strong and solid underneath her, and she loved it when he wrapped his arms around her and held her that way.

"Kiss me," he said.

She pressed her lips to his and dipped her tongue into his mouth. "Like that?"

"Just like that," he said, pulling her in for another.

For lunch, they picked up sandwiches from Mona's because Kate won the coin toss after stating she could not eat Thai food one more time. Ian insisted the sound of the TV wouldn't bother him, so she watched a movie after they finished eating. Kate knew he was telling the truth because he was so immersed in his work he didn't look away from the screen when the movie ended and she stood up to stretch and go to the bathroom. The sunken whirlpool tub caught her eye when she was washing her hands. A nice, relaxing bath would be an excellent way to pass the time until Ian was finished.

She searched the cabinet under the sink while the tub filled, but Ian didn't have any bubble bath. She'd have to remember to bring some the next time she visited. When the water reached the level she desired, Kate undressed and lowered herself into the tub, hitting the button to turn on the jets.

Now *this* was a bathtub.

It was big enough for two, even if one of those people was a six-foot-four-inch man. Kate could see herself buying one of those little air-filled pillows and maybe a tray where she could set a book and a glass of wine. She'd suggest to Ian that they should spend more time at his place, and that he need not look farther than his bathroom if he wanted to find her.

After ten minutes of the pulsing water massaging her body, Kate felt incredibly relaxed. She turned down the jets and rested her arms along the side of the tub, eyes closed. She opened them when she heard the door open.

"You don't have any bubble bath," she said, knowing he could see her body clearly under the water.

"Thank God." He stripped off his T-shirt and unbuttoned his jeans in one fluid motion. After he removed the rest of his clothes, he eased in behind Kate and wrapped his arms around her.

"I wasn't trying to distract you," she said. "I just couldn't resist this tub."

"It's okay. I'm officially done for the day."

She rested her head on his chest and angled her neck so he could reach it. He kissed it and laughed.

"What's so funny?" she asked.

"I was not specifically invited to join you in the bathroom, but here I am. Pressed up against you, even." He skimmed his palms down her breasts.

"You are *not* a good rule follower."

"The worst," he said. "It's the hacker in me." He kissed her neck again and gave it a little nip that made her shiver despite the warm water.

"Kate, I have to go."

Her body tensed and he tightened his hold. "When?"

"Soon. Within a month or two."

That meant the end of April at the latest.

"Once the arrests are made, those who managed to elude us will be extremely motivated to find out who brought down the forum. I'll be on borrowed time."

"Do you know where you'll go next?"

"No. The only thing I know for sure is that I want you to come with me."

Their commitment to one another was deep enough that Kate had already known he'd ask. She thought she'd been prepared for it. But the reality of packing up and leaving everything behind was something she'd have to carefully consider.

"How would it work?"

"We'd pick a destination. Someplace large enough to get lost in. Preferably warmer this time."

"Texas?"

"Anywhere but Texas," he said, and his tone left no doubt about whether he had any desire to return to his home state. "I'd shift to my private-sector clients for a while. You could do whatever you wanted. You could find another nonprofit to work for, although you wouldn't have to work at all if you didn't want to. You could volunteer somewhere if that's what you'd rather do. The possibilities are endless."

"Would we ever stop moving?"

"I hope so. Living in rented apartments at thirty-two isn't the same as twenty-two. Someday, maybe soon, I'll say no to the next government assignment and put down roots somewhere. Buy a house. Share it with a beautiful brown-eyed girl. But even so, the risk of someone finding out who I am will always be there."

She was silent for a moment. "You said you'd asked two women in the past ten years to come with you. Why did they say no?" Kate knew Ian had been single for about a year when he met her and had been with his previous girlfriend for nine months. But she didn't know anything about the two women he'd asked before asking her, and she was curious about their reasons for declining.

"I dated the first woman for three years. She'd actually moved with me twice by that point, but when it was time to move again, she said she wouldn't come unless I married her. I understood her reasoning, but I was only twenty-four and I couldn't fathom settling down at that point. After we broke up, I dated but didn't get serious with anyone until a few years later. What I discovered when I asked the second woman to come with me is that the only aspect of my lifestyle she was willing to tolerate long-term was my income, so I moved on."

Kate did not need an engagement ring in order to make her decision, nor was she interested in Ian's money. She turned around so they were facing each other.

"It's a lot to ask of you," Ian said. "Selfish, even."

"Wanting to be with someone doesn't mean you're selfish. It just means you want them."

"What do you want, Kate?"

"To be with you."

"Is there a certain place you'd like to live?" he asked.

"I've always thought North Carolina was beautiful."

"If you decide to come with me, that's where we'll go."

"Just like that?" She sometimes forgot that anything was possible in Ian's world.

"Sure. Why not? But you still have time to make your decision. I don't want you to feel pressured." But his yearning expression belied his true feelings on the matter.

"I don't feel pressured."

She owed it to herself and to Ian to make sure this was what she wanted. It wasn't that her feelings for him were in doubt, because they weren't. But Kate would be starting down an unfamiliar path, and life as she knew it would change. For all Ian's talk about turning down the FBI's next assignment, there was something about it that he loved. She could see it in the way his eyes lit up when he talked about it.

He kissed her then. His arousal had been evident since he'd climbed into the tub and pressed it against her, and now her body responded in kind.

"How do you feel about drying off and moving this to my bed?" He rubbed his thumbs across her nipples, and her skin felt electrified under his touch.

"That depends. Will there be a number seven kiss included with this offer?"

"Absolutely. And if you give me half an hour to recover between them, you can have two."

"Half an hour? Boy, you're not fourteen anymore, are you?"

"I can probably cut it down to twenty minutes if you do that thing I really like."

She smiled. "Don't I always?"

"I'm a lucky man in more ways than one. Don't think for a minute that I don't know it." He stroked her cheek and looked at her longingly. "Please think about coming with me."

"Of course I will."

She *would* think it over—carefully—because it was a big decision that deserved contemplation. But deep down she already knew she'd go with him. She'd go despite the things she'd be leaving behind. She'd go regardless of what she'd have to give up, because she couldn't imagine telling him good-bye and watching him leave without her.

He'd stayed because he loved her.

She'd go because she loved him.

CHAPTER TWENTY-SIX

KATE WAS SITTING AT HER desk going over her to-do list.

"Can you do a client interview?" Helena asked. "There's a gentleman asking for you by name. He said he was referred by a friend."

"Of course."

She picked up her clipboard and an intake form and walked to the room where they interviewed new clients. It was hardly bigger than closet-sized, but at least it was private.

A young man was waiting there for her. He was wearing a flannel shirt, jeans, work boots, and a worn-looking coat.

She smiled brightly. New clients were often a bit hesitant when visiting the food pantry for the first time, and she wanted to put him at ease. "Hi, I'm Kate Watts."

"Zach Nielsen," he said and shook Kate's proffered hand.

"Please have a seat."

Kate went through the intake questionnaire. Zach was twenty-seven, lived with his disabled mother, and also cared for a younger brother. The family currently received food stamps but still came up short at the end of the month.

"My little brother is fifteen," Zach said. "My mom can't keep him filled up. He's growing so fast. I've got a part-time warehouse job, and I'm trying to get on full-time. Maybe in the next month or so, they say."

"It'll be okay," Kate said. "We can help you."

Kate noticed the relieved look on his face and the way he seemed to relax in the chair. "Do you have ID?"

His smile faltered. "Yes, but I don't have it with me."

"Don't worry about it," Kate said reassuringly. "Just bring it next time, okay?"

"Okay."

When the interview was complete, Kate helped Zach fill a box with a three-day supply of food for each member of his household.

"Come back next month and we'll fill the box again."

"Thank you," he said.

When she finished with Zach, she started another list, jotting down the things she'd need to take care of if she left with Ian. Breaking her apartment lease and turning in her resignation to her board of directors were the two biggest things she'd need to address. Though he'd mentioned that Kate didn't need to worry about finding a job unless she wanted one, she knew she wouldn't be happy without something to fill her days and give her a sense of purpose.

Helena's voice interrupted her thoughts. "Earth to Kate. I've said your name three times."

"Sorry," Kate said. "I was thinking about Ian."

"If that man were my boyfriend, I'd never get anything done. I'd just sit and stare off into space thinking about him."

"Helena Sadowski, listen to you."

"Well, it's true."

Kate walked over and sat down on the edge of Helena's desk. "Ian may need to relocate for one of his clients. He's asked me to come with him."

"It would take me approximately four seconds to make up my mind if I were in your shoes."

"Did Bert ever ask you to make a choice? Follow him somewhere, do something you hadn't planned?"

"When we were first married, he wanted to move to California. I thought it was the dumbest idea I'd ever heard. We were so young, both of us barely out of high school. Our families were here. What could California possibly give us that we didn't already have other than maybe a little more sunshine? Then the babies started coming, and Bert stopped talking about leaving. It wasn't until much later, after the fog of parenting started to lift, that I realized staying had taken some of the spark out of him. I asked him once if he was unhappy we didn't go, and he said he wasn't. But I know California would have been an adventure for him, and who doesn't want that? If I could rewind time, you and I wouldn't be having this conversation because living in Minnesota would be nothing but a distant memory for me."

"I feel like we're doing such good work here. Like we've finally hit our stride." The food pantry was currently in great shape, and not all of that was due to Ian's assistance. Donations were up, and they were successfully meeting the needs of their clients. Things seemed to have fallen into place, and Kate wondered if the rough patch they'd experienced had been an unlucky fluke. "I guess I'm struggling with the idea of giving up something I already gave up my law career to do."

"You have the rest of your life to work, and taking a break from something doesn't mean you're any less passionate about it. You've done a fantastic thing here, Kate. The progress you've made won't disappear because you're not here to oversee it. People will continue to receive assistance long after you're gone. But love. Love is not guaranteed. Love will still be there for you when you're too old to work and the company you worked for all your life shuffles you out the door with a nice gold pen. Always choose love. Always choose the adventure. You'll never regret it."

That night when Ian came home, she met him at the door. "I'm coming with you when you go."

"Really?" There was no denying the relief she heard in his voice.

"I love you. I can't imagine watching you leave and not going with you."

"I love you too, Kate. So much."

Okay then," she said, smiling. "I guess we're moving to North Carolina."

CHAPTER TWENTY-SEVEN

MARCH CAME HOWLING IN LIKE a lion. Mother Nature dumped a foot of snow on Minneapolis, and the city came to a temporary standstill. Kate and Ian had decided to ride out the storm at her place and were snuggled up under the covers in bed, eating leftover pizza and listening to the wind rattle the windows. Kate slipped her bare feet between his calves.

"Gah! Your feet are freezing."

"I know. I'm trying to warm them up. You're lucky I didn't wedge them up any higher. They'd be nice and warm there."

"That would be very… jarring for me. Your toes are like ice cubes."

"Maybe I should put some clothes on."

He squeezed her feet between his calves. "That's crazy talk."

"What about Charlotte?" Kate had been researching North Carolina cities at work and had decided that Charlotte sounded like an ideal place for them to live. There were plenty of things to see and do, the weather was warm, and the people seemed friendly.

"Charlotte would be great."

"I'd love to live on Roanoke Island, but it's probably too small."

"Bigger cities are ideal, but we can always plan a weekend getaway to Roanoke Island whenever the mood strikes."

"When do you want to leave? I need to give notice to my board of directors, and I'd like to be involved in the process of hiring my replacement." Kate had worked too hard on opening the food pantry to leave without knowing it would be in good hands.

"Mid-April? Is that enough time? I really don't want to stay any longer than that." Ian had mentioned that the task force had almost all the evidence they needed to start making arrests.

"It should be."

"I'll handle the logistics and arrange for movers to pack and transport our things. I've done it so often I've got it down to a science." Ian finished his pizza and set his empty plate on the nightstand. "Have you said anything to your parents?"

"Not yet. I thought I'd tell them you'd accepted a long-term assignment with a client and that neither of us wanted to do the long-distance thing."

"You can tell them the truth."

"I'm not sure how that would go over."

He didn't say anything, and Kate reached for his hand. "I'm a grown woman and perfectly capable of making my own decisions. This is my life. Soon to be *our* life. If I didn't want to do this, I wouldn't."

He squeezed her hand. "I'll do whatever it takes to make sure you don't regret it."

By Saturday they were both going stir-crazy after being cooped up for almost two days. But the sidewalks had been cleared, the sun was shining, and the temperature had risen twenty degrees. Kate was leaving for Pilates soon and Ian was going to run back to his place to grab some clothes. She was in the kitchen loading the dishwasher and waiting for her laptop to boot up while he worked on the couch.

"Kate?" he called out.

She popped her head into the living room. "Yes, lover?"

He looked up from his computer and laughed. "Is there any more coffee?"

"For you? Sure." Kate took his empty mug, went back into the kitchen, and returned with his coffee and her laptop. "Can you take a look at my computer when you have a minute? It's running really slow."

He set his laptop on the coffee table and reached for hers. "How long has it been running slow?"

"I don't know? A week, maybe? I kept forgetting to say something."

"What have I told you about clicking on those how-to links?"

She snorted. "Like I'm still doing that. But don't look at my browsing history, okay? No reason."

Kate went back into the kitchen to finish loading the dishwasher. She was about to join Ian on the couch when he walked into the room holding her laptop.

"What was wrong with it?" Kate asked.

"You're low on memory. I can take care of it for you at my place. I'll bring your laptop with me and install it for you while I'm there."

"Wow," she said. "Having a hacker boyfriend is turning out to be quite handy."

Ian appeared deep in thought and didn't respond.

"Ian?" She waved her hand in front of his face. "Are you with me?"

He grabbed her hand and kissed it. "Yes, just making a mental list. What did you say?"

"I said you're handy to have around."

"Yeah." He still seemed quite distracted. "When are you leaving?"

"In half an hour or so."

"Let's grab some lunch at Tug's when I get back. I should be done by noon or one."

"Sure."

"Okay." He kissed her good-bye and put on his coat. "Gotta run."

When Ian returned, they went to lunch. Once they were seated, he stared down at his phone which had pinged repeatedly on the walk over.

"It's crowded here today," Kate said. "I guess we're not the only ones who wanted to get out of the house."

When he realized she was waiting for a response, he looked up. "What? Sorry," he said slipping the phone into his front pocket.

"You can respond to the messages if you need to. I don't mind."

He shook his head. "It can wait."

The waitress took their order, and Kate told Ian that Paige had called and asked if she wanted to see a movie later. "It's a rom-com."

He grinned. "Of course it is."

"Strangely, Jason is not burning to see it, but she knew I would be. We're going to the early show, so I should be back by nine thirty."

"Okay." He'd put his phone on vibrate, but she could still hear the sound of it buzzing in his pocket every couple of minutes.

"Are you sure you don't need to answer whoever's texting and calling you?"

He reached across the table for her hand. "Nope."

"Is it work?"

He nodded. "A problem came up. I'm trying to figure out how to solve it."

"I'm sure you'll figure it out," Kate said with a wink. "You *are* the best."

When they got home from lunch, Ian spent the afternoon switching back and forth between sending texts and typing on his laptop. When it was time for her to meet Paige for the movie, he was still hard at work, his brow furrowed in concentration.

"Hey, hacker. I'm leaving now," she said.

He looked up sharply as if she'd startled him. But then his expression softened into a smile. After setting his laptop on the coffee table, he crossed the room to take her in his arms.

"Don't work too hard while I'm gone," she said, pressing her body against his.

He pulled her closer and kissed her. "Hurry back."

***

When she returned, he was still in the same spot on the couch.

"How was the movie?" he asked.

"It was good. You might not have enjoyed it quite as much. There were no car chases or explosions."

She went into the kitchen and returned with a glass of bourbon. "You look like you could use a drink."

"You always know just what I need," he said, taking a sip.

She sat down next to him. "Which client is having the problem?"

"FBI," he said putting his glass down on the table. "We encountered a problem with the forum."

"Will you have to go to headquarters again?"

"No. I can work on it from here."

"Did you figure out how to solve it?"

"Yeah. I just wish I knew if it was the right solution."

Half an hour later he silenced his phone, powered off his laptop, and set his glasses down on the coffee table. Kate walked out of the bedroom as he swallowed the last of the bourbon. She was wearing a thin camisole without a bra and a pair of boy shorts, her long legs on full display.

His eyes tracked her as she walked toward him. "Remind me to buy you some more of that underwear."

She gave him a pointed look. "You like boy shorts?"

"I like them on you."

When she reached the couch, she started to sit sideways on his lap the way she always did, but he said, "No. Straddle me."

She obliged, and he held her face tightly and kissed her.

"I love the way you taste when you drink bourbon." She placed her hands underneath his jaw, running her thumbs along his scruff and kissing him again.

"You are *mine*." He said it with conviction while looking into her eyes.

"Yes," she said with equal conviction. "And you're mine."

He put his hands on her hips and pulled her closer. She felt his hardness between her legs and pressed down on it, making him groan. He kissed her, gently at first and then slowly progressing to a rougher, almost bruising, meeting of their lips.

There was something possessive about the way he claimed her mouth, and she responded with equal fervor as their tongues collided. He wound his fingers in her hair, tugged hard on it, and left a searing trail from her mouth to her throat. The pain and pleasure left behind by the scrape of his teeth made Kate ache. The next kiss was slow and whisper soft, and he lightly brushed her cheeks with his thumbs. The back-and-forth between rough and gentle, taking and giving, set Kate on fire.

He fluttered kisses along her collarbone, her shoulder. With agonizing slowness, he reached for the hem of her camisole and then pulled it over her head, baring her to the waist. He nuzzled his face in her breasts, cupping their soft weight and licking them until she was writhing under his touch. He began to suck, gently at first, but then Kate felt a stab of exquisite pain as he increased the pressure, sealing his mouth around her nipple in a way that would surely leave visual proof he'd been there. Only rarely did he mark her, and the few times it had happened had been accidental. But Kate thought he'd meant to do it this time and was shocked by how much she liked it.

He put his hand down the front of her boy shorts, groaning when he discovered how aroused she was. As he stroked her, she arched into his hand, inhaling sharply and then sighing softly. His touch was light, teasing, and Kate thought she might fall apart right there on the couch.

"I love watching you, listening to the sounds you make." He took his hand out of her shorts, and without removing her from his lap, he stood.

She was never more aware of his size and strength than when he picked her up like that, as if she weighed nothing. She wrapped her legs around his waist as he walked toward the bedroom, his hands gripping her backside. After laying her down, he stripped off his clothes and dragged the boy shorts down her legs. Lying between them, he braced one of his elbows against her thigh, holding her open as his tongue traced a pattern and his fingers stroked her. She writhed underneath him, holding him in place, taking what she wanted, what she needed.

Kate was glad they'd taken the time to get tested and no longer needed condoms because as soon as she came, he entered her as if he couldn't possibly wait another second. His thrusts were urgent, relentless, and there was something about the way he covered her body with his, pinning her underneath him without worrying he'd break her, that she loved.

His groans and his ragged breathing told her it wouldn't be long for him. Another minute or two and she'd be able to get there again herself.

"Harder," she gasped, and it was like throwing gasoline on an already raging fire as he complied.

"Kate," he said, and she knew he was barely hanging on.

She answered him with her cries, and seconds later he joined her. It was the closest they'd ever come to finding their release at the same time, and she felt every pulse of his as the aftershocks of her own washed over her.

"I've never loved anyone the way I love you," Ian said.

"Neither have I," Kate said, trying to catch her breath.

He clung to her tightly. "Don't ever lose faith in me."

"I won't," she promised.

Why was he mentioning that now? He'd won her over, and she believed in him wholeheartedly. He was nothing like the man he'd seemed when she'd met him, and she understood it now. Knew why he'd come on so strong. It would take a certain kind of woman to be with him. Strong, fearless. Tolerant. Just like he'd told her in the beginning.

She *was* that woman.

And he was the man she hadn't known she'd needed until the day she'd crashed into him on the sidewalk.

CHAPTER TWENTY-EIGHT

KATE RECEIVED A TEXT FROM Ian shortly before she left work on Monday.

Ian: *I'm going to take the Shelby for a spin. I hope she starts and that those boneheads at the storage facility haven't been joyriding in her all winter.*

Kate: *Better do it soon. It's supposed to snow. Again.*

Ian: *I love you, sweetness. So much.*

That made her smile.

Kate: *I love you too.*

By four thirty, when Kate walked home from the Pilates class she'd taken after work, the sky had turned dark and rain was falling. She'd forgotten to bring an umbrella and the icy drops pelted her cheeks. Ducking her head, she quickened her step, but by the time she walked in the door of her apartment her hair was soaked. In the bathroom, she stripped off her wet clothes and turned on the water, waiting until it turned hot and steamy. After her shower, she wrapped herself in her robe and sat down on the couch, throwing a blanket over her lap. She clicked on the TV and listened to the Channel 5 meteorologist issue a winter storm warning for the overnight hours. Kate groaned. March snowstorms were the worst: icy, slushy, heavy, and wet. The rain would soon be changing to snow and the

National Weather Service predicted totals of six to eight inches for the area, along with high winds.

> Kate: *Looks like you got that drive in right under the wire. I hope the Shelby has now been returned to its spot at the storage facility. Come home and keep me warm! Let's order in.*

She watched the rest of the newscast, and when it was over she picked up her phone. Ian hadn't responded yet, and Kate hoped that meant he was on his way. She was excited to talk to him about North Carolina. The food pantry had been slow that day, and she'd spent some time in the afternoon reading about Charlotte. She dreaded turning in her resignation, but she was starting to look forward to the move and planned on breaking the news to her parents in the next day or two. Her mother would be happy for Kate, and even if she did have a few reservations, she probably wouldn't utter them. Her dad might be a different story, but telling him she was going with Ian would likely go over better than when she told him she was going to stop practicing law. He'd probably try to convince her to return to it now that she'd no longer be responsible for the food pantry.

Kate felt a slight prickle of unease when Ian had not arrived by seven. She opened the app on her phone to track him and clicked on Ian's Phone. But instead of a pinpoint on a map she got the word Offline. Her forehead creased in confusion. Was there a problem with the app? He wouldn't have turned off the location function, would he? She called him, but it went straight to voice mail.

Kate set the phone on the coffee table and went to the window. The rain had changed to snow and was coming down hard, but it was nothing he couldn't handle in his SUV. The Shelby, however, would be a different story. The temperature had plummeted and the wet streets would be icy under the layer of snow. The rear-wheel-drive car would be helpless in those conditions.

She fidgeted, unable to keep still, and she paced as the hours crept by. At eleven she drove to his apartment. The roads were horrible, and she had to fight to keep the TrailBlazer from fishtailing and sliding through intersections. When she arrived, she went to the main entrance to buzz him since she didn't have a key. She pushed the button on the intercom for fifteen seconds straight and waited a full minute between each attempt. There was only silence in return.

Finally she went home.

She spent the night in the chair by the window, watching the snowflakes as they passed through the beam of the streetlight, her emotions cycling rapidly between frustration and fear, confusion and resignation. She wanted to heave something at the glass, feel the satisfaction and hear the crash when it shattered.

Every twenty minutes, she'd tap Ian's Phone on the app.

Every time it said Offline.

Though he'd promised he wouldn't, he'd left without telling her. There was no other logical reason for why he was not curled up on the couch in front of the fireplace with her.

She watched the sky lighten as the sun came up. At seven, she decided she would try his apartment again. Fighting tears, she pulled on her boots and wrapped a scarf around her neck. The roads were still a mess, and it took longer than usual to get downtown. She drove carelessly, her mind occupied by more important things.

A man wearing a dark gray sweatshirt with the hood up was sitting on a bench in the entryway of Ian's building. Kate ignored him and crossed to the bank of intercoms, angrily jabbing the button for Ian's apartment. No buzzer sounded in return, no voice spoke to her through the speaker.

Goddamn you, Ian.

She stood there, trying to figure out what to do next. Should she wait? If she called the rental office and told them she was worried about him, would they let her in? Tears filled her eyes, and she exhaled in frustration and swiped at them with the back of her hand. The man in the hooded sweatshirt was watching her, and Kate turned away because she didn't want him to know she was crying. If he asked her what was wrong, she'd probably break down sobbing. Kate decided that if she didn't hear from Ian by noon, she *would* call the rental office. And if they let her in and she discovered his things were gone, she had no idea what she'd do.

On the West River Parkway, traffic came to a crawl at Second Street South near the Stone Arch Bridge. It was a little before eight, and at first she attributed the delay to the street conditions and morning rush hour. But as she inched closer, she noticed the people standing in front of a chain-link fence and how the fence was mangled like something had driven right through it. She hadn't come this way last night, had chosen instead to reach downtown via Hennepin Avenue.

Behind the fence was an embankment, and below that the Mississippi River. Traffic had all but stopped by then, and a few curious motorists, frustrated with the delay, got out of their cars and went to get a closer look. Kate wished she hadn't taken this route. She wanted to get home. What if Ian was there now?

Kate pounded the steering wheel and threw open her door. She pushed through the crowd, elbowing her way closer to the fence where she hoped to find a policeman who would tell everyone to get back in their cars and clear the way so she could leave.

Bystanders were pointing at something, and Kate craned her neck to get a better view. Her knees buckled when she saw the blue car with white racing stripes, its raised bumper attached to the chain of a tow truck that was parked at the edge of the riverbank.

The voices became a roar in her head as she caught snippets of their conversations:

—"Truck slid on the ice and hit him from behind."

—"Crashed through the fence and disappeared under the water."

—"Road conditions were horrible. No reason to be out driving in that."

—"It must have happened fast, caught him off guard."

—"Someone said they found him downstream."

Kate zeroed in on the man who had made the last comment, her heart soaring. *He had crashed but someone had found him! He was hurt. That's why he hadn't called.*

"Where? Where is he now?" Kate screamed, yanking on his sleeve.

"The morgue, probably. Not much they could do for him at that point."

An anguished cry tore from her throat, and she fled.

The man shouted after her. "Miss? Are you okay?"

There had never been a time in all her years on earth when she'd felt such visceral pain. It was as if the loss was physical, her heart torn in half, beyond repair. The beat itself seemed irregular, and Kate thought she might be going into shock. When she reached her car, she slid behind the wheel and closed the door as sobs wracked her body.

The man was wrong. Someone had found Ian. Taken him to their home and given him a blanket. Warmed him up and called him a cab. He was probably on his way home to her right now. He would walk through the door and say, "Gotcha, Katie Long Legs! Boy, did that suck."

It's twenty-two degrees outside, and even colder in the water. If he was okay, he would have called.

The crowd had dissipated and traffic was moving freely by the time she felt capable of driving. Numb, Kate put the car in gear and shivered uncontrollably all the way home. When she entered her apartment, she looked around expectantly, praying desperately that she'd find Ian on the couch with his laptop and a cup of coffee.

Silence greeted her.

She sat on the couch, rocking back and forth, running her hands up and down her arms because she couldn't stop shaking, couldn't get warm. She turned on the TV. Channel 5 was covering the story, and just before nine the newscaster announced that a body had been recovered and the victim identified as thirty-two-year-old Ian Merrick.

His last name is Bradshaw. It's not him!

But Kate knew it was him. She ran to the bathroom where she emptied the paltry contents of her stomach, the bitter taste of bile coating her mouth. She flushed and wiped her face with the back of her hand.

For as much as she'd worried about the things Ian was involved in and those who might want to find him, she'd never once worried about the one thing she should have: that he was not actually a superhero and was no less mortal than she or anyone else. In Kate's mind, Ian was invincible. Larger than life. To lose him in something as ordinary as a car accident was perhaps the most unexpected blow of all. Feeling hollow and empty, she laid her head on the floor and wished she could disappear. Just wither up and float away.

But floating made her think of water, and it was then she realized that the reason Ian hadn't called and the app said Offline was because his phone had likely been carried away by the current of the cold and muddy Mississippi River.

CHAPTER TWENTY-NINE

AFTER SITTING ON THE FLOOR of the bathroom for an inde-terminable amount of time, Kate called her mom. She needed Diane's comfort more than anything, but she knew the minute she made the call everything would become real.

"Ian's dead," she said when her mother answered. She was crying so hard she wasn't sure Diane could understand her.

But she must have, because Diane choked back a gasp and said, "Ian? What happened? Were you with him? Are you okay?"

Kate interrupted her, the words tumbling out in one long sentence. "Mom, I don't know anything other than someone hit him and it was icy and his car went over the embankment into the river and I need you to come right now please please come okay?"

"Honey, listen to me. I'm going to hang up and call the air-line. Is there someone who can stay with you until I arrive?"

She hadn't contacted any of her friends because she knew the last name of Merrick would not tie Ian back to her, so there was no reason to start making calls quite yet. Although she barely remembered doing it, she *had* called Helena and was overjoyed when she got her voice mail. Kate had marshaled her strength and managed to leave a message about being sick and asked Helena to take over until she felt better.

"I don't want anyone but you," Kate said.

"I'll be there as soon as I can."

When Kate hung up, she reached for the phone Ian had given her. She had been waiting for it to ring. Surely someone would call her, would deliver the news personally. It wasn't fair that she'd had to drive by the aftermath, see it on the news.

But no one would know to call her because she was not linked to Ian in any way.

He'd made sure of that.

Even if his phone had been recovered, which was doubtful, it probably wouldn't work. Had someone from the FBI field office identified Ian? Had they heard about the crash and recognized his vehicle? Would they know how to contact his mother? Ian said she'd remarried, but Kate didn't know her current last name or if she still lived in Amarillo. She didn't know what to do, where to start. Maybe she should go to the police. Tell them who she was and what she knew? She thought of Ian's body lying in a drawer somewhere, alone and so cold. She squeezed her eyes shut, but the image remained.

He preferred texting over calling and rarely used voice mail. But Kate had saved one of the few messages he'd left her, and she hit the button to listen to it.

"Hey, sweetness. Just left my place. I've been thinking about you all day. Be there soon. Love you."

She listened to it over and over and cried for the next hour.

In the bedroom she found one of his sweatshirts in the hamper and pulled it out. She put it on over her shirt and tucked her face down under the neckline, breathing in the smell of him. It was the wrong thing to do and only brought on a round of fresh sobbing because Kate would never smell him again.

Never feel his arms around her.

Never kiss his lips.

Never see his smile.

Never hear him call her sweetness.

She spent the rest of the afternoon and early evening lying on Ian's side of the bed, her head on his pillow, hating how cold the sheets felt without him in them. Though it only made her cry, she listened to his voice mail repeatedly. When she got up to go to the bathroom, she passed her closet where many of his clothes hung. In the bathroom, she looked at his things on the counter: his toothbrush, his razor, his cologne.

No one would come for his possessions. They were hers to keep, and she'd never get rid of them because they were all she had left.

Diane Watts arrived at 8:15 p.m. She had elected to drive because by the time she waited for the next available flight, sat through a layover in Chicago, and landed in Minneapolis, driving would get her there sooner with the added bonus of not having to worry about delays or cancelations.

Kate had known when to expect her because her mother had called on the hour to check up on her. Kate had calmed down enough to tell Diane what she knew about Ian's death, giving her the information in bits and pieces.

"He should have never taken that car out," Kate had cried during one of her mother's calls. "I don't know why he didn't do it earlier like he'd planned."

Maybe he'd gotten caught up in his work and had been running behind. Maybe he'd noticed the declining road conditions and was on his way to her place to park the Shelby in her lot overnight instead of driving it back to the storage facility. Kate would never know the reasons behind Ian's decision.

Now that her mother was with her, Kate broke down completely. Diane held her as she cried, and when Kate grew quiet, she wrapped her in a blanket and rubbed her back. She made a steaming pot of tea, and she made the calls Kate hadn't been able to—to Kate's friends, to Kate's board of directors, and to Helena to explain what had really happened.

Her dad called, but for some reason his soothing words made her cry harder, so Diane took the phone out of Kate's hand and said they'd try again in a little while. Chad and Kristin called, and her brother's sentiments were heartfelt and supportive. Kristin had broken down and cried with Kate.

"Do you know anything about a funeral service?" Diane asked gently.

"I don't know anything. I don't know who to call. I don't know if anyone's contacted his mother."

"Maybe there'll be something online. Let's not worry about it tonight. We can look for it tomorrow."

Kate needed the closure of Ian's funeral. She desperately wanted to say her good-byes and know he had a final resting place, even if that place was in Texas.

At midnight, Kate's mother put her to bed, assuring Kate that she'd be fine on the couch. When the door closed, Kate automatically rolled to her left side, but she had to turn onto her back because the absence of Ian's arms around her, his back pressed up against her, was more than she could handle.

She cried.

She listened to his voice mail message again.

She lay awake for hours.

Eventually she slept.

CHAPTER THIRTY

KATE WOKE WITH A HEADACHE and eyes so swollen she could barely see. Her mother coaxed her into the shower.

"You'll feel better," Diane said, laying out warm, comfortable clothes on the bed for Kate.

Kate wouldn't feel better because she missed Ian with every ounce of her being and a shower could not possibly put a dent in her grief. But she went into the bathroom and turned on the water, and when she undressed the first thing that caught her eye was the mark Ian had left on her breast. It had faded considerably since Saturday night, and she placed her palm flat on it. Soon there would be nothing left of it or of him. She stepped under the warm spray and cried, and when she was done she dressed and joined her mother in the living room because there was nothing else for her to do.

Her mother had made coffee, and Kate sat down on the couch and accepted the cup Diane handed her. "Paige called this morning to see how you were doing. She said she thought Ian's last name was Smith, not Merrick. Your dad and I did too."

"Actually, it's Bradshaw." Kate was too emotionally exhausted to provide the details surrounding Ian's real name. "I'll explain later."

Diane looked confused, but she didn't press her daughter for more information.

Kate booted up her laptop, which still ran slowly even after Ian had added more memory. She googled Ian Merrick, but the search returned only his website. Kate clicked on it, but there had been no change in content. She took a deep breath and googled "Ian Merrick Amarillo Texas death notice." If the search came back empty again, she'd try Ian Bradshaw. If she still couldn't find anything, she'd go to the police and ask them to put her in touch with whoever had identified Ian's body. They might not give her the information, but she would try.

But the search wasn't empty this time.

When Kate clicked on the link, it took her to the death notice section of the online edition of the *Amarillo Globe-News.*

Merrick, Ian, 32, self-employed, died Monday. The body will be cremated. No services are planned.

Diane tried to comfort her, but Kate was inconsolable. She clung to her mother, soaking her shirt with her tears. Diane dug a Xanax out of her purse. Her oral surgeon had prescribed it to help her relax before dental surgery, but she'd found she hadn't needed it.

She put one of the pills in Kate's mouth, held a glass of water to her lips, and said, "Swallow." Then she helped her daughter back into bed where Kate remained, asleep, for the next six hours.

The first thing Kate did when she woke up was ask for another pill.

"They only gave me two, and I think we should hold on to the last one for now," Diane said.

Kate didn't agree. She'd found the effects of the Xanax highly preferable to being awake.

"Did you eat anything yesterday?" Diane asked.

"No."

"You have to eat, Kate. I can heat up some soup or go out and pick up something."

"You decide. It doesn't matter to me."

Diane heated up some soup and managed to get a little of it into Kate. She'd convinced her to try a cracker when someone knocked on the door. Kate looked up quickly, her heart soaring.

But Ian wouldn't have knocked.

And Ian was also dead.

Diane had observed Kate's hopeful expression and looked worriedly at her. "I'll answer it."

Kate thought it might be one of her friends, but when Diane opened the door, she heard a man's voice and caught only fragments of the conversation.

When Diane returned to the couch, she said, "You have a new neighbor. He moved in right down the hall. He seemed very nice. He left a card and said you should stop by sometime and introduce yourself." Diane set the card on the coffee table, but Kate ignored it.

"Now can I have one of those pills?"

"It really is the last one, honey. I'll give it to you, but there are no more after this."

"I don't care."

Kate wanted oblivion. Kate wanted nothingness. Kate wanted to wake up and find the whole thing had been a bad dream.

Her mother gave her the pill and Kate swallowed it.

She slept.

The next day there was another shower, more soup, and no pills.

"I'm going to wash the sheets," Diane said.

"No," Kate said. "Just leave them." Those were the sheets she'd slept on, made love on, with Ian. She was not ready.

She spent most of her time sitting in the chair by the window, staring out at the gray sky and listening to Ian's voice mail message. Diane went to the store. She cooked, she cleaned, and she made sure Kate got out of bed.

"I know it's hard to fathom right now, but you'll get through this," Diane said.

"No, I won't," Kate replied.

She brushed Kate's hair out of her eyes and said, "Yes, you will."

On their fifth night together, Diane opened a bottle of wine and poured them a glass. She built a fire and sat down on the couch next to Kate.

"You told me you didn't like Ian when you first met him and promised that someday you'd tell me the whole story."

Kate's eyes instantly filled with tears. "I can't, Mom."

Diane squeezed her hand. "Talking about him will help."

The only thing that would truly help was Ian walking through the door and calling her sweetness. But her mother was trying so hard, and it was the least Kate could do considering Diane had dropped everything to rush to her side. "Ian was a hacker."

"I thought he owned a computer security company," Diane said.

"He did. But mostly he loved to hack into things. He said no one could keep him out if he wanted to get in because he was the best. I didn't really buy it at first. But after he hacked air traffic control at O'Hare, I started to believe him."

Diane's eyes widened. "He hacked air traffic control?"

"I needed time to get to a different gate after my flight got canceled. He fixed everything after I got on the plane."

Kate took a sip of her wine and found it went down better than she'd expected. "I told you his last name was Smith because when I met him he wouldn't tell me what it really was. Referring to him as Ian Smith became our little inside joke."

"You didn't know his last name?" Diane asked.

She shook her head. "Not right away." Kate went back to the beginning and told her mom about the donations and how Ian had tracked her to the café by hacking her credit card account. "And then he told me he'd stolen the money he'd donated but thought we could still be friends. I told him I didn't think so."

Diane's shocked expression conveyed how alarming she found this revelation.

Kate took another sip of her wine. It wasn't as effective as the pills, but it calmed her a little. "He'd stolen it from cyberthieves who shouldn't have had it in the first place, like some kind of modern day Robin Hood. It was his version of vigilante justice." Kate explained the cause of Ian's dad's suicide, and the reasoning behind Ian's actions.

Diane took a rather large drink of her wine. Under any other circumstances, Kate knew her mother would have had plenty to say about Ian. But Kate's grief was too raw, and she wouldn't have been able to handle hearing anyone say one negative thing about him. Diane kept her thoughts to herself.

"Not only had he hacked my credit card account, he'd hacked my personal computer. That's why I said I didn't like him at first. He was just so cocky and arrogant, and he had no concept of boundaries. But he was charming as hell, and he went to work on winning me over right away."

"But what about the money he stole?"

"I no longer cared about that. Ian never once made excuses for it. He'd look you in the eye and tell you he was a thief. Said it wasn't an ethical struggle for him at all. By then I knew he was a good person, and I knew he would never treat me badly. And he didn't. I fell in love with him so hard, and I never saw it coming."

Kate took another drink of her wine. Her mother had been right. It did feel good to talk about Ian.

"He didn't tell me right away, but in addition to his regular clients, he also did some hacking for the government, working with the FBI to fight cybercrime. That's why he protected his identity so carefully. He didn't want the hackers he was trying to catch to know who he was or where he lived. He moved around a lot so they wouldn't find him. He was getting ready to leave Minneapolis, and I was going to go with him. To Charlotte, North Carolina."

"You were going to move?" Diane said. "What about the food pantry?"

"I was going to resign. I loved Ian and I wanted to be with him." Kate started crying again.

Diane kissed Kate's temple and smoothed her hair the way she had when Kate was a little girl.

"He was the one I was supposed to spend the rest of my life with. When people talk about a once-in-a-lifetime love, I thought I knew what they meant. But I didn't. Ian was the man I didn't know I needed until I met him. The whole time I was with Stuart, Ian was out there, waiting. And we found each other, but then I lost him."

"I promise you'll get through this."

Kate wiped her eyes. "Right now I'd settle for not feeling quite so much pain."

"It's going to take time," Diane said gently.

Her mother spoke the truth. It's what Kate would have said to anyone who had suffered a similar loss. "I think I'll go to bed," Kate said. "I don't want any more of my wine."

She kissed her mother and then went into the bedroom and lay down on Ian's side of the bed, clutching her phone and listening to his voice mail message as she cried herself to sleep.

CHAPTER THIRTY-ONE

DIANE WENT HOME A WEEK after Ian died. Kate had convinced her mother she'd be okay on her own, not that she actually believed it. But she couldn't keep using her mother as a buffer, a crutch. It was time to see if she would sink or swim.

"I can come back in a few weeks," Diane said.

"We'll see," Kate said. "I love you, Mom. Thank you so much for being there for me."

After Diane left, Kate continued with the routine Diane had set for her: sleep, shower, dress, try to eat. Now she added work, and walking through the door of the food pantry on her first day back was the most difficult thing she'd had to do since losing Ian.

She owed it to her clients not to look like she was at death's door and to try to function like a real human. But her eyes were constantly swollen and red-rimmed, surrounded by dark circles. She kept a bottle of eyedrops in her desk drawer, and she stopped wearing eye makeup. Her complexion, normally so healthy and bright, looked dull and ashen. Styling her hair in anything other than a ponytail seemed like a waste of time. Acting as if nothing was wrong took a monumental amount of energy, and she felt physically drained by the end of the day, a brittle shell of her former self.

Her smiles were forced and she could only maintain them for so long, but she tried her best, especially for new clients.

She didn't want them to think there was something wrong with her although many probably wondered if there was. When Samantha came in with the kids, Kate held Georgie on her lap and tried not to cry. Only Helena knew what had happened to Ian, and she treated Kate like one of her own daughters, fussing over her, hugging her, doing whatever she could to help.

Two weeks after Ian died, Kate was having a particularly hard day and had been hiding out in the back room so no one would see her cry. That morning, she'd found a note Ian had once left for her and that she'd shoved into a drawer in the kitchen and forgotten about. But then her smoke alarm had started to chirp while she was getting ready for work—the relentless, grating noise almost sending Kate over the edge—and the note was in the drawer where she kept the batteries.

Picking up dinner. Back soon, baby. xoxo

She'd put the note in her pocket and had reached for it throughout the morning. It had the same effect as Ian's voice mail message, which she listened to constantly. It only heightened her sorrow, but Kate couldn't stop reading his words, couldn't stop rubbing her fingers across the paper. She promised herself that tomorrow she'd leave the note at home.

Helena stuck her head into the back room. "Kate?" Her tone was gentle, the way it always was with Kate now.

She looked up. "Yes?" Her voice sounded raspy and hoarse.

"A client is asking for you."

"I'll be right out."

Everyone at the food pantry had been picking up her slack, Helena especially. Feeling like she wasn't pulling her weight only contributed to Kate's sadness and general unhappiness. She needed to work harder on pulling herself together, and she promised herself that she would. It was just that getting through the day felt like wading through quicksand.

There wasn't time for eyedrops, but Kate smoothed her hands over her hair and tightened her ponytail. Zach Nielsen, the young man who'd been so worried about his younger brother, was waiting for her by her desk.

"Hi, Zach," she said.

"Hey. My mom wanted me to stop by and say thank you. She's been so worried about my brother, and she said you really saved us."

"Please tell her it was my pleasure. We're happy to help."

He looked at her curiously, and Kate became painfully aware of her appearance. "Um, are you okay?"

She felt the tears forming again and blinked rapidly as heat flooded her face. Many of Kate's clients had shed their own tears at the food pantry. They would come to her hungry and destitute, but when they left they would be smiling. They deserved an executive director who was strong and mentally healthy and would take away their troubles and save them from their dire circumstances.

Not a broken woman who looked like she was the one who needed saving most of all.

Mustering a weak smile, she attempted to convince him he was in good hands. "I'm fine," she said, fooling no one.

"Okay," he said, looking embarrassed to have caught her in such a personal display of emotion. "I guess I'll see you in a few weeks."

"Take care, Zach."

Kate's shoes kicked up plumes of muddy water as she marched through the puddles left behind by the melting snow.

Spring in St. Anthony Main was a dirty, sodden affair, as if Mother Nature's brushstrokes had come from a palette of gray, black, and white. The pastel colors of spring would not arrive for another month at least, and that's only if the season arrived on time in Minnesota.

Kate had been staring at the ground and didn't notice the man until she was halfway up the steps to her building's front door. Stopping suddenly when she sensed him, she swerved to the left, her arm brushing the fabric of his suit coat. He was leaning against the metal handrail, the same one Ian had once leaned against while waiting for his cab. He looked like he was in his early fifties. His hair was light brown with a sprinkle of gray, and his eyes were blue.

"I'm sorry," she said. "I wasn't paying attention."

"No problem," he said, and his smile was kind. "My name is Don Murray. I'm your neighbor, by the way. I've seen you in the hallway a couple of times. I dropped off a business card when I moved in. I gave it to the woman who answered your door."

"You did?" Kate didn't remember that. He must have come by when her mother was there because Kate rarely received unannounced visitors and hadn't opened her door to anyone since Ian died. The man fished a card out of his pocket and handed it to her.

"In case you can't find the other one," he said. "Let me know if you ever need anything. I'm right down the hall from you."

"Sure. Thanks" A quick glance at the card revealed his name and phone number, but there was no business listed, no occupation. Kate shoved the card into her pocket. "Sorry, I'm Kate. Kate Watts." She held out her hand and he shook it.

"Nice to meet you."

"You too." She didn't want to be rude, but she didn't have the energy for small talk and her head was pounding. "Well. I'll see you around."

"Have a nice day, Kate."

She made her way up the steps and disappeared into the building.

CHAPTER THIRTY-TWO

STUART STOPPED BY THE FOOD pantry on what would have been Ian's thirty-third birthday. Kate was hiding in the back room again, this time under the pretense of doing inventory after experiencing a particularly intense and sudden crying jag, which she feared might recur at any moment. She was momentarily confused when she looked up from the cans she'd been rearranging and noticed him standing there.

"Hi," he said. Stuart had once spent a considerable amount of time at the food pantry helping to unload food, build shelves, and carry in desks and office equipment. Whatever Kate had needed in the early days of the food pantry, Stuart had been there to lend a hand.

"Hi."

He approached her slowly, as if she were a wounded animal that might strike out at him, and hugged her. Stuart might not have been the most stimulating man she'd ever known, but she'd once found safety and comfort in his arms and she found it again now.

"I was walking by and thought I'd stop in and see if you were okay. I ran into Paige and she told me you were dating that guy who crashed into the river, except she said his last name was Smith and I don't really understand that. Anyway, I wanted to tell you I was sorry about what happened to him. If you ever want to get together, for a drink or dinner or whatever, just let me know, okay?"

"Thanks, Stuart. That's really nice of you."

Kate had wanted excitement. She had wanted an adventure.

But maybe safe was better.

Maybe safe wasn't so boring after all.

He'd almost reached the door when Kate spoke. "Stuart? Maybe I'll give you a call sometime."

He smiled and said, "I would really like that."

Kate went for a walk after she locked up the food pantry. She'd been doing that a lot lately because her apartment seemed too quiet and empty now that it was just her again. She set off toward the pedestrian walkway of the Stone Arch Bridge that spanned the Mississippi River below the St. Anthony Falls.

Once she reached the bridge, she pulled out her phone and listened to Ian's voice mail message. *"Hey, sweetness. Just left my place. I've been thinking about you all day. Be there soon. Love you."*

She knew that listening to his message so often wasn't healthy.

She knew it was preventing her from starting the healing process.

She thought she might be losing her mind because of her attachment to it, and that scared her a little.

Instead of playing the message again, she chose the only contact in the phone and dialed. The call went to voice mail as she knew it would. His cell was either resting at the bottom of the river or had been carried downstream. Even if it had stayed in his pocket, it would have been damaged beyond repair, the corrosion starting immediately upon the phone making contact with the water.

Kate listened to the generic outgoing message that had come with the phone and began to speak after the beep. "Today is your birthday, and I'm having a really hard time. I miss you, Ian. I loved you so much, and I don't know what to do. I listen to your voice mail message every day, multiple times. I listen to it at night when I'm lying in bed, and I cry because you're not there. I found a note you left me, and I keep it in my pocket and I can't stop touching it."

She was crying hard, wedging the words in and around her sobs. A man walking his dog gave her a concerned look, but she ignored him.

"You were supposed to be the one I would spend the rest of my life with. I'm so mad at you for taking that car out. I will never get over the loss of you, and all I have are the things you left behind. Sometimes I wear your clothes, and I know that's weird, but they smell like you and when I'm wearing them I feel close to you. I will never love anyone the way I loved you, and I will never stop loving you. My heart hurts so much and I'm trying to be strong, but it's so hard. You were the best thing that ever happened to me, and it's not fair that I didn't get more time with you."

A beep sounded in her ear when she ran out of time and the recording cut her off. She rested her head on the railing of the bridge, her shoulders shaking as she cried.

When she was all cried out, she looked up and hesitated only for a moment before heaving the phone into the Mississippi River.

That night, Kate reached into the cupboard for one of the glasses she'd given Ian for Christmas. She filled it halfway with bourbon and sat in the chair by the window where she had waited for Ian to come home. But he would never come home again no matter how long she sat there.

She took a drink and winced at the taste. She would never truly be a whiskey girl, but since Ian wasn't there to celebrate his birthday she'd decided she'd drink it for him. The second mouthful went down a little easier, and the alcohol warmed her, which she welcomed because she felt cold all the time.

When the glass was empty, she poured another. Her tears flowed freely because at home she didn't have to hide them or pretend everything was okay. She drank and she cried, and her longing for him was as bottomless as her glass.

Earlier that day, shortly after Stuart left, Samantha had come into the food pantry alone. She'd pulled Kate aside and whispered, "I got some money. This is the second time it's happened. The bank traced it to one of those charitable websites where you can ask for help and people can donate anonymously. But I never went to that website, and I never asked for help. I spent it because I needed it so badly. Do you think it's okay to spend this one too?"

Kate had scared Samantha when she'd grabbed her hands and started crying.

"What is it?" Samantha had asked. "What's wrong, Kate?"

"Nothing," she said. "I'm just so happy for you. You should definitely spend the money."

"If you think it's okay, then I will."

Kate finished the second glass of bourbon, head spinning and tears rolling down her face. She didn't know why some people could have everything and others had to struggle and fight. Why some people lived to one hundred but others would not see thirty-three.

The only thing she knew for sure was that Ian had not been granted enough time on this earth, and she'd give anything to have him back.

CHAPTER THIRTY-THREE

IAN HAD BEEN DEAD FOR thirty-one days when Kate received the message. She'd been walking home from work in the pouring rain, umbrella turned inside out from the gusty wind that had accompanied the downpour, when her phone sounded an alert to let her know she'd received a new e-mail. She forgot all about it until she went to call her mother an hour later and couldn't find her phone. After finally tracking it down in the front pocket of the soaked jeans she'd removed immediately upon her arrival at home, she remembered the alert. When she hung up with Diane, she scrolled through the unread e-mails. A message from the dating site she no longer used caught her eye.

The subject line said, *You have one new message.*

Kate would have to log on to her dating account to read the message, but since she had no desire or interest in doing so, she deleted the e-mail notification.

The next day while sitting at her desk, she received another notification. *You have one new message.*

At Ian's request, Kate had not deleted her account. But the thought of dating anyone made her physically ill, and the last thing she wanted was a constant reminder of her single status. She opened a browser on her phone and logged on to her account. Kate had modified her preferences so that she'd no longer receive alerts, but all the notification settings had been turned back on. She jabbed at the drop-down menu to turn them off again. Deciding it was time to remove her profile permanently, she went in search of the delete button.

"Kate? Can you unlock the back door for a delivery?"

"Sure," she said, setting the phone aside to dig the keys out of her pocket. She walked to the back and forgot about deleting the account until the next day when she received another notification shortly after returning to her apartment after work.

You have one new message.

Once again, she logged on to her dating account.

Once again, all notifications were back on.

Irritated, she clicked over to the actual messages, wondering who was being so persistent. After taking a look, she would delete the account as planned. Kate expected to find dozens of messages, but there were only three, all of which had come in since she'd received the first alert two days ago, and all from the same person.

Someone named Rion Bodoh.

Rion? Kate thought.

She went to his profile, but there was no picture and no bio.

She clicked on the first message:

I would really like to connect with you.

Kate deleted it and the second message filled the screen.

Please, I would really like the chance to get to know you.

Kate deleted that one too.

The final message filled the screen.

All I'm asking is for a simple response to let me know you're receiving my messages. If you're not interested in getting to know me, please tell me and I won't write to you again.

Kate tapped out a short reply, hoping it would end his attempts to engage her in conversation.

Yes, I've received your messages. I have no interest in meeting or dating anyone. I am deleting this account.

The sound of the e-mail alert chimed in her hand almost immediately.

You have one new message.

In the interest of being polite, she'd done what he'd asked. But of course "Ryan" with the weird spelling hadn't held up his end of the bargain.

They never did.

I can't tell you how happy I am that you responded. I'd really like to get to know you. I like your glasses. They make you look very smart.

Her glasses?

Kate clicked over to her profile. Her bio was still the one Ian had written, but she inhaled sharply when she noticed the picture, remembering exactly when Ian had taken it.

She'd been lying in bed next to him, hair tousled, eyes half-closed, lips turned up slightly in a satisfied smile, naked under the covers. He'd reached for his phone on the nightstand and snapped the picture. When he showed it to her, he said, "This is my new favorite picture of you. I love it because I'm the one who put that look on your face. God, Kate. You are so beautiful."

She remembered how after he'd shown her the picture, he'd pulled back the covers and asked if he could take one more. "For my eyes only," he said.

She'd said yes.

Now the picture had been cropped to show only her face and rotated so it appeared she was sitting upright.

And she was wearing glasses.

Nice, normal glasses.

How long after New Year's Eve—when her profile photo had still been a picture of her driving the Shelby—had Ian changed it?

It made sense he'd choose his favorite photo of her, especially because he was the only one who knew the circumstances behind it.

But when had he added the glasses?

And why?

Her irritation was replaced by curiosity. She'd never needed glasses in her life, so what significance did they bring to the photo? Ian was the one who wore glasses, not her. She thought back to the first time she'd seen him wearing them.

"Are the glasses a disguise? Because I totally knew it was you."

"The glasses are real. I often suffer from eyestrain since I spend so much time on the computer, and I was up late last night, working."

"They make you look very smart."

It's a coincidence, she told herself. That's all it is.

Her phone chimed again. *You have one new message.*

Kate clicked over to her account, her finger shaking slightly.

Please don't delete your account. I'll wait.

Wait for what? Wait until she figured it out? She set the phone on the coffee table and leaned away from it, hugging her knees to her chest. Believing the messages had anything to do with Ian was a dangerous line of thinking and would rip off the scab that had only recently formed over her grief. Did she think he had somehow figured out how to communicate from the grave?

I'll wait.

For my eyes only.

Rion Bodoh

The name stumped her even more than the glasses. It was too odd not to have significance. There was something she was supposed to *see*.

She stared at the name.

Rion Bodoh.

When she clicked over to her account preferences, they'd been turned off again. Whoever was sending the messages no longer wanted an e-mail alert to accompany them.

That night, when Kate was lying in bed wide-awake, it came to her so suddenly she couldn't believe she hadn't been able to see it before. Her heart thundered in her chest and goose bumps covered every inch of her skin.

Please don't be wrong, please don't be wrong, please don't be wrong.

She threw back the covers and ran into the living room, turning on the lights on her way. She grabbed a piece of paper and a pen, crossing out each letter as she wrote them down in a new order.

Rion Bodoh.

Robin Hood.

Kate's spirits soared and she began to cry.

After a sleepless night and a call to Helena to let her know she'd be in around eleven, Kate arrived at the storage facility in Bloomington shortly before nine o'clock. A little voice inside her head warned that if she was mistaken, or worse yet—if this was some kind of trick—the agony she would experience would be ten times harder to bear than the initial news of Ian's death. But her hope was a snowball rolling downhill, gaining speed and momentum and strength, and she was powerless to stop it.

She walked through the front door of the storage facility wearing a pencil skirt, a push-up bra, and high heels. She carried a leather satchel.

The young man behind the counter looked about nineteen and very bored, but he perked up a little when she took off her coat, revealing a blouse that had one button too many undone.

"Good morning," she said. In a matter-of-fact tone, she pulled a sheaf of papers from the satchel and clicked open a ballpoint pen. "I need a copy of a rental agreement. The name is Ian Merrick. M-E-R-R-I-C-K. Do you have that name in your system?"

He typed the name into his computer and looked up.

Bingo, Kate thought.

"I'm working to settle Mr. Merrick's estate. If I can get a copy of that agreement, I can move forward. You can imagine how comforting that would be for Mr. Merrick's family."

"I can't give it to you. Our records have to be subpoenaed. People store stuff here they don't want anyone to know about. We can't just give out that information."

"Yes I know. I'm an attorney." Kate pulled one of her old business cards out of her satchel and held it up just long enough for him to see the writing. "But waiting on the proper forms so I can draft the subpoena is something I don't have time for. The family is devastated, as you can imagine."

"Sorry," he said. "I still can't give it to you. I could lose my job if I don't follow the rules."

Kate looked into his eyes, holding his gaze a beat longer than necessary. When she slid the business card back into her satchel, her elbow knocked a rack of brochures off the counter and they scattered on the floor.

"I'm so sorry. I guess I can tell what kind of day it's going to be." She crouched down to pick them up.

"No big deal." He came out from behind the counter to help her pick them up, stealing a good long look down her gaping blouse in the process.

"You can probably get that subpoena, right? Seeing as you're an attorney and all? I feel bad that I can't help you."

"It's okay. I'm sure your adherence to company policy is one of the things that make you such a valued employee. How long have you been in charge here?"

"Almost a year," he said. "I'm not really in charge. Not yet anyway."

Kate smiled. "It probably won't be long until you are. They've undoubtedly taken notice of your dedication."

He stood up and put the brochure rack back on the counter. "You're a lot nicer than that guy who came in here asking questions," he blurted.

"Was he rude to you?" Kate's tone was sympathetic, caring. She leaned against the counter as if she wasn't in a hurry to leave.

"Nothing I couldn't handle. I know everything that goes on around here, but I didn't feel like telling him on account of what a dick he was being to me."

"What did he want to know?"

"He wanted to know when the FBI had come for Mr. Merrick's other car. The one he left in the parking lot while he was out driving that cool old car. That's when I knew he was crazy. They'd barely pulled the body out of the river at that point. Why would the FBI be interested in a car accident, you know? That didn't make any sense."

Kate kept her expression neutral. "That does seem a little odd. Was he dressed like me? Maybe he was from the insurance company or something."

"He was just some punk wearing ripped jeans and a hoodie."

Her pulse quickened. "A purple one? Vikings fan, maybe?"

"No. Gray I think. Or maybe it was black."

"Thank you for your time today." She rested a hand on his arm. "You've been very helpful."

He stood a little taller. "You're welcome. You can come back if you need anything else. I'm here all the time."

She smiled. "I'll keep that in mind. Bye now."

Kate had never been interested in the rental agreement. There was nothing on it that would help her, nothing she even remotely cared about knowing. She'd just needed an excuse to start a conversation. Because if anyone outside the FBI had shown up, it likely meant Ian's cover had been blown and there was enough doubt surrounding his death to warrant a visit. And it was any mention of another person who'd been nosing around, especially someone who might have been a hacker, that she'd been after from the start.

CHAPTER THIRTY-FOUR

BACK AT HER APARTMENT, Kate kicked off her shoes and rubbed her temples.

For my eyes only.

The glasses had definitely been his way of helping her figure out who the messages were from. But the picture itself must have been his way of telling her to use caution regarding their communication. If Ian was contacting her via her dating account, did it mean he'd been hacked? Was this the only secure connection between them? She supposed he could have used the cell phone he'd given her if she hadn't thrown it in the river.

She thought back to the days leading up to Ian's death. The way his phone had pinged on the way to lunch. The problem he'd mentioned not being sure how to solve. She remembered how desperate he'd seemed when they'd made love and what he'd said afterward.

Don't ever lose faith in me.

Maybe she'd misunderstood him. Maybe he'd been trying to prepare her for a future event. Kate began to question things. Why was the tracking turned off on his phone? Why had he taken the Shelby out when he knew the roads would be bad?

She logged on to her dating account and drafted her reply carefully:

The glasses do make me feel very smart. I'm able to understand things so much better when I'm wearing them.

She waited thirty seconds and refreshed the screen. A new message appeared, its header bolded to signify it hadn't been opened yet. Kate clicked on the message.

Smart and beautiful. Promise me you'll wear the glasses on our date.

Kate's heart was thumping when she replied.

You seem very nice, but I'm not interested in going on a date. I recently lost someone very important to me. He was the love of my life, and I'm still mourning him. I'm sorry.

She waited two minutes and refreshed the screen.

I completely understand that you're not ready for another romantic entanglement, but maybe we could go to lunch. I happen to know of a restaurant that serves the best charcuterie in Minneapolis.

Mentioning the charcuterie was Ian's way of assuring her it was really him. Tears ran down Kate's face as she typed her reply.

I suppose lunch wouldn't hurt.

He sent a reply immediately.

I predict you'll be so taken with me you'll be more than willing to move on to the next stage. I have that effect on women.

Kate typed her response: *You seem very confident. If you're so successful with women, why are you single?*

I'm currently between lovers.

She wiped away tears.

I see. Kate wanted him to know that she understood.

I knew you would.

Kate knew he must have a plan but that it would need to be revealed carefully.

What would happen if things were to go well on our first few dates?

He replied immediately.

I was hoping you would ask. If things go well, maybe you'd consider a romantic weekend away. We could board a private plane on a Saturday afternoon and go someplace where we could be alone.

A Saturday afternoon.

Kate was fairly certain he meant for her to meet him at the airstrip *this* Saturday. As in, two days from now.

What if I'm afraid to take this step? I've been hurt very badly.

She refreshed the screen.

Please know that everything is under control. I would never harm you, Katie. Never. So I'll see you on Saturday? Around two?

Yes. I'll be ready.

Make a couple of stops on the way and take a cab.

His message threw her for a minute, but then she realized what he meant—shake whoever might be following you—and fear gripped her.

I understand.

She took a deep breath, and when she refreshed the screen, the messages were gone. That night, when she finally fell asleep after lying there for hours, all her dreams were of him.

CHAPTER THIRTY-FIVE

ON SATURDAY, KATE PULLED a large tote bag from the top shelf of her closet. She placed her wallet, keys, phone, a few toiletries, and a change of clothes inside it. Time seemed to drag, but at one thirty she walked to Wilde Roast Café—fighting the urge to look over her shoulder the whole way—and ordered a sandwich. She was trembling slightly and didn't dare order anything containing caffeine to go along with her food. Fifteen minutes later, after forcing down as much of her meal as she could, Kate paid the check. She exited the restaurant and walked slowly down the street as if she had no particular place to be. After ducking into the tunnel that linked SE Main Street with the St. Anthony Falls parking ramp, she took out her phone and called a cab, waiting just inside the ramp's exit onto Second Street until it pulled to a stop at the curb. Then she walked quickly to the waiting car and slid into the back seat.

"Where to?" the driver asked.

She gave him the address of the airstrip and tried to calm her breathing.

The plane was sitting on the tarmac when they pulled into the parking lot, the same one she'd seen Ian get into when she'd dropped him off. Still she hesitated. What if it wasn't him?

"This is your stop, miss," the driver said.

"I know. Give me a minute please." With shaking hands, Kate dug her phone out of her bag and sent a message via the dating site.

I'm not sure if I should meet you today. What if it's a mistake to go out with you?

Her stomach was in knots, and she thought the sandwich might have been a bad idea.

It isn't. I promise. Just get out of the car. You can do this. I'm waiting for you.

Kate took a deep breath and let it out. The only thing standing between them was her fear. She handed the money to the driver and gripped the door handle, throwing it open. Committed now, she strode across the parking lot and through the open gate. She faltered a bit on the tarmac because there was no one waiting in the open door of the airplane.

I'll stop at the top. I won't get on the plane if I don't see him.

Slowly she climbed the stairs, heart pounding. Too many emotions were competing for Kate's attention. There was fear and anxiety, but most of all there was hope. That's where she drew the courage to climb the final step and peer around the opening of the plane.

And there he was, standing there like some kind of ghost.

He lunged toward her and caught her right as her knees buckled. She wrapped her arms and legs around him, clinging to his body as she broke down, sobbing hysterically.

"Please don't hate me," he said, holding her so tightly it hurt, as if he was trying to meld her body to his.

She didn't mind the pain because it grounded her and proved to her this was real. He lowered them into a seat, and she curled into a ball on his lap, her face pressed into his chest, fisting his T-shirt tightly in her hands. She couldn't stop crying, couldn't still the massive shaking of her body.

"What's happening to her, Phillip?" Ian said.

"Just give her a minute," a voice said somewhere off to her right.

"Sweetness, I'm sorry," Ian said rubbing her back.

"Kate, my name is Phillip Corcoran. I work for the FBI, and I'm a friend of Ian's. You're safe, and everything is going to be okay. I want you to take a few slow, deep breaths."

The words and the tone in which Phillip had delivered them helped to calm her a little. Ian's arms were still wrapped tightly around her, but he loosened them slightly, allowing her to inhale fully. The smell of him, still so familiar to her, filled her nose as she breathed in. She nuzzled her face into his neck, feeling his warm skin against her lips as he stroked her hair.

"Everything's okay," he whispered. "I'm right here." He held her for a long time, neither of them speaking, until gradually her shaking subsided. The shock and adrenaline rush had left her physically exhausted.

"The pilot is ready to take off," Phillip said. "I don't suppose you'd be willing to buckle her into her own seat."

"No," Ian said, holding her tighter.

He didn't let go of her when they taxied down the runway or when the plane rose into the air. He never stopped rubbing his hands up and down her back, and he whispered in her ear, telling her he loved her, telling her how much he'd missed her.

Kate had never been so emotionally spent in her life. Though she tried, she couldn't hold her eyes open, and she fell asleep in his arms.

The slight thumping of the wheels making contact with the runway roused Kate from an exhilarating dream in which Ian was alive.

Except that it wasn't a dream because Ian was holding her on his lap, and the first thing he did when she opened her eyes was kiss her gently on the forehead.

"Where are we?" she asked.

"Just outside DC."

"I can't believe this is really happening," Kate said. She touched his face, fingers skimming over his eyes, nose, mouth.

"Believe it, sweetness. It's happening." He wiped the tears that had filled her eyes and spilled onto her cheeks. "Phillip and I will explain everything when we get to the house."

Phillip Corcoran lived in an older, well-maintained colonial-style home an hour outside the nation's capital. His wife met them at the door.

"My name is Susan. Come in, dear," she said, taking Kate by the hand. "Can I get you something to drink?"

Kate's throat felt raw from crying. "Could I have some water, please?"

"Of course." Susan patted her shoulder and gave it a quick squeeze before disappearing into the kitchen.

Ian was holding Kate's hand, and he followed Phillip into the living room and led Kate to the couch. Phillip sat down across from them.

"Thank you," Kate said when Susan returned and handed her a glass of water. She took a drink, and it soothed the burn in her throat.

"I'll be upstairs if you need me," Susan said.

Phillip smiled and nodded at her. Kate set the glass on the coffee table and turned to Ian. Dark circles rimmed his eyes, and he seemed exhausted.

"They found you," she said. When she'd finally allowed herself to believe he might actually be alive, she'd started putting it all together. "That's why you put your car in the river. You wanted them to think you were dead."

"Yes," Ian replied. "They found out who I was and where I lived." Ian and Philip shared a glance. "But even worse than that, and the reason I did this, is because they found *you*."

CHAPTER THIRTY-SIX

KATE FELT AS IF THE wind had been knocked out of her. "Me?"

Ian nodded somberly. "I realized it when you asked me to look at your computer. Your firewall had been turned off, you had a backdoor, and there were several shell scripts running simultaneously. I couldn't do anything about it. If I had, they'd have known I'd discovered it."

Kate's mind was reeling, and she felt like a weight was pressing down on her chest. The room was suddenly too warm. "Do they know where I live? Where I work?"

"They know everything," Ian said.

"How?" Kate asked. "How did they find you?"

"We're not sure," Ian said. "My computers are all clean. I would have known immediately if they weren't. Phillip and I have some theories, but nothing we've been able to prove. But they would have seen us together as soon as they started watching me. Then it would have taken them no time at all to identify and hack you.

"You said if they ever found you there would be threats," Kate said, her voice rising. "Disturbing threats."

"They wanted me, Kate. Not you. The fact that they hadn't made any direct threats yet meant they were probably planning to use you to draw me out, to force me to react in some way. And I would have. I'd have done anything they asked if it meant they'd leave you out of this. Even so, there's no way I would leave you unprotected. Your new neighbor, Don Murray, is an FBI agent who works out of the Minneapolis field office. So does the man who follows you to and from work every day, and the two men who keep an eye on your street and the food pantry."

Kate sat in stunned silence. How had she gone from running a nonprofit organization to being under FBI surveillance? She could not wrap her brain around it no matter how hard she tried. It was simply too surreal.

"We had to act fast," Ian said, "before they could put whatever they were planning into motion. We got lucky because we didn't have to wait long for another storm."

"How were you able to convince the police, the media?"

Phillip answered her. "Ian abandoned the car on the side of the road. The streets were fairly empty because of the road conditions, and it didn't take much to stage a collision that pushed the Shelby over the embankment. We called 911 ourselves and reported a car in the river. No one would have survived something like that, not in a vehicle without airbags and not in freezing-cold water. Then we leaked to the media that a body had been recovered and identified. The FBI claimed jurisdiction, and the only information we shared was what we wanted to make public."

"There was a death notice," Kate said.

Ian's expression remained blank, but his features hardened and Kate detected a slight clenching of his jaw. "I wrote it."

"After you found out about Ian's death, did you google Ian Merrick on your laptop?" Phillip asked.

"Yes. I did a general search and then a more specific one. That's how I found the death notice."

"What about Ian Bradshaw?"

"Not on my laptop. I googled him once on my special phone after Ian said I wouldn't be able to find him, but that's it."

Phillip nodded and seemed happy with her answer.

"What if I had? Would that have ruined everything? Why leave such an important thing to chance?"

"It wouldn't have ruined anything, Kate," Ian said softly. "Phillip just wants to know what we're dealing with so we can do some long-term planning."

"Within an hour of the crash, we blew Ian's cover ourselves," Phillip said. "We made sure the name Ian Merrick, and the news of his death, was all over the forum. We made sure they knew he was working with the FBI."

"Did they buy it?" Kate asked. "After everything you did, did they believe you?"

"Anytime a hacker with any notoriety dies, there's immediate suspicion that it's a hoax and a call to arms for any hacker within a ten-mile radius to help verify the information," Phillip said. "It's the oldest trick in the book, and the only way it would work was if your reaction was genuine."

Kate didn't know what to say. They'd started following the steps of their carefully laid out plan before she'd even known there was a problem.

"Do I still have a backdoor?" she asked.

"Yes. That's why Ian had to contact you the way he did. And even then it was quite risky. I wanted him to hold off a little longer before he reached out, but he said he couldn't wait. Did anyone ever approach you, Kate? Ask you anything that might have seemed strange?"

"No."

"Do you remember seeing anyone who looked out of place?"

"When I went to Ian's apartment the morning after he didn't come home, there was a guy near the bank of intercoms. He was young, midtwenties probably. It was hard to tell for sure because he had his hood up. I remember thinking at the time that he seemed to be watching me, but I thought it was because I looked upset. I was trying not to cry, and I didn't want him to see, so I turned away. Then when I went to the storage facility I learned that someone had been there asking about when the FBI had come for the Escalade. Some young guy wearing a dark hoodie."

"You went to the storage facility?" Phillip said.

"Yes. After I got Ian's message on my dating account I got nervous and wanted to do some investigating of my own. See if anyone had shown up there and asked questions."

Kate told them how she was able to get the storage facility employee to share the information. "But that's it. I don't remember seeing anyone else."

Susan walked into the room and announced that dinner would be ready soon. Kate had no appetite, but Susan was kind so Kate smiled and gave her a slight nod.

"We'll have to handle your move from Minneapolis a bit differently than Ian had planned," Phillip said.

Kate looked away. They'd assumed she would go along with their plan for moving forward now that they'd brought her into the fold, but all she could think was *no*.

Because now that she'd recovered slightly from the initial shock, other thoughts had started to materialize.

Emotions were starting to bubble their way to the surface.

What Ian had done was not on the same level as hacking her credit card and computer or walking in on her in the bathtub.

He had let her think he was *dead,* which was the worst kind of hell you could put anyone through, and she was not done processing it.

Philip was too focused on what would happen next to notice Kate's reaction. But Ian—a man who missed nothing—sure had. She could feel the weight of his stare, and as soon as she looked up, he locked eyes with her, comprehending.

"I need some time alone with Kate," Ian said.

"Of course," Phillip said. "I'll call down when dinner is ready."

A small guesthouse sat behind the main property. Ian carried Kate's bag as they made their way along the flagstone path, neither of them speaking. Once they were inside, there was no mistaking the fact that the space belonged to Ian. The main room had a couch and a coffee table on which sat a laptop computer and an empty coffee mug. His tennis shoes were on the floor, and his favorite MIT sweatshirt, the one that was faded red and soft and that Kate had sometimes worn, was lying across the arm of the couch.

"How could you do something like that to me?" Kate said as soon as Ian shut the door and turned around. Her face crumpled as she started to cry. "You promised you wouldn't leave without telling me, but you did it anyway!"

"I couldn't tell you. If they saw you looking like your world had ended, they'd leave you alone. But if they spotted you walking down the street just once, laughing, wearing a smile, it would only draw them in closer, and I wouldn't have been able to protect you. If I thought I could have done it any other way, I would have."

"You left me behind," she said.

"Would you have come? If I told you we had to leave immediately, no good-byes, no time to submit your resignation, no preparation, would you have done it? Lived on the run? How long would it have been before someone decided to start watching your family, Kate? All those texts I got, all that time I spent on my computer the day I discovered they'd hacked you? I was trying to come up with another way to pull this off, and I couldn't. They found my weakness and named their price. I paid it, but I paid it on *my* terms."

"I paid too," she cried, "and it would have been easier to bear if I'd known about it. Because of you, I experienced the worst pain I have ever felt in my life. How can we be a team if only one of us knows what's going on?"

Tears rolled down Kate's face. Ian led her to the couch and held her as she cried. He waited until her tears had tapered off and she'd gone limp in his arms.

Stroking her head tenderly, he began to speak. "Leaving you behind was the hardest thing I've ever had to do, but I did it because I thought it was the only way to solve the problem permanently. Phillip made me promise that I'd wait until things died down and it was safe to contact you. In the meantime, I made those agents tell me about every single observation they made. I knew all about your tears and your shell-shocked expression, and it killed me."

Kate's mind was racing and her thoughts were jumbled. She was torn between the comfort his arms provided and the turmoil his actions had caused. His phone rang, and Kate lifted her head off his chest.

"That'll be Phillip," Ian said. "He's the only one besides you who has this number." He reached out and wiped away her tears. "We don't have to go up there if you'd rather not."

"You still have the same phone?"

He nodded.

"I left you a message on your birthday."

"I know. I listen to it every day so I can hear your voice, and every single time I think about what I did to you and wonder if it was the biggest mistake I've ever made. I know you paid, but I wouldn't have asked it of you if I didn't think you were strong enough to handle it. I'm so sorry, Kate. I'm sorry for the pain I caused you. I'm sorry for what you went through. I'm sorry for all of it."

During dinner, everyone tried to pretend there was nothing out of the ordinary about the circumstances that had brought the four of them together. Susan fretted over her and Ian, offering more salmon, more rice and vegetables, even though they'd yet to finish what was already on their plates. For the first time, Kate noticed how thin Ian looked. She'd dropped at least ten pounds herself and appeared worn and drawn, as if she'd recently suffered an illness and hadn't fully recovered.

"Our home is open to you for as long as you'd like to stay," Phillip said.

"I'd like to leave tomorrow, please," Kate replied. As much as she hated the thought of being separated from Ian again, he'd raised the stakes and she needed time to contemplate what a future with him would truly be like.

The sound of silverware clinking seemed especially loud in the silence that followed, and neither Ian nor Kate even pretended to eat much after that. When the meal was over, Kate thanked Susan and Ian announced they were going to turn in early.

"It's been a very long day I'm sure," Susan said. "Please let me know if there's anything you need."

"Thank you," Kate said. "I'm sure I'll feel better after a good night's sleep."

Once they'd returned to the guesthouse, Ian gave Kate one of his T-shirts to sleep in and they got ready for bed. They had to take turns because the tiny bathroom barely had enough room for one. Looking at Ian's toothbrush in the holder and his razor made Kate think of the identical items that were still sitting on her own bathroom counter. The equally small bedroom contained a queen-size bed and a nightstand. Ian stripped down to his underwear, pulled back the covers, and lay down next to Kate.

"I know you're upset with me, and you have every right to be, but I really want to hold you."

"I want to hold you too," she said. Regardless of how hurt and betrayed she felt, she couldn't help but think of the dark days after Ian's death when she'd mourned the loss of him. How she'd cried when she thought of never being able to touch him again. How she would have given anything to feel his arms around her.

Ian was *here*.

Not dead and cold, but warm and alive and holding her in his arms.

It was pitch-black in the small room. Kate couldn't see Ian, but she could feel him—his strong arms around her; his bare chest underneath her; his legs entwined with hers. He kissed the top of her head, lips lingering in her hair.

"Is this where you've been the whole time?" Kate asked.

"Yes. Whenever I'm between apartments I always end up here. I'm the only one who really uses the guesthouse, and over the years it's become a second home to me. Phillip and Susan are like family to me." It made Kate happy to know that Ian wasn't quite so alone in the world, but except for one brief mention of Phillip, Ian had never talked about the Corcorans.

He began to stroke her head and her body relaxed. "I missed you so much," he said. "I missed talking to you. I missed walking to dinner with you and hearing about your day."

"I missed those things too," she said and tears flooded her eyes.

"Kate," he said when her tears overflowed and trickled on-to his skin. He adjusted their position so they were lying on their sides facing each other and wiped her tears away. "I'm so sorry. Please don't cry." He kissed her, and his lips were warm, gentle, fleeting.

But she couldn't hold back the tears even if she'd wanted to. "Tonight at dinner I was thinking that no one loses some-one and then gets them back like this. When someone dies, it's all you wish for, but it never actually happens. Except that it did. You will never know what that feels like, but I do."

"I know." He was holding her tightly, but she wanted more, wanted him to squeeze her like he had on the plane. She wanted to know this was *real*. This time, it was Kate who brushed her lips against his.

He responded with a kiss of his own, raising his hand to the back of her head to hold her in place, deepening it. She didn't want him to stop kissing her. He would if she asked him to, but she didn't.

Their breathing grew ragged as they crushed their mouths together. He moved his hand to her backside and cupped it, pulling her closer until she was pressed tightly up against him. She could feel how much he wanted her, and she needed to make a decision about what would happen next.

She didn't want to talk or cry or think.

She wanted to *feel*.

"Kate?" His voice trembled with need.

"Yes."

He peeled off her T-shirt, slid his fingers under the elastic of her underwear, and dragged them down her legs. Starting at her neck, his fingers moved softly over her collarbone to the slope of her breast, his hands lingering as if he was learning the contours of her body for the first time again. When he closed his mouth around her nipple, she moaned.

His hand drifted lower, skimming over her belly and coming to rest between her legs. She took off his underwear, and he opened her legs enough to enter her. As soon as he did, Kate closed hers around him, holding him tight. They moved together, their movements frantic, desperate, and she cried out his name because it felt so good.

Maybe she shouldn't have wanted to do this. Maybe she should have told him no. There were decisions to be made, and Kate still had some long, hard thinking to do. But she missed him desperately, and right then he was what she needed.

He groaned, and Kate knew this wasn't going to take long for either one of them. Already she could feel the sensations building, and she moved faster, chasing them. She caught up to them and found her much-needed release a minute or two later, and he must have been right there with her because he groaned again, longer and louder this time, and then shuddered and shook inside her as he came.

After, he held her tight, and their heated skin warmed Kate from the outside in, reaching a place that had not been warm since she lost him.

"I love you," he said.

"You hurt me," she whispered.

"I didn't want to."

They slept facing each other that night, Kate's head nestled under Ian's chin, arms around each other, a tangle of legs. Shortly before sunrise, she got up to go to the bathroom, and when she climbed back into bed, he stirred and pulled her back into his arms, holding her as if he couldn't bear to let her go.

CHAPTER THIRTY-SEVEN

BREAKFAST WAS MARGINALLY LESS AWKWARD than dinner had been the night before. Kate attributed this to Susan and Phillip's easygoing nature and the ten hours of solid, restorative sleep she'd had. They'd gone to bed so early that Kate had awakened feeling, if not back to normal, at least well rested and a bit calmer.

When they were done eating, Susan declined Kate's offer to help clear the table. "Relax. Have some more coffee," she said, placing a carafe halfway between her and Phillip. "I'll get the rest when I return. Ian is going to drive me to the garden center. Now that it's getting warmer, I'm looking forward to getting my plants organized."

"I'll grab my keys," Ian said. He bent down and kissed Kate's forehead. "Back in a little bit."

"The pilot can take you home later this morning," Phillip said. "We'll need to leave in about an hour."

"That'll be fine. Thank you."

Phillip poured Kate some more coffee.

"Did Ian ask you to talk to me?" His departure had seemed a bit too convenient.

"Yes," Phillip said, looking sheepish. "I'm not here to argue on his behalf. That's between you and him. But maybe I can help you understand where he's coming from."

"How long have you known Ian?"

"Since he was twenty."

"How did you meet him?"

"I arrested him."

Kate choked on her sip of coffee. "You arrested him?"

"I had to. He'd hacked the Pentagon, and he hadn't tried to hide it all that well. I knocked on the door of his dorm room, flashed my badge, and led him away in handcuffs."

"I don't know why I'm surprised. That sounds exactly like him."

Phillip chuckled. "I could tell right away he wasn't a bad kid. He's brilliant, but he didn't have a lot of impulse control back then."

Kate smiled. "Sometimes he still doesn't."

"I scared him pretty good that day. Then I gave him a choice. He could show us how he'd done it and tell us what we needed to do to make sure it never happened again, or he could go to prison. He opted not to go to prison of course, and we were blown away by what he could do. When he was younger he liked showing off just to make sure we hadn't forgotten what he was capable of, but now I think his involvement gives him a sense of purpose. Pride even. He won't work *for* us although we've tried countless times to recruit him. But he's continued to work with us long after he paid for his transgression, and I hope he never stops. He's gone places we couldn't get to on our own. Places where the stakes were high and there was considerable risk."

"And you know about the money he…?"

"Steals from cyberthieves?" Phillip nodded. "I pick my battles. That one isn't worth fighting."

"Ian told me last night that you and Susan are like family to him."

"My wife and I never had any kids of our own. It just wasn't in the cards for us, I guess. Susan treats Ian like the son she never had. Considering his own mother isn't in the picture much, it suits them both. Our relationship is a bit trickier. Sometimes I'm his friend, sometimes his mentor, and when he'll let me, a father figure."

"It sounds like you really care about him."

"I do. I try to give him his space, especially now that he's older. But I offer advice when I think it's warranted. When he told me what he wanted to do after he discovered you'd been hacked, I tried to talk him out of it. I argued that it would be too much for you, but Ian said you were strong enough to handle it. Putting that car in the river would require a considerable amount of FBI resources, which aren't always easy to obtain. He'd also be throwing away a company he loved and that he'd spent ten years building and would have to start over from scratch. He was undeterred. He couldn't get past the fact that his enemies knew who you were. He's not easily rattled, but I've never seen him that distraught."

"So it's true he has enemies."

"He's been working with us for far too long and angered too many people to not have them. Frankly I'm surprised no one had found him yet. I disagreed with Ian about several things. But the one thing we unanimously agreed upon was that if we did this, your reaction had to be genuine because we knew they'd be watching. Ian would have never put you in any kind of physical danger, and the FBI surveillance was purely a precaution. I told Ian I thought one agent would be plenty. He argued for two." Phillip smiled. "We compromised with four. He's very driven, Kate, but he needs a strong woman by his side. Not just because he's headstrong, but because he needs a partner who's as strong and smart as he is. Someone he can confide in. Build a life with. He's going to have to open himself up completely, and he's never really had to do that. For as much as he likes being in charge, I think what Ian wants the most is to belong to someone. To know that someone loves him unconditionally. That's hard to find in a woman, especially when you consider his line of work. His love for you is immeasurable, and he trusts you."

Kate was not one to hold a grudge, and in time she could forgive Ian for what he'd done. He and Phillip had explained why they'd kept her in the dark, and though their actions had hurt her, she understood them. But being with Ian in any kind of permanent capacity required a level of trust and tolerance Kate wasn't sure she possessed. Her mind was still reeling, and she needed time to regroup.

"It's a lot to consider," she said.

"I understand. Well, if you'll excuse me, I'm in the middle of the rather delicate process of sorting out an insurance claim on a seven-million-dollar car owned by a man who's not actually dead. The red tape is ridiculous."

Kate nearly dropped her coffee cup, and it clattered onto its saucer. "The Shelby was real?"

"Oh," Phillip said, looking alarmed. "I thought you knew."

"I assumed it was a replica. I didn't know his company brought in that kind of money."

"His company was extremely profitable, but Ian's also very technically gifted. I don't know of many hackers who can code like he can. When he was in college, he did a lot of the early programming for a social network start-up. There may be a bit of rivalry between MIT and Harvard, but if I told you the names of some of his friends, you'd recognize them. Those

Cambridge boys don't mind helping each other out. But Ian had no interest in being a part of someone else's company, so he accepted a small stake in lieu of any named credit or involvement. That company went on to be worth billions."

"I told him once that he used his money to excuse his behavior. He agreed and said there weren't many problems his money couldn't solve."

Phillip smiled, looking thoughtful. "I think he might have been wrong about that, Kate."

CHAPTER THIRTY-EIGHT

KATE CLEARED THE COFFEE CUPS from the table and took them into the kitchen. Susan was unpacking her seeds and bulbs.

"Did you find everything you needed at the garden center?" Kate asked.

"Yes. It's a little early yet, but I'm really looking forward to planting everything."

"Do you know where Ian is?"

"I think he's out front."

She found him on the porch. "Hi," she said, sitting down in the empty chair next to him.

"Hi."

"That was nice of you to help Susan."

He smiled. "It's nothing compared to when she'll want me to unload an SUV full of forty-pound bags of dirt. That'll be next."

"Phillip said the plane will be ready to take me home soon."

"Okay."

"It's not... it's not your plane, is it?"

"No. But I paid the charter fee. The FBI puts up with a lot from me, but I don't expect them to fly in my girlfriend."

He reached for her hand. "Right before you came out here, I was thinking about when I saw you on TV. I told you that the Shelby had broken down, and when I went to pick her up, I was waiting in the lobby of this repair shop. They had a TV mounted in the corner. I was looking right at it when you started talking, and there was something about you that absolutely captivated me. The first thing I noticed was how beautiful you were, and the second was that you seemed so down-to-earth and so real. You were asking for money, but not for yourself. I wanted to know if your passion was genuine and if you were really as kind as you appeared. When I got back to the hotel I was staying at until I could move into my apartment, I pulled up the clip online and watched it an embarrassing number of times. When I was in Canada, I'd started feeling something that I thought was restlessness, like I wanted to get away. But after seeing you on TV, I realized that what I was feeling wasn't restlessness at all. It was loneliness. I don't remember ever feeling that way in my twenties, so maybe it was because I was getting older. I wondered how it would feel to have a girl like you by my side. Someone who was beautiful and selfless and wanted to help people the way I did. I thought maybe if I met you in person I'd feel differently. Maybe you'd be dull or standoffish or even rude. But then you came crashing into me on that sidewalk and you were none of those things. I told myself, 'Do not drag her into your fucked-up world,' and then I did it anyway. I pushed every limit you had, and every time you gave me an inch I turned around and took a mile because I knew there weren't very many women out there who would be able to handle me. But you could. And even after all that you still saw the good in me. And you still wanted to be with me. You made it so damn easy for me to love you, and just as easy for me to like you. You just kept doing everything right." He turned to look at her. "Have you stopped loving me?" His voice was low and raw.

"No." She looked into his eyes as the tears ran down her face. "But maybe I'm not cut out for this after all," she whispered.

"Maybe you're not." His eyes were dry, but she had never seen such sadness in them.

Phillip opened the door and stepped onto the porch. "I'm sorry to interrupt, but we'd better get going."

At the airport, when the three of them got out of the car, Phillip turned to her and said, "Please be aware of your surroundings at home, Kate. If they're still watching and you're seen smiling or laughing, it could undo everything we've done."

Kate didn't think she'd be doing much of either, but she said, "I'll be careful."

Phillip nodded and then reached out and shook her hand before getting back into the car.

Ian walked Kate onto the tarmac, and they stopped at the foot of the stairs. He pulled a phone from the pocket of his jeans and handed it to her. "If there's anything you need or anything I can do, I want you to call me. Okay?"

Kate nodded and slid the phone into her bag. She glanced toward the plane, feeling foolish that they were waiting on her.

"Don't be afraid," Ian said. "Don and the other agents are still going to be watching you."

Kate blinked back the tears that were already filling her eyes. She wished they could go back in time to when things weren't quite so complicated. Kate could argue that this wasn't what she'd signed up for, but that would be a lie. Everything Ian had done was faithful to his nature, whether it was hacking her computer, walking in on her in the bathroom, or faking his own death.

You know that saying, "Act now, apologize later?" I'm pretty much the poster boy.

He pulled her close and held her tight. "I love you. I will never stop loving you."

"I love you too."

"Don't go." He whispered it quietly but fiercely into her hair.

"I have to. I need some time to think. To figure things out." She kissed him one last time, and then she did leave, her legs heavy as stone as she walked up the staircase and disappeared into the plane.

CHAPTER THIRTY-NINE

SHE TOOK A CAB HOME from the airport, making sure to ask the driver to drop her off three blocks away. Kate didn't know if they were still watching her, and she could barely handle the thought of someone observing her every move as she navigated the streets of her neighborhood.

After taking a hot bath, she crawled into bed with the phone he'd given her. She clicked on the unnamed plain blue app and selected Ian's Phone. It showed Phillip's address, and Kate wondered if Ian was with them or if he was down in the guesthouse, thinking about her the way she was thinking about him.

She fell asleep that night with the phone in her hand. And the next morning, her first thought upon awakening was a jubilant *He's alive* and her second was *I miss him so much.*

On her walk to work, every man wearing a suit was an FBI agent; everyone else was a hacker.

That afternoon, Kate booked an airline ticket to Indiana after making sure that Helena didn't mind covering for her again. Her parents—especially her mother—deserved to know the truth about Ian, but Kate decided it was the kind of news that should be shared in person.

"I'm sorry," Kate said. "My mom really wants to see for herself that I'm doing okay. She's spent so much time here already, I feel like it's my turn to go home."

"Of course," Helena said. "When are you leaving?"

"Friday after we close. I'll be back late Monday."

Helena put her arm around Kate. "Are you okay? You've been really quiet today."

"I'm fine. I just have a lot on my mind and didn't sleep well last night."

For the next few days, Kate went through the motions as if she were on autopilot, similar to the way she had after Ian died. But when she took a shower in the morning, she couldn't stop thinking about how they'd always showered together. When she picked up dinner, she automatically recalled what Ian would have ordered. The absence of his hand holding hers felt like phantom pain. Sleeping on her side without his arm around her made her feel sad and hollow.

You could be doing all those things with him again, she thought. *Because he is alive.*

She was responding to e-mails shortly before closing time on Thursday afternoon when Zach Nielsen stopped by her desk. It was not uncommon for Kate's clients to visit for a while after they'd filled their box with food, and they'd tell her what a difference she was making for them and their families. Kate thought of Zach often and hoped his younger brother was doing okay and getting enough to eat.

"Hi," he said.

"Hi, Zach. How are things going?"

He sat down on the edge of her desk. "They're going great. I got on full-time at the warehouse. I may not even need the pantry next month. I think I can buy enough food for all of us with my paycheck."

Though she was feeling pretty low, she forced herself to smile. "That's wonderful."

"How are things with you?" he asked. "I hope you don't mind my saying something, but last time I was here you seemed a little, I don't know, sad maybe?"

She hated that he'd noticed how upset she'd been on his last visit and doubted he was the only one of her clients who had. Kate probably didn't look much better this time around because her last good night of sleep had been in Phillip and Susan's guesthouse with Ian. Her bed felt cavernous without him in it, and she lay awake for hours thinking of him.

"I was going through a very rough patch personally. I'm sorry if I appeared unprofessional." Feeling the warmth on her cheeks, she bent her head, gathering the papers that were lying on her desk and organizing them into a neat pile.

"No, it's fine. I was just wondering if things were better now."

When she looked up to answer him, she noticed his eyes were a little red, as if he were tired.

And his hair was on the longer side.

He'd asked for her by name the first time he'd come in, saying he'd been referred by a friend. But he'd never mentioned the name of the person.

She held his gaze just long enough for her eyes to fill with tears, and then she glanced away. "Not yet. Maybe someday they will be. At least I hope so." She pulled a Kleenex from the top drawer of her desk and dabbed at her eyes. "Do you have your ID with you today, Zach?"

He took one hand off his box of food and patted his pocket, and her eyes tracked his movement. A brace peeked out from the cuff of Zach's shirt. It was the same type of brace Ian sometimes wore when his wrists became sore from spending too much time on the computer. "Left it at home again. Sorry."

"That's okay," she said. "Just make sure to bring it next time."

"I will." He rose, hoisting the box a little higher in his arms. "I'll see you next month. Unless I don't need to come in."

"Take care."

"Thanks. You too."

As soon as he left, she walked to the file cabinet and retrieved Zach's intake form. She called the phone number he'd given her during the intake interview, but it wasn't a valid number. When she put his address into Google Maps, nothing came up.

She told herself she was being paranoid. Lots of people had tired, red eyes. Lots of men let their hair grow a bit long. It would not be unusual for someone who worked in a warehouse to wear a wrist brace. New clients *did* ask for her by name, all the time. People didn't always carry their IDs on them, and occasionally her clients would falsify their personal information.

But a hacker would protect his identity at all costs.

Especially one whose sole reason for visiting the food pantry had been to catch her in a lie.

CHAPTER FORTY

KATE LANDED IN CHICAGO AT seven, which left her with forty-five minutes to kill before her flight to Indianapolis. The phone Ian had given her pinged as she was walking down the aisle to exit the plane, and seeing his name on the screen filled her with happiness. He'd given her the time and space she needed, which had been wise of him because the longer she'd been home, the more the hurt had faded, and in its place was a feeling of persistent and aching yearning.

Ian: *Cinnabon?*

Kate: *Thinking about it.*

Ian: *You should.*

Kate: *Not the best choice for dinner, but maybe I will.*

Ian: *Have some wine too. That'll make it better.*

Kate smiled, weaving her way around the passengers as she walked and typed.

Kate: *Wine makes everything better.* 😊

Ian: *How are you?*

Kate: *I'm okay. How are you?*

Ian: *I've been better. I miss you so much.*

Kate: *I miss you too.*

Ian: *Have you been thinking about us?*

Kate: *I think about us all the time.*

The interaction made her feel good, and she wanted to prolong their conversation. She pictured him sitting on the couch in the guesthouse, typing out a text. After stopping at Cinnabon, she sat down at a nearby table, ignoring her cinnamon roll as she stared at her phone, waiting for him to respond and wondering why it was taking so long. She was so deep in thought that the scrape of a chair being pulled back startled her.

"Here's what I think," Ian said, sitting down next to her. "You *are* cut out for this, Kate. You're smart and you're fearless. I understand that being with me comes with a unique set of challenges, but I firmly believe we can overcome them."

Kate stared at him in shock. Even if he'd left the minute he realized she was on her way to the airport, her flight was shorter than his. "How did you…?"

"I figured you'd go home, so I waited for you to book your ticket and made sure to take off an hour before you did. I'm seriously going to pitch my services to American Airlines. They have no idea how much they need me."

He reached for her hands. "I wanted to see you. I wanted to talk to you again. I love you, and I know we can make this work."

Passersby gave her worried glances when she started to cry.

"They were out of her favorite," Ian explained. "I'll get her something else." He pulled her in close and rubbed her back, and the way he smelled and the feel of his arms around her was so familiar and good and *him*. She wanted to stay there forever. Finally she lifted her head and reached into the Cinnabon bag for a napkin to wipe her eyes.

"You okay?" he asked, brushing the hair back from her face.

She nodded and clasped Ian's hands in hers, running her fingers over his knuckles. "A hacker came into the food pantry yesterday. He'd been in twice before."

He looked alarmed. "How did you know he was a hacker?"

"I didn't at first, and I'm still not sure. His story was good, and he'd obviously put some thought into it. He was quite friendly. Really had me fooled." She explained the ruse Zach had used and how he'd asked for her by name but had never mentioned who'd given him the referral.

"I checked the dates on his paperwork. The first time he came in was right before I asked you to look at my computer. I was my normal self that day. Happy, smiling. If he was a hacker, that means they were already watching me. The second time he came in, I was a complete mess. Red eyes, tears. The whole nine yards. When he came in yesterday I thought I was being paranoid, but he always had an excuse about why he couldn't show me his ID, and he was wearing a wrist brace the way you sometimes do. After he left, I discovered the phone number and address he'd given me were bogus. I was feeling pretty down, so I don't think I aroused any suspicion."

"I'm sorry, Kate. I never wanted anyone I love to be messed up in this." He wiped the tears that were running down her face. "I've been thinking a lot about the future, and I've decided to start a new company. I'll have plenty to keep me busy because I'll have to start over and build it from the ground up. Phillip needs someone to do pentesting on government systems so they can be strengthened, and I told him I'd do it. There's no infiltration. Nothing undercover. Just hacking and coding. It's not nearly as warm as I'd hoped, but the DC area makes sense because I'll have to spend more time at headquarters than I did before. I don't want to live in the guest-house forever, so I'm going to buy a house. For us."

"Can you do that?" she asked. "Can you just move some-where and start over?"

"A dead man can do whatever he wants. But I don't know who doxed me and hacked you. I don't know if they'll ever truly believe I'm gone, and they may never stop trying to find me."

"When did you know you loved me? You said one day you'd tell me and then we'd see who was first." When she thought he was gone forever, the answer to that question had haunted her and she'd regretted not asking him.

He smiled as if the memory made him happy. "When I went to DC the first time, I got your text saying you were thinking about me and missed me. It made me feel good to know you were waiting for me. I told you I didn't remember much about coming home, but I do remember thinking, 'Go to Kate.' I had a vague recollection of this soft voice speaking to me and wondered if I'd dreamed it. When I woke up, I was in your bed and knew it was your voice I'd heard. My phone was plugged in next to me, and you'd put a glass of water on the nightstand. I was already crazy about you, but as I lay there, I thought to myself, 'I'm in love with this woman. I want to be with her always.' When we were watching the Christmas fire-works, I said I was falling for you because I thought it was too soon to tell you I loved you. But on New Year's Eve I couldn't wait any longer. What about you? When did you know you loved me?"

"When you told me about your dad. You hadn't shared many personal things with me at that point, and I felt really close to you that night. But you're right. You did fall in love first."

"That's because I'd given myself a pretty big head start. By the time we actually met, I'd already built you up into something special, and it didn't take long for me to realize I was right. You *are* special. I meant what I said when I told you I've never loved anyone the way I love you. But I've never hurt anyone the way I hurt you. I can't undo it, but I'll never do it again, and I'll spend the rest of my life trying to make it up to you."

"Why didn't you tell me about your money?"

"Because it's ridiculous to have been paid so much for doing something I love, and I knew you didn't care about it."

"I don't, but it's part of who you are. So is your relationship with Phillip and Susan. You said I knew everything, but I didn't."

"You do now, and I promise I will never keep anything from you again."

He wiped a stray tear and glanced at his watch. "They'll be boarding your flight soon." He held her hand as they walked to the gate, and then he led her over to a row of chairs. "Want me to bump you up to first class?" he asked, pulling his phone out of his pocket. "There might still be time if they're not full."

She shook her head. "I'll be fine in coach."

A voice came over the loudspeaker announcing the start of the boarding process.

"You're the best thing that's ever happened to me, Kate. If you can forgive me and let me love you again, all the pain you're feeling will go away. If you can't, I'll get out of the way and let you live your life. Any man would be lucky to have you." His voice caught on that last sentence.

"What if you hurt me again?"

"I won't."

"How can I be sure?" Kate asked.

He looked into her eyes, and this time they were hopeful. "Because we're a team."

The final boarding call came over the loudspeaker, and she glanced anxiously toward the door.

Another plane waited for Kate.

Another decision needed to be made.

"Maybe you don't want the guy who broke your heart to be the one to help put it back together, but I would be grateful if you'd give me the chance. It's not often that I don't have the upper hand, Kate. But this is one of those times. Let me know what you decide." He kissed her like it was the last time he'd ever have the chance to do it, and then he walked away.

She made her way onto the plane and found her seat. When she thought about being with him again, an incredible feeling of happiness swept over her. He was right: the pain did go away. A future with Ian would require putting her faith and trust in his hands, but he would be hers again and she would be his. They would talk and laugh and love, and every night they would sleep in each other's arms.

Or she could get on with her life. She could call Stuart and meet him for that drink. See if there was anything left to rekindle, and if there wasn't, she could start over completely and hope she'd be fortunate enough to find another man she could love the way she loved Ian. But neither of those options filled her with anything other than sadness.

She dug her phone out of her purse and started typing.

Kate: *I choose you.*

She only had to wait a few seconds for his response.

Ian: *I will spend the rest of my life making sure you never regret it. I love you, sweetness.*

Her seatmate noticed the tears rolling down Kate's face. "Are you okay?" the woman asked.

Kate smiled and said, "These are happy tears."

She patted Kate's hand. "Honey, those are the best kind."

CHAPTER FORTY-ONE

KATE RESIGNED FROM HER POSITION as the executive director of the Main Street Food Pantry, citing personal reasons and her desire to move closer to her family. Ian had told Kate he was taking a few months off before starting his new company and the work he would be doing for Phillip and proposed that they spend the summer on Roanoke Island before settling in the DC area.

"I thought Roanoke Island was too small," Kate said.

"It would be if I was working on a government assignment, but I'm not. I checked your computer and the computer at the food pantry. There was nothing in your browsing history that would lead anyone there."

"Do you think they'll try to look for us in Charlotte? I used my laptop to do a few searches."

"Your history didn't have anything too specific. If they were really motivated they might try anyway, but Charlotte's a fairly large city and it would be tough for them to know where to start without at least a few details. The Washington metropolitan area will be an even harder place for them to find us, especially since they have no way of knowing that's where we're headed. For all they know, we could be anywhere."

Ian had made arrangements for most of her things to be transported to a storage facility in DC, and everything she needed for the summer would be sent to the house he'd rented on the island. The movers had arrived that morning, and as soon as they left, Kate would begin the nine-hour drive to Indiana where she would be reunited with Ian.

To say Kate's parents had been flabbergasted when she sat them down and told them the truth about Ian would be an understatement. Her mother kept saying, "I just don't understand this at all" over and over, and her dad had gone on a bit of a rampage about the legal ramifications of faking one's death. It had taken a considerable amount of effort to convince them she was making the right decision.

When Chad heard the news, he'd called Kate. "Your life is like something out of a movie. You know that, right? Kristin is freaked out. She keeps calling Ian a ghost."

"My life is a bit unconventional. That's all," Kate had said.

"I can't believe he put that Shelby in the river."

"Now I'm really going to blow your mind, Chad. The Shelby was real."

"He's nuts, Kate."

"Yeah, I know."

Though Kate had told him it wasn't necessary, Ian insisted he needed to make things right with her parents. He'd spent last night in a hotel in Zionsville and planned on spending the day with Steve and Diane while Kate was on the road. Then they'd drive to Roanoke Island in Ian's car, leaving hers in Indiana for Kate's parents to sell. Ian had already begun erasing her Internet presence, and once she no longer owned the TrailBlazer, there'd be one less public record for Kate Watts.

She'd gone to the food pantry the day before to say her final good-byes to the volunteers and staff, and she'd pulled

Helena aside. "I'm going to miss you so much. You've been absolutely wonderful to me."

"I'll miss you too, but I can understand why you'd want to be closer to your family." She'd reached for Kate's hands. "I know things have been hard for you. You're far too young to experience the kind of loss you went through. I know you're not ready, but someday when you are, there will be a man out there who will make you every bit as happy as Ian did."

Kate had smiled. "I'm sure there will be. Will you do me a favor, Helena?"

"Of course. You know I'll do anything."

"I tried to say good-bye to as many clients as I could, but if anyone should ask where I've gone, can you tell them I suffered a personal loss and decided to move on, but you're not at liberty to say where. I feel like the only way to get back on my feet again is to cut ties and start fresh. I don't want anything from my old life in Minneapolis to follow me to my new one."

Or anyone.

"Of course, Kate."

She gave Helena a final hug. "You'll hear from me soon. You can count on that."

She met Paige and Audrey for a good-bye lunch at Aster Café. If they hadn't quite known what to say after Kate and Stuart broke up, they really didn't know what to say to a friend who'd suffered such a devastating loss, and who could blame them? They'd fumbled their way through predictions of future happiness, and their sympathetic expressions touched Kate and made her feel bad for her deception. She'd longed to tell them Ian was alive, but that was a can of worms she'd promised never to open. Kate would miss getting together with them, but she'd stay in touch.

"My computer is having some problems," Kate said. "Viruses. You know how that goes. I hate responding to e-mail on my phone, so once I get settled I'll buy a new laptop and send you a message."

When lunch was over, they'd shared a final hug, and then Kate walked the streets of St. Anthony Main for the last time.

"Miss?" One of the movers held a clipboard. "I think that's everything. Can you sign here please?"

Kate scribbled her signature on the form.

"You have a good day now," he said.

Before she left, she took one last look around her apartment and smiled. Chad was wrong. Clearly, Kate was the one who was nuts.

Two hours into the drive, she stopped for gas and sent a text to Ian while she waited for the tank to fill.

Kate: *How are things going?*

Ian: *Boy, is your dad PISSED.*

Kate: *As long as he doesn't bring up all the different types of fraud caused by faking one's death, you should be okay.*

Ian: *Yeah, HE OPENED WITH THAT.*

Kate: *You are so screwed, man.*

Ian: *I've only been here for forty-five minutes, and his face has turned red twice. He went into the den a while ago. Pretty sure he's drafting some sort of legal contract that says he'll have my balls if I ever fake my own death again.*

Kate: *If you ever fake your own death again, I'm the one who will have your balls (and not in the way you like).*

Ian: *I'm thankful you have not lost your sense of humor.*

Kate: *It's only recently returned and is still a bit skittish. Please don't do anything to scare it away.*

Ian: *As soon as your dad calms down a little, I'm asking him for your hand in marriage.*

Kate: *I'll take Victorian mating rituals for eight hundred, Alex! Also, did I hit my head or something, because I don't remember discussing marriage with you?*

Ian: *A beautiful woman once told me that when it comes to men, you either break up with them or you marry them. We did not break up. And I'm fully aware that you're a modern woman, but I'm not positive your dad won't actually veto our union. This is a sticky situation and needs to be handled... carefully.*

Kate: *Aren't you putting the cart before the horse? You haven't actually proposed to me. I AM NOT A SURE THING, IAN.*

Ian: *You will have a proper proposal, but first your dad and I need to conclude this extremely uncomfortable meeting.*

Kate: *Ask him how much my dowry is. I'm just curious.*

Ian: *How about I don't poke the bear right now? The only reason your dad might actually ENTERTAIN the idea of having me for a son-in-law is because I'm kind of a big deal at the FBI. I've done too many good things in the name of national security for him to completely discount me.*

Kate: *Oh! Tell him about the time you got arrested for hacking the Pentagon.*

Ian: *I'm going to save that particular anecdote for another time.*

Kate: *Like the holidays.*

Ian: *I hear your dad coming. I should probably put my phone away in case he's not done yelling. If he did draft a contract, he'll probably make me sign it in blood.*

Kate: *I'm certainly going to.*

Ian: *I can't wait to kiss that smart mouth of yours. Drive carefully (but please don't dawdle). I'll be tracking you and eagerly awaiting your arrival. Love you.*

Kate: *Love you too. Here I come. xoxo*

CHAPTER FORTY-TWO

KATE WAS TWO HOURS FROM home when she spotted the first message. It was on one of those electronic Department of Transportation signs mounted over the highway.

I CAN'T WAIT TO SEE YOU KATIE

All she could do was shake her head and laugh. Fifteen minutes later, she drove under the next one.

YOU'RE GETTING CLOSER

Kate couldn't wait to see Ian. She still had moments when she wanted to kill him herself for what he'd done, but then she'd think about the miraculous turn of events that had brought him back to her, and her anger would dissipate. She couldn't wait to fall asleep in his arms tonight, and every night after that.

It was another forty miles before she spotted the next sign.

HI KATE IT'S YOUR MOM

Kate reached for her cell phone. When Ian answered, she said, "Exactly how long did it take you to bring my mother over to the dark side?"

"Not long at all. I have to tell you, she is fascinated by hacking. I convinced her to open a bottle of wine, and after her second glass she insisted we hack into something."

"Does she know hacking road signs is a felony?"

"I'm going to go with no. But don't worry, they'll never catch us."

"How's my dad?"

"Still a little frosty. I tried to give him his own special phone. That did not go well *at all*."

"Give it to my mom. It sounds like she won't have a problem with it. And please tell me you haven't checked out of your hotel yet. I'm really looking forward to our reunion, but I'd like it to take place somewhere other than my parents' home. I don't think my dad could handle overhearing us, and I'm telling you right now I plan on being loud."

"The hotel room is waiting for us, and I will definitely be giving you something to yell about. I thought we could take your parents out for breakfast tomorrow and then hit the road."

"I think that sounds like an ideal plan." Kate noticed a sign in the distance but couldn't yet make out the words. "Still hacking, I see."

"This next message is my favorite," he said.

As she got closer, a smile spread across her face.

I'VE GOT A NUMBER SIX WAITING HERE FOR YOU SWEETNESS

"Do you see it?" he asked.

She laughed. "I see it. The six is my favorite."

"Mine's the seven."

"That does not surprise me at all."

"I can't wait to see you, Kate."

"It won't be long now. Tell my mom not to drink all the wine."

CHAPTER FORTY-THREE

THE TWO-BEDROOM COTTAGE on Roanoke Island was aptly named the Endless Summer. The exterior was sunshine yellow with white trim and a picket fence, and four Adirondack chairs sat grouped together on the small brick patio.

"What do you think?" Ian asked after he unlocked the door and they went inside.

Kate looked around. The interior was a perfect blend of kitschy beach house and modern amenities. "What an adorable love nest."

"It's cozy, that's for sure," he said, laughing. "At least it's bigger than Phillip and Susan's guesthouse."

"It's perfect for the two of us." She slipped her arms around his neck and kissed him.

"What do you say we christen this place? It won't really feel like ours until we do."

Kate had not had her fill of him yet, so she said, "That sounds like much more fun than unpacking."

Once they'd finally emerged from the bedroom and brought everything in from the car, they explored the quaint streets of downtown Manteo, walking hand in hand as they checked out a gift shop, bookstore, and art gallery.

"Hot enough for you, hacker?" Kate asked. The temperature was hovering somewhere in the mid to upper seventies, which was typical for early May. Not as hot as it was going to be, but warmer than Minneapolis.

"Not quite. Maybe by July."

"It'll be in the high eighties by then."

"Good. Maybe the only thing you'll feel like wearing is a bikini."

They crossed the street and stopped in front of the Tranquil House Inn, which had a sign that read 1587 Restaurant.

"Are you as hungry as I am?" Ian asked.

"Starving." They'd left Kate's parents' house around noon the day before and had broken up the thirteen-hour drive from Zionsville to Roanoke Island by stopping in West Virginia for the night. They'd gotten back on the road right after breakfast and hadn't stopped for lunch. Having been sidetracked upon their arrival, they were now more than ready to eat.

A hostess escorted them to a table near the window and took their drink orders. They had a stunning view of Shallowbag Bay and the boats in the slips that lined the dock. Kate shielded her eyes from the sun that reflected off the water and streamed into the dining area, filling it with light.

When their drinks arrived, Ian lifted his glass. "Cheers to an endless summer, Katie."

She smiled, clinked his glass with hers, and said, "Cheers."

Roanoke Island was good for Kate. Ian treated her like a cherished treasure, and he handled her with the utmost care.

Every night he slept with his arms around her and his body pressed up against hers.

Every day he told her how much he loved her.

She had cried an ocean of tears in the preceding months, more than she'd ever had a reason to shed in her adult life, and she was determined that there would be no more crying.

They explored every inch of the island as well as all the towns along the Outer Banks, making their way north to Duck and south to Hatteras. Each day brought a new choice, and they'd discovered early on that they both preferred spending their time near the water. Kate loved lying on the beach, watching the ghost crabs scuttle along the sand while she read a book until she got too hot and had to submerge herself in the still slightly chilly ocean. She took long walks before breakfast every morning, but on Roanoke Island the air smelled like the ocean instead of the Mississippi River.

Ian had taken up windsurfing on Pamlico Sound as his preferred form of exercise. His dirty-blond hair was longer and had lightened considerably from the daily exposure to the sun. With his deep tan, he looked more like a surfer than a hacker, especially when he came out of the water, board shorts hanging low on his hips and sand clinging to his feet.

By the middle of June, only the slightest sadness remained from the emotional trauma of thinking she'd lost him forever. But every now and then the events of the previous months backed up on her and escaped without warning.

"This house is too small for a man who is six foot four," Ian said one day after nearly hitting his head on the doorframe.

"I like this small house and this small island because I always know where you are," Kate said and then burst into tears.

"Sweetness, come here," he said, pulling her to him. He held her tight, stroking her hair until she calmed.

"I'm sorry," she said, holding on to him until her heart stopped racing. "I don't know where that came from."

"You don't ever have to apologize to me. And I promise I will never leave you again."

To celebrate the Fourth of July, they decided to spend the evening at Nags Head.

"One of the locals told me they're shooting fireworks off from the pier. We should have a great view from the beach," Ian said as he put the cooler in the car.

When they arrived at the public access point, they walked along the path and up the wooden stairs until they reached the top of the dune, Ian pulling a beach cart behind him with their supplies. Below, the beach was filling up fast.

"Let's head over that way," Ian said, pointing toward an area that wasn't quite as crowded.

He hadn't let Kate help him with any of the preparations. He'd filled the cooler, gathered up the rest of the things they'd need, and loaded everything in the car. Now, after they shook out the blanket and set their low beach chairs down side by side, he reached into the cooler.

"Wow, champagne," Kate said when he held up the bottle. "Fancy."

He popped the cork and filled two flutes. "Nothing but the best for you."

"What else do you have in that bag of tricks?"

"Chocolate-dipped strawberries, of course."

"Of course," she said, opening her mouth so he could feed her one.

They ignored the beach chairs in favor of stretching out on the blanket. Around them, children built sand castles and chased each other holding sparklers. The sun began to dip lower on the horizon, its fiery reddish-gold color fading as the light slowly disappeared from the sky. A strong breeze was blowing in off the ocean, and Kate shivered. Ian reached for his faded MIT sweatshirt and pulled it down over her head, freeing her hair while she put her arms through the sleeves.

"Ah, much better," she said.

When it was fully dark, he sat down in one of the beach chairs and tucked Kate in front of him, nestling her between his legs. "While we're waiting for the fireworks, I thought I'd tell you a story."

"A story? I'm intrigued."

"Once upon a time there was a hacker. He saw a woman on TV and he thought she was beautiful and selfless and kind. And even though he'd hacked her, she agreed to go out with him. He tried to play it cool, but he was really happy about that. He didn't even mind when she whipped out her pepper spray and made him take off all his clothes."

"You wanted me to see your naked body, which I will concede I now enjoy having unlimited access to. God, you were so cocky that night. I can't believe I agreed to go out with a man who'd hacked my computer and wouldn't tell me his last name. What was I thinking?"

"I have no idea. Frankly I thought you'd run." He reached around with the champagne bottle to top off her flute. "So when this hacker was younger, he never thought much about settling down or having a wife."

Kate took a sip of her champagne and smiled.

"But one day he started thinking about it. He was deeply in love with the girl he'd seen on TV and wanted a future with her. Unfortunately, things didn't go as planned and he was scared that he'd lost her forever. But one of the things he'd always admired was her tolerance. Though he'd really pushed it, she found it in her heart to forgive him for what he'd done. And after several tense hours of negotiation, her dad reluctantly agreed to give the marriage his blessing."

At this point, Ian turned Kate around so that she was facing him.

"I want to spend the rest of my life with you. Katherine Watts, will you marry me and make me the happiest man in the world?"

Tears rolled down Kate's face despite her resolution that there would be no more crying. "Nothing would make me happier than marrying you, Ian. I would be honored to become your wife."

He embraced her, and she pressed her face to his chest. She had never felt more sure about a decision in her life. Feeling movement between their bodies, she pulled back slightly and wiped her eyes. "Are you trying to put your hand down my shorts?"

"I'm trying to dig your ring out of my pocket."

"There's a ring?"

"Of course there's a ring." Once he'd managed to remove the box, he told her to close her eyes, and he turned on the flashlight app on his phone so they'd have enough light to see by. "Now give me your hand."

She worried that he might have spent too much. Any man who could pay seven million for a car could have easily gone overboard in the ring department. But when he slipped it onto her finger and told her to open her eyes, she gasped because it was exactly the type of ring she would have chosen. At approximately two and half carats, it definitely wasn't small, but it wasn't ostentatiously large either. A halo of smaller diamonds surrounded the center princess-cut stone, giving the ring a vintage feel that she loved.

"Oh my God."

"Do you like it?"

"It's perfect. Have you had it the whole time?"

"It was a custom design. FedEx just delivered it yesterday."

"Let me guess. Right around the time you asked if I'd run back to the coffee shop to grab you a muffin."

"I was tracking the delivery on my phone."

Kate laughed. "Of course you were."

"Remember the day I spent with your parents while you were driving from Minneapolis? I really wanted to get it right, so I asked your mom to help me design the ring. It made her cry."

"It's amazing. I love it."

"You were worried it might be too big, weren't you?"

"No, not at all."

He laughed. "Kate."

"Maybe a little."

Just then the fireworks began, and as the colors streaked across the sky, the future Mrs. Bradshaw snuggled with the man she couldn't wait to spend the rest of her life with.

The next night, when they were seated at a table at 1587 Restaurant, which had quickly become one of their favorite places to eat on Roanoke Island, Ian said, "My fiancée would like a glass of chardonnay and I'll have a bourbon."

"You are so sweet," Kate said, smiling back at him because his happiness was palpable.

"Congratulations," the hostess said. "When's the big day?"

"We haven't gotten that far yet," Ian said.

"We do weddings at the inn. You should stop by the front desk and pick up some information on the way out."

"Really?" Ian said.

"Yes. People get married here all the time. I'll be right back with your drinks."

"We cannot elope," Kate said once the hostess had walked away. "Underneath my mother's sweet and mild-mannered exterior lies a woman hell-bent on immersing herself in the planning of her only daughter's wedding. She's been looking forward to it my whole life. She won't admit it, but when I broke up with Stuart she mourned the loss of that ceremony. She hasn't been able to scratch her itch with Chad because Kristin's mom is just as cuckoo about weddings as she is. If she doesn't get the chance to make her wedding fantasies come true with me, she'll come unglued and then my dad will kill you for real."

"Oh, I know all about your mother's wedding obsession. After she helped me with your ring, we sat on the couch with my laptop for *hours* while we were waiting for you. She showed me flowers and dresses, we looked at tuxedos and wedding cakes. I know we can't elope. But what about inviting everyone to come here? It shouldn't be hard to plan, especially with your mom's help."

"That's actually a really good idea."

"Do you think she'll be upset that we can't have a large wedding?" Ian said. They'd already discussed the fact that only Kate's parents and Chad and Kristin could know what had happened with Ian.

"She'll be fine. And considering we'll have to pull it together quickly, she'll have her work cut out for her."

"What about you? What do you want?"

"As long as my immediate family is here and you're waiting for me at the end of the aisle, that's all I care about. Maybe everyone could spend some time with us on the island before the wedding. You could meet Chad and Kristin. Just a heads-up: my brother thinks you're crazy."

"I'll win him over. You'll see. I'd want to invite Phillip and Susan too."

"Of course," Kate said. "Maybe we could also invite your mom."

"Yeah, maybe."

But Kate didn't think he would.

Diane had thrown herself headlong into planning the wedding, and she'd already made a trip down to meet with the wedding planner and go over things with Kate. They'd decided to get married at the inn as their hostess had suggested. It was such a small affair that everything came together easily, which was exactly the way they wanted it. Kate bought a dress online, which had almost sent her mother over the edge, but once Diane saw a picture of it she calmed down considerably. The ivory bias-cut silk sheath with narrow straps was simple and understated and would look beautiful on Kate.

"Has Ian seen the dress?" her mother asked one day when they spoke on the phone.

"No. I told him he had to wait until our wedding day. He did ask about my hair. I said I was going to wear it up and attach the veil underneath. I have no idea why he wanted to know."

"I know why," Diane said.

"You do? Tell me."

"Absolutely not. I've been sworn to secrecy."

"You're just giddy about it, aren't you?"

"I can't help it," Diane said. "You're going to be so surprised."

"What do you feel like doing today?" Ian asked one morning a week before the wedding. They had walked to the Coffeehouse to pick up breakfast and were now sitting in the Adirondack chairs on the patio, drinking coffee and eating, the air around them growing steamy and humid. "Beach day at Nags Head? Lunch in Rodanthe?"

"It's supposed to storm later, so I vote Rodanthe," Kate said. "We can have lunch at Good Winds and then come back here and crawl into bed while it rains."

"I like the way you think."

"Heard from Phillip lately?" Kate asked, taking a drink of her coffee.

"I actually got a call from him this morning while you were on your walk. He said he was losing hair at an alarming rate and that what was left was turning white. He sounded worried."

"He should be basking in the glow of a job well done now that the forum's been shut down."

"Phillip doesn't bask. Despite the stress, he's not happy unless he has a new problem to solve."

The carding ring had been fully dismantled, but the arrests had all been carried out after Ian had been doxed, leaving him to wonder if it was actually a carder who'd discovered his identity. He'd admitted to Kate that the possibility of it being someone with a different motive worried him immensely.

"What's got him so rattled?" Kate asked.

"Hacktivists. They'll rattle anyone, even Phillip."

"Hacktivists? Hackers who are activists?" Kate knew the combination of those two words couldn't be a good thing.

"That's exactly what it means. They're socially and politically motivated. Largely nonviolent, but they care deeply about their agenda and will pursue it at any cost. It's keeping Phillip awake at night."

"Are they really that bad?"

"They make the carders look like Boy Scouts. But unlike cyberthieves, they're not profit oriented, which makes them much harder to stop. They just want to be heard."

"So if they don't steal, what do they do?"

"They launch denial-of-service attacks, which send so much traffic to a website that it crashes. They help themselves to confidential information because they believe very strongly in free speech. Government agencies are frequent targets, which is why Phillip asked me to do the pentesting. He doesn't feel the current systems are as secure as they need to be."

"What do you think?"

"I think he's right to be worried."

"Sounds like it'll be quite a challenge," Kate said.

"I'm looking forward to it. I've never gone this long without hacking into something."

"Frankly I'm surprised you don't have the shakes."

"When did that mouth get so smart?" he asked, grinning and pulling her toward him for a kiss.

They'd brought their laptops to the island, and Ian had secured an anonymous network connection for them. Kate had been relieved to learn that he could no longer detect the presence of a backdoor on her computer, but she still felt uncomfortable using it.

"The longer you use it, the more convincing it will seem, in case they check back," Ian said. "We'll gradually phase it out and I'll set you up with a new one."

They were planning on returning to Washington a few days after the wedding, having decided that a summer on Roanoke Island was the perfect honeymoon and neither of them minding that they'd done things out of order. "Let's go someplace tropical in January," Ian had said. "I'll be itching to get out of the cold by then."

Kate was looking forward to the next phase of their lives, and she knew Ian was eager to get back to work. Though he swore to Kate that the time they were spending at the cottage was everything he wanted and needed, it was the most idle he'd ever been in his life. He was ready to buy a house and wanted to connect with a Realtor as soon as possible; in the meantime, they'd live in Phillip and Susan's guesthouse, which did not thrill him.

"It won't be long before we have our own place," she reassured him. She didn't mind the guesthouse for the same reason she didn't mind the small cottage they were currently living in. She needed closeness more than she needed space. For a little while longer at least.

Kate's family and Phillip and Susan were due to arrive on the island the next morning, and Kate and Ian had booked them rooms at the Tranquil House Inn. Ian had invited his mother, but she'd left a voice mail saying she'd be unable to attend and hadn't given a reason. Ian shrugged it off, and Kate didn't press him about how he really felt. Someday maybe she'd be able to facilitate a reconciliation between the two of them.

Kate had expected to be busy, maybe even a little stressed out, but Diane had triple-checked every detail, leaving Kate with nothing to do but relax.

"I'm going out to get a haircut," Ian said.

Kate looked up. "You don't have to do that."

"I would expect any man marrying my daughter to get his hair cut before the most important day of his life."

"This is the second time you've mentioned your daughter."

"Shelby is *our* daughter."

"You've already named her?"

"You can name our son."

"William."

"Oh, sweetness. How long have you had that picked out?"

"Since I was about twenty-three. William Ian Bradshaw has a nice ring to it, don't you think? We can call him Will for short."

"William was my dad's name, but everyone called him Bill."

"Then William would be a perfect name for our son."

Ian nodded and smiled, looking quite touched. "What name did you have picked out for a girl?"

Kate shrugged her shoulders. "I can't remember. What name did you have picked out for a boy?"

"Didn't have one."

She smiled.

Ian enveloped her in a bear hug. "We are such a good team, Katie."

"I couldn't agree more."

CHAPTER FORTY-FOUR

IAN WAS WAITING FOR KATE at the end of the makeshift aisle on the deck overlooking Shallowbag Bay. Phillip and Chad stood next to him, all of them sweltering a bit in their tuxedos. An August wedding might not have been their best move, but neither he nor Kate wanted to wait for cooler weather.

Kate and Steve's arms were linked, and she held a bouquet of raspberry-colored roses in her left hand as they waited for the ceremony to begin. Ian had never seen anything more breathtaking than Kate in her wedding gown. Three months of lying on a beach and swimming in the ocean had turned her skin golden brown. The diamond headpiece he'd surprised her with, which had made her cry, shot out brilliant prisms of light and only added to her radiance. Looking at her reminded him how close he'd come to losing the best thing that had ever happened to him, and he was going to get choked up if he thought about it for too long. There weren't many things that scared him, but not having Kate by his side was one of them.

There had been moments during their stay on Roanoke Island that had sliced through his heart, like the time Kate burst into tears after saying she liked the confines of their cottage and the island because she always knew where he was. Before he'd received the tear-filled voice mail she'd left him on his birthday, he'd never heard her cry. Before she'd stepped onto that plane and realized he was alive, he'd never *seen* her cry. Every single one of the tears she'd shed had been his fault, and he vowed not to ever make her cry again unless they were happy tears.

The faint notes of the wedding march filled the air, and Kate and Steve walked slowly down the aisle. When they reached the end, Steve bent down and whispered something in Kate's ear. Ian hoped it wasn't a last-minute plea for her to run, but he wouldn't be at all surprised if it was. Steve kissed his daughter, and then he and Ian shared a look. An unspoken agreement passed between them: You will not hurt my daughter again. You will not put her in harm's way. Earning Steve's trust would take time, and Ian would be on probation with him for a long time, maybe forever. The reasons were justified.

Diane had convinced them to write their own vows. After the wedding officiant welcomed everyone and completed the invocation, he nodded at Ian. Phillip handed him a folded sheet of paper, and Ian recited the words he'd written.

"I love you, Kate. You're beautiful and kind, and from this day forward I vow to be your partner, your lover, and your friend. I will be faithful, devoted, open, and honest. I will cherish you, I will keep you safe, and I will provide for you. I will never hurt you, and I will do everything I can to show you that you made the right decision when you chose me. I promise that life with me will never be boring. You mean the world to me, and my love for you will never waver."

Her big brown eyes were swimming in tears by then, but the smile never left her face.

Now it was Kate's turn. She gave her bouquet to Chad in exchange for her vows. "I love you, Ian. More than I've ever loved anyone. I promise to be your faithful partner no matter what life throws at us. I want you to know that I love you just the way you are because it's part of what makes you special to me. I promise to always believe in you and support you and love you. I trust you and will stand proudly by your side. You are my one true love, and from this day forward, and all the days of our lives, you will have my heart."

A tear ran down her face, and he let go of her hands just long enough to wipe it away. The sound of Diane, Susan, and Kristin sniffling could be heard as they proceeded to the exchange of rings.

"Kate, I give you this ring as a sign of my love and commitment," Ian said as he slid the diamond-encrusted wedding band Phillip handed him onto her finger.

Chad gave Ian's ring to Kate.

"Ian, I give you this ring as a sign of my love and commitment." She slid the matching platinum band onto his finger.

"I now pronounce you husband and wife. You may kiss the bride."

Ian leaned down and whispered in Kate's ear. "This is our first kiss as husband and wife, and it will forever be known as the number eight."

He held her face gently in his hands and gave her a deep openmouthed kiss with tongue. But he dipped her at the end, just so she wouldn't confuse it with the number five.

She loved that.

Their guests applauded loudly.

He had never been so happy in his life.

They moved inside to the comfort of an air-conditioned reception room where they dined on fresh seafood and beef medallions. After a few drinks, Chad announced he was going to give a speech.

"Oh no, here it comes," Kate said softly.

Ian laughed and put his arm around her.

They were sitting at a long table set for eight. Chad was sitting next to Kate, and he stood and cleared his throat. "First of all, on behalf of Kristin and myself, I'd like to congratulate Kate and Ian on their special day. May you have many years of wedded bliss. To my little sister, Kate: I love you and I wish you a lifetime of happiness with Ian. Clearly, you love this guy *a lot*. To my new brother-in-law: you have impeccable taste in both automobiles and women. You've brought excitement to the Watts family, the most we've seen in a long time. Or ever, for that matter. Something tells me there's more to come, and I'm okay with that as long as Kate is. It's kind of cool having a hacker in the family, even if you are a bit of a wild card, and I look forward to getting to know you better. Take good care of my little sister."

Ian smiled, nodded once, and raised his glass. Chad leaned down and clinked it with his.

Kristin clapped her hands together and laughed. "Okay, let's wrap it up."

After dinner, there was dancing. Kate and her dad shared a father-daughter dance. Steve was actually smiling as he and Kate swayed to the music, so maybe he hadn't drawn up the rough draft of an annulment just yet. Then Ian and Kate shared their first dance—and several slow, deep kisses.

"Have I told you how beautiful you look?"

"More than once," she said, and that earned him another kiss.

He ran his hands down the soft silk of her wedding gown until they rested on the small of her back. He loved Kate's body. Naked, she was truly a sight to behold. But there was something about seeing her covered in bits of tulle and lace that drove him wild. He knew what it was hiding. Knew what was waiting there for him and how it would feel.

Her soft skin.

Her warmest places.

"I can't wait to see you in your lingerie." Kate had insisted that he not see her in her wedding gown until right before the ceremony, which meant he hadn't been around to see how she looked in what was underneath it.

"You really outdid yourself this time. It's absolutely gorgeous."

He'd given her La Perla again. The bustier was the same off-white color and tea rose pattern as the Chantilly lace babydoll nightie he'd given her for Christmas, and the Brazilian lace thong was likely going to drive him out of his mind. He'd also included a tulle garter with a silk-and-satin ribbon that he pictured encircling her long, slim thigh. When he took everything off later, he was going to leave that on.

After they cut the cake, Ian ditched his tie and shared a piece with Kate who was now sitting on his lap. She twirled the stem of her wineglass between her fingers and opened her mouth so he could feed her.

When they'd finished the cake, he set the plate on the table and reached for her hand, clasping it tight.

"I will be such a good husband to you." He said it with conviction, and he meant it.

Her response was every bit as resolute. "And I will be a good wife."

"My wife." He kissed her tenderly. "You are my future, Kate Bradshaw."

"And you, Ian Smith Merrick Bradshaw, will be my adventure."

THE END

WHAT'S NEXT?

Follow Kate and Ian to Washington as the next chapter of their lives together unfolds in *White-Hot Hack*, the full-length, dual-narrated sequel to *Heart-Shaped Hack*. Publication details coming this fall. Sign up for my newsletter at www.traceygarvisgraves.com to get the latest updates.

ACKNOWLEDGMENTS

I am deeply grateful for the contributions, assistance, and support of the following individuals:

My husband, David, because his encouragement means more to me than he'll ever know.

My children, Matthew and Lauren. Thank you for being patient—again!—while Mom spent all that time with her laptop. I love you both.

Amanda Tadych. Thank you for your expertise on Northeast Minneapolis and for giving me the perfect neighborhood for Kate to reside in. Special shout-out to the gang at Twin Cities Live.

Elisa Abner-Taschwer, Stacy Elliott Alvarez, Trish Kallemeier, Hillary Faber, and Tammara Webber. Thank you for your encouragement and for helping me to see what I could not.

Peggy Hildebrandt. Even though you're not a fan of reading a book in chunks, you agreed to read the first sixty pages of *Heart-Shaped Hack*. Your heartfelt enthusiasm and immediate request for additional pages encouraged me more than you'll ever know. You are a true friend.

Megan Simpson. Thank you for answering my questions about public interest law. Your assistance was greatly appreciated.

Erika Stone Gebhardt. Thank you for every bit of your beta feedback and for coming to my rescue in Dallas. I'm sure swinging through the Walgreens drive-through to pick up my emergency Rx before meeting me in person for the first time wasn't weird at all.

Sarah Hansen at Okay Creations. Your talent is immeasurable. This is truly my favorite cover and I spent a ridiculous amount of time just staring at it.

Anne Victory of Victory Editing. Thank you for your eagle eye and your words of encouragement. You helped me in more ways than one.

Jane Dystel, Miriam Goderich, and Lauren Abramo. You are truly the trifecta of literary-agent awesomeness.

Special thanks to the book bloggers who have been so instrumental in my ability to reach readers. You work tirelessly every day to spread the word about books, and the writing community is a better place because of you.

I want to express my sincere appreciation to the booksellers who hand-sell my books and the librarians who put them on their shelves.

My heartfelt gratitude goes out to all of you for helping to make *Heart-Shaped Hack* the book I hoped it would be. Words cannot express how truly blessed I am to have such wonderful and enthusiastic people in my life.

And last, but certainly not least, my readers. Without you, none of this would be possible.

ABOUT THE AUTHOR

Tracey Garvis Graves is a *New York Times, USA Today,* and *Wall Street Journal* best-selling author. She lives in a suburb of Des Moines, Iowa, with her husband and two children.

She can be found on:

Facebook at www.facebook.com/tgarvisgraves

Twitter at https://twitter.com/tgarvisgraves

You can visit her website at http://traceygarvisgraves.com

She would love to hear from you!

OTHER BOOKS BY TRACEY GARVIS GRAVES

ON THE ISLAND
UNCHARTED (ON THE ISLAND, 1.5)
COVET
EVERY TIME I THINK OF YOU
CHERISH (COVET, 1.5)